THE HUBRIS OF AN EMPTY HAND

THE HUBRIS OF AN EMPTY HAND

stories

MAHYAR A. AMOUZEGAR

UNIVERSITY OF NEW ORLEANS PRESS

Cover illustration by Xuxu Ariya Amoozegar-Montero
Cover and book design by Alex Dimeff

Library of Congress Cataloging-in-Publication Data

Names: Amouzegar, Mahyar A., author.
Title: The hubris of an empty hand : stories / by Mahyar A. Amouzegar.
Description: New Orleans : The University of New Orleans Press, [2021]
Identifiers: LCCN 2021020072 (print) | LCCN 2021020073 (ebook) | ISBN
  9781608012213 (paperback) | ISBN 9781608012220 (ebook)
Subjects: LCGFT: Short stories.
Classification: LCC PS3601.M679 H83 2021 (print) | LCC PS3601.M679
  (ebook) | DDC 813/.6--dc23
LC record available at https://lccn.loc.gov/2021020072
LC ebook record available at https://lccn.loc.gov/2021020073

First edition
Printed in the United States of America on acid-free paper.

UNIVERSITY OF NEW ORLEANS PRESS
2000 Lakeshore Drive
New Orleans, Louisiana 70148
unopress.org

To my mother

Stay, you imperfect speakers, tell me more:
By Sinel's death I know I am thane of Glamis;
But how of Cawdor? the thane of Cawdor lives,
A prosperous gentleman; and to be king
Stands not within the prospect of belief,
No more than to be Cawdor. Say from whence
You owe this strange intelligence? or why
Upon this blasted heath you stop our way
With such prophetic greeting? Speak, I charge you.
    —*Macbeth*

The secret *things belong* unto the Lord our God: but those *things which are* revealed *belong* unto us and to our children forever, that *we* may do all the words of this law.
    —Deuteronomy 29:29

"[*amesha spenta*] Lord of broad vision, disclose to me for support the safeguards of your rule, those which are the reward for good thinking [*Vohu mano*]. Reveal to me, by reason of my [spenta ara-maiti], those conceptions in harmony with truth [asha]."
    —*The Gathas of Zarathustra*, Yasna 33.13

"O, Ye who art in search of knowledge . . . [my] message is not pleasing to those who destroy the world of truth through their lures of devils. . . ."
    —*The Gathas of Zarathustra*, Yasna 31.1

Table of Contents

TELL ME MORE

.

.

.

Joseph . . .
Immediate . . .
Spenta . . .
Knowledge . . .
Elios . . .
Oblivion . . .
Misery . . .
Erudite . . .
Judah . . .
Empathy . . .
Joseph . . .
Amani Parker continued with his steady drone of seemingly random words as I sat at the kitchen table, dutifully writing each one down on a yellow legal pad. I didn't know what else to do or how to respond to him, so I continued carefully copying every single thing that crawled out of his mouth, hoping to find a pattern in Amani's brewing madness.

The only word that had been repeated more than once in his litany of abstruseness was Joseph. He had said it earlier in his slow rant and then twice just now. I had underlined the word the first time, and now again, as he said it twice more—"Joseph, Joseph . . ."—though this time, he announced the name with the same monotone, steady voice that had filled the kitchen for the past two hours, and not with the careful, pointed pronunciation of the first mention.

Ordinarily, the feat of listing two hours' worth of names and places with only one repetition would have been rather remarkable though not overly strange. Amani could list all the states and their capitals in reverse alphabetical order. However, today was turning into anything but ordinary.

*   *   *

Before I got to Amani's, there were no signs that the day would be anything but predictable. One would expect, or at least hope for, some type of premonition when one's life was about to change forever. And perhaps if I were more pious or, as my mother puts it, a better person, I would have received a sign from a deity. But as it were, my day started out like any other.

I woke up early, fully prepared to start my everyday life of going to work, then coming home to get ready for my date—the third date with the same person, going out for a nice dinner and then coming home alone, or not, depending on how the night went—and then have a leisurely weekend—definitely alone, no matter what. I should have put calling my mother on my to-do list for the week. Perhaps that would have bought me some reprieve from the hell that I'd enter at the end of the day.

It started ordinary, as these events tend to be inconspicuous and versed in hiding their core intentions; mine began with a simple phone call. I was about to put on my makeup when the phone rang. Don't answer, I told myself, but I never listen, not that it would have mattered this time. I picked up the phone.

"Can you come over?"

Okay, I need to pause here.

The person on the line was Dalia Smart, and she never called me. I mean, never. So, my response was not as rude as it may sound.

"What? Now?"

I heard Dalia take a deep breath, and I knew she was trying hard to check herself. She never really liked me and calling me so early in the morning to ask for a favor meant she was desperate. And I was in a mood to make her feel that way even more.

Don't judge me yet.

I waited, and she waited.

"Amani needs you," replied Dalia finally in a managed voice, invoking the trump card.

"Is everything okay?" I asked, now worried.

"No, of course not. Would I have called you if everything was fine, Jackie?"

I ignored the outburst but then again, I knew she was right. She wouldn't have called me if she could have called someone else. "What's wrong, Dalia? Is Amani ill?"

I wasn't trying to be nonchalant about it, but Dalia had made it clear from the minute she and Amani were married that I wasn't welcome in their house, and more pointedly, in their life.

Their life!

They had become a singular organism that seemed to have no more room for me. Dalia Smart would tolerate my presence when it was absolutely necessary, like at large parties when all of Amani's friends, including me, had to be invited. But other than that, my longtime, close friendship with Amani had to be curtailed to accommodate Dalia's immense presence. Amani wasn't happy about it, but he'd married her and not me, so no more occasional late-night chats or weekend runs in the park. No more us. Just them.

Do you find it strange, as I do, that you can spend a decade with someone, share your most intimate thoughts with that person, and then, within days and months, that's all gone, as if there was never an *us*, and little or no room for you? And, therefore, using Dalia's own logic, no place for Amani to need me, right?

Dalia and Amani had known each other for five years and have only been married for three; I've been Amani's friend for almost twenty years, since our first day in college. I wasn't a threat to Dalia, as there was nothing one could describe as romantic between Amani and myself (anymore).

It would have been just fine, and Dalia and I would have kept a cordial but not so close relationship if Amani had not, in one of his one-should-never-have-any-secrets moments, divulged our love affair that had ended almost a decade earlier, before asking for Dalia's hand in marriage. This imprudent confession effectively ended any possibility of friendship between Dalia and me. The worst part of the whole thing, if there is anything less than the worst in this sordid affair, was how he did it.

He did it right in front of me and without any advance warning. So, one minute, I'm chatting with Dalia, keeping things light, trying to be nice to her for Amani's sake, and then the next minute, Amani is on one knee, his arms outstretched, blathering about honesty in relationships and his everlasting love for her. Saying that it was awkward for Dalia and me would be putting it very mildly. It was horrific, watching us melt away.

Imagine this: I was standing next to the handmade kitchen table that Dalia had finished a week earlier—the same kitchen table that I am sitting at now while transcribing pages and pages of Amani's ramblings—pretending to admire her workmanship. For her part, Dalia was describing, ad nauseam, every single detail of chiseling and sanding and the arts of tongue and groove, when suddenly my best friend drops to one knee and tells her everything about us, and I mean everything. And within minutes *the us* that was private and sacred became public and ugly, and decimated.

As I tried to comprehend Amani's confession of love for Dalia, she was trying to grasp Amani's abrupt revelation of his past love affair with me. The image and feel of that moment have stayed solidly with me, as I'm sure they have with Dalia. My mouth froze open midsentence, as did Amani's impervious grin, as did Dalia's look of horror. I looked at Dalia and kept repeating with an utter sense of desperation that it was nothing, and it was a long time

ago and that Amani only loved her. And Amani, oblivious to the
terror he had caused, kept on grinning, and then followed the
first act with the coup de grâce of pulling out a beautiful ring
from his pocket and, to my mind, putting salt on the wound he
had opened so callously. He wanted to profess his devotion in
front of me because he thought of me as family, as a best friend,
but Dalia only saw years of conspiracy. In the end, they were
married, but I was out.

But then Dalia had never called me for anything, even before
that fateful day in her kitchen. So, if she was contacting me this
early in the morning, it meant she hadn't managed to solve whatever problem that had the gall to exist in her perfect world.

I heard Dalia take a deep breath on the other side of the line. I
could tell she hated this phone call as much as I did. "Amani has
gone mad, and he doesn't listen to me," Dalia said, keeping her
voice slow and even, trying hard to be calm, though not really
succeeding. "He's been ranting for days and won't eat or sleep."

I wasn't sure how to respond. "What happened?"

I don't think she was listening to me, and knowing her, I am sure
she was trying hard not to betray her sense of desperation. But she
finally gave up. "I don't know what to do, Jackie. I asked him to see
a professional but he refused and I don't want to force him."

Amani is an intense and sensitive man, and he may be passionate about many subjects, but he was certainly not the kind of
person in the habit of ranting. Dalia never really liked his passion
and had, in the past, stopped him amid a discourse on social
issues or politics to talk about something light and happy. That
is not the full truth if I am honest. Dalia can be rather intense
as well, and she can get into serious conversations of her own.
Perhaps she didn't like Amani's kind of passion. This is where
they were different. Amani invited penetrating discussions where
Dalia was more inclined to lecture the audience. Their distinctive
mode of engagement was on full display only a few days earlier
at a party with several of our friends—he was undoubtedly passionate then, but sane.

So, I still couldn't take Dalia seriously. Especially if it apparently wasn't serious enough to take Amani to the doctor. "Are you sure there isn't anything else?"

"Fuck you, Jackie," was her calm but rather venomous reply before hanging up on me.

So, it was real.

I called her back, but she didn't respond, so I called again and then again. I told myself one more time and then no more, but unfortunately, she answered on the third try.

"He has locked himself in the bedroom and says he doesn't want to see you."

"How does he know you're talking to me?"

"He overheard us."

"Do you still want me to come?"

"Yes. . . . Please."

"I'll be there in thirty minutes," I replied and hung up without waiting for her response.

*   *   *

As I turned the corner, I could see Dalia pacing in front of her house, his house—their home—like a caged animal. Absorbed in her thoughts, she hadn't seen me coming, and I was sure she was in pain because she had to call and seek my help. It was an indication that her life was out of control. But I was wrong, of course. Life itself was out of control.

I admit Dalia is beautiful, smart, and talented. She is thirty-four, five years younger than Amani and me, but she has a powerful job and makes ten times as much as I do. She has long, beautiful hair with light brown eyes and has one of those angular faces you only see on models. So, I admit it: Dalia is perfect, where I'm just a regular person, with a regular job and regular looks. To be truthful, it gave me a sense of satisfaction knowing that Dalia wanted me to rescue Amani in his hour of need. Of course, I'd turn out to be wrong there, too. Amani was beyond help, and neither I nor anyone else could have aided him. But that's not what you think when you rush to support a friend, is it? You are confident you can step in and alleviate whatever ails him. You have done it before, so why not now? Huh.

Dalia was startled when my old car made a screeching sound coming to a halt in her driveway. She was dressed in her powerful, don't-fuck-with-me business suit, but at that moment, it was a weak armor. I turned off the engine and stepped outside, and she watched my movements without blinking. She gave a timid smile but didn't move, waiting for me to go to her.

"How is he?" I asked as soon as I came close enough.

"The same," she replied but still didn't move, expecting me to say something else, but when I didn't, she added, "It's serious, Jackie. He's gone mad."

"I'm sure he's fine," I assured her with a certainty that wasn't justified.

"You don't get it, Jackie. He's not fine. Do you think I'd have called you if he was fine?"

I had to admit that she was right. "I'm sorry, Dalia. I'm just trying to be helpful."

"I know," she offered, and there was some warmth in her voice, like the way she was when we first met. She used to say that Amani and I were like siblings, the way we fought and interacted. But with Amani's confession, I moved from a friendly sister to the fraudulent bitch who had slept with her boyfriend and then lied about it. It didn't seem to matter that Dalia wasn't even in the picture when I was romantically involved with Amani.

"I know you want to be positive, Jackie, but he's in bad shape," Dalia said, and then she took a step forward, and for a second, I thought she was going to hug me, and perhaps she was, but at the last moment, she stepped back and opened the front door.

I walked in the house expecting to see chaos, remnants of a lunatic annihilating any sign of order, but the hallway was spotless as usual with polished hardwood floors and fresh-cut flowers on the side table. I could see the kitchen from where I was standing as the sun shone brightly, putting Dalia's table under a spotlight. I walked up the stairs trying hard to ignore Dalia and Amani's myriad photos, capturing them in their happy moments. The door to the bedroom was closed, so I knocked gently, but there was no response.

"Amani. It's Jackie," I called out. No response, no reaction. Dalia had followed me upstairs and was standing there, staring at me—neither helping nor hindering.

"Amani?"

Nothing. I had expected Amani to open the door as soon as he heard me or at least acknowledge me. I thought no matter what ailed him, no matter how bad he was, my voice would at least soothe him enough to respond.

I knocked again. "Come on, Amani. Open the door, now!"

"No." I heard a thin voice from the other side of the door.

Feeling emboldened, I urged him on, "Come on, sweetheart, open the door." I felt the icy cold stare of Dalia on my back, and I knew I should not have used a term of endearment, but it was too late now.

"I know," Amani called out.

"What do you know?"

"He knows. He knows," cried out Dalia. "That's all he says." She walked closer and knocked on the door hard. "What is it? Tell me or tell Jackie. Tell someone. Please."

"I know. . . . I know . . . but I can't. . . ." moaned Amani with a voice filled with such frustration and pain that both Dalia and I took an involuntary step back.

"You can tell us anything. We're both here for you, darling," offered Dalia generously.

"Please, Amani," I added as if a polite word might penetrate him.

"I can't take it anymore. . . . It's too much. . . ." He trailed off and we waited.

And when nothing else came out of him, we knocked a few more times, but there was no response.

"Darling," Dalia said, "I've made some orange muffins. The kind you like. Please let me bring some for you. You don't have to talk, but at least let us give you something to eat."

She then looked at me. "Amani hasn't eaten for days, and you know how much he loves my muffins." She said the words in a wistful voice, as if she couldn't believe he wouldn't open the door for her muffins. I shared her pain, and despite myself, I couldn't disagree with her. Dalia is a fantastic cook. Her muffins were not mere, orange-flavored baked goods; they were, to use a cliché, a symphony of crystallized ginger and subtle essence of orange. Despite Amani's predicament, and to my shame, I wanted to walk down to the kitchen and grab a muffin, whether she could convince Amani or not. I looked at Dalia, and she looked at me, and then we both stared at the door, hoping the offer of muffins would miraculously open it.

It didn't work, and we both stood there in silence for a long time. And I really wanted to have one of those muffins.

"I have to go," Dalia said finally, avoiding my gaze.

"What?"

"I'm sorry, Jackie, but I have a big meeting today, and I'm already late. I really can't miss it, not today. I was home all day long yesterday, nursing him."

That's your job, I thought but then again, of course. Dalia is an investment banker and manages millions, if not billions. She is a superb carpenter and can make little birds from scrap metal. Who am I but a simple book cover designer? Not even that. I'm the second assistant to the book cover designer. I could do most of my work at home, but I choose to go to the office because I have a one-bedroom apartment, but I hate working and living in the same place. I like interacting with my colleagues and my boss, who is fantastic and smart. I love my job, even if it pays nothing and I can only afford a small, one-bedroom apartment on the edge of San Francisco. So, I pretend I'm living in the city that I could never truly afford. And I have an understanding, supportive boss. So, of course, Dalia should go, and I should stay.

"Okay. You go ahead, and I'll stay here," I offered.

"Are you sure? Thank you, Jackie."

"No problem."

"No, I mean it. Thank you. I'll be back in a few hours."

Dalia put on her high heels to match her powerful outfit and left. I knew that despite what she'd said, she wouldn't be back until late in the evening. So, I sunk to the floor and leaned against the door that separated Amani from me. For the longest time, I stayed there.

*   *   *

After a while, there was a bit of shuffling on the other side. "Are you there?" Amani asked.

"Yes."

"You shouldn't have come."

I leaned closer and put my ear against the door, so I could hear his barely above-whisper voice. He sounded like himself, calm and rational.

"Come out, Amani."

"No."

"Why not?"

"You shouldn't have come," he insisted.

"Well, I'm here. Open the door and let's talk."

"No."

"Just open the door, and we don't have to talk," I offered.

"No."

"Tell me what's troubling you, sweetheart."

I could be myself with Dalia gone. I could be generous and kind and let him open up. I knew him better than anyone. I could defeat his demons, no matter how strongly they'd possessed him.

"I know. . . ." Amani repeated the mantra that was getting tiresome.

"I know too," I offered, and my earnest voice made him chuckle. It was a small step but I became more hopeful. "I know," I said again, "and I will tell you."

There was no response.

"Amani."

Nothing.

"Amani?"

Nothing.

I pulled myself up and knocked hard on the door. "Stop it. Stop it now. You're scaring me," I cried out, and despite myself I could feel tears rolling down my cheeks. And I sobbed in frustration.

Still nothing, so I waited patiently like a mother would, like a sister might, like a lover could. I sat down again, leaning against the door, thinking that he might be doing the same on the other side of this thin wooden barrier. I thought I heard him sob too, so I started to cry again, as quietly as possible, but this time for him and with him.

Minutes passed, and my legs felt numb, so I stretched them in front of me and banged my head on the door in frustration.

"You shouldn't have come. Please leave," Amani warned.

"Open the door, and let me see you, and then I'll leave."

I needed to make sure. I just wanted to see Amani's eyes. I told myself that I'd console him if I could only get the door open, and I would be comforted in return. I told myself the simple act would prove Dalia wrong.

"Please, Amani."

"I know . . . and . . . and it is killing me, Jackie. Go away or it will kill you too."

"What, darling? What's it with you?" I was beginning to think Dalia was right and Amani had gone mad in the few days since I'd last seen him.

"I want to. . . . But I can't."

"If you ever loved me, you will open the door this very moment."

I didn't want my anger and frustration to get ahold of me, but I couldn't help it. I was about to say something else, to take back the love requirement, when I heard the door unlock. I stood up quickly and fixed my dress. The door opened excruciatingly slowly as if the act of unlocking it had exhausted him. Amani was sitting on the floor like I'd been, but not against the door as I had hoped. He was leaning against the wall and away from me.

Amani looked up. He looked like an animal that had been caged so long that it feared freedom, the open door a trap. Amani's large brown eyes had sunken so deep in their sockets that they looked like small black rocks at the bottom of an abyss.

"Amani," I exclaimed in shock but found enough courage to reach down and pull him up on his feet. He was wearing his suit and tie, like a man ready to go to work, though he was barefoot, and his clothes were disheveled and dirty. He stood up effortlessly and allowed me to hold his hands. They felt warm and dry in mine, and I gently led him out of the room.

"You should go home now before it's too late," he warned me.

"I will, sweetheart, but let me clean you up a bit, and then make you something to eat," I commanded, and it seemed to work; Amani nodded and followed me to the bathroom.

I cleaned his face with a small towel and walked him to the kitchen and made him sit at the table, all without saying a single word, even though I was dying to know what he knew and why he could not share it. I made a fresh pot of coffee and put a muffin in front of him and took one for myself from a perfect row of perfectly sized orange muffins.

Amani stared at his food but didn't move, whereas I took mine and practically put the whole thing in my mouth. He stared at me and gave a tiny smile. I went to the refrigerator, poured some cold milk, and drank it heartily while he watched my every move. It felt good to eat voraciously. For some reason, it gave me a sense of power. I took mauling Dalia's perfectly shaped muffins as an act of rebellion, no matter how petty the action was. I walked over to Amani and cut his muffin into little pieces and put one in his mouth, which he accepted like a little bird and chewed softly. I gave him a second piece, then another.

Then I poured some coffee, and we drank and ate one more muffin each and drank another cup, again all in silence. And it seemed the quiet and the food and the coffee had made Amani calm. I thought all was well, and I was successful where Dalia had failed.

Of course, I was wrong.

*   *   *

I crawled under the table and sat next to Amani, who seemed to be in a trance. I took his hand in mine, rubbed it gently, and then laced my fingers into his like we used to do long ago.

When I'd had enough of silence and coffee and muffins, I tried again to get him to open up. After a few minutes of my relentless questioning, Amani had screamed like an insolent child, edged himself under the table, and refused to come out since, as if that had become his new sanctuary. He again started insisting that I had to leave, and when we reached another impasse, I crawled under the table and joined him.

I didn't know what else to say, so we sat under the table, and neither of us spoke for a long time, repeating the cycle of brooding silence, followed by relentless appeals from each of us. Then, without any prompting, Amani started his litany of names and places, and after a few seconds, when I realized that he was not going to stop, I came out from under the table and started carefully writing down his list on the yellow legal pad that was already on the table.

After more than two hours, he stopped, and his last word was Joseph, his fifth repetition of the name in a list of hundreds with no duplication. I only knew of one Joseph, a friend of a friend whom we had recently met. I asked if Amani meant the same Joseph, but he ignored my question. It didn't make any difference anyway.

I took off my glasses and rubbed the bridge of my nose and waited, thinking that Amani might go on again, but nothing happened, so I brought him a glass of water and made him drink it before crawling under the table again. We played the silent game for a few more minutes, but then I couldn't take it anymore.

"Let me help you, darling," I offered, as we both stared straight ahead. "What do these names and places mean? Just tell me." I squeezed his hand, trying to give him some comfort.

He looked over and stared at me and then leaned even closer, as if to kiss me. My heart stopped beating for a second, but then it started again in disappointment as he withdrew back to his shell. He was still looking at me, but it felt like he was looking through me, as though I had become transparent, a ghost that had no right to be there.

"I know. . . ." Amani declared again.

"What is it, you know, sweetheart?"

"I know! I know! But I can't tell you," Amani cried out with a pained voice, and I could see his eyes welling up with tears.

"You can trust me. You know that, don't you?"

"Yes, but . . ."

"No, sweetheart. Just trust me," I said, hoping that he held the same faith that I had in him. We have been lifelong friends, and I trusted him with my own life.

"You should've told me."

"Told you what?"

He continued staring at me and beyond me at the same time. I could see a hint of his inner struggle in his eyes as if he was already regretting the little information he had revealed. He looked down for a moment and then, deciding, focused his eyes on me and said, "You should've told me about your hysterectomy."

"What . . . Who told you?"

I don't know why, but I burst into tears even though this had happened a decade ago, and I was over it—or at least I'd thought I was over it.

*   *   *

When Amani and I were together, we both wanted children, and when I got pregnant, I was over the moon. But I kept the pregnancy to myself. I'd had a miscarriage in college when I became pregnant by my no-good boyfriend at the time. Then, I welcomed the miscarriage as a gift, as it spared me from making one of the most challenging decisions any woman could face. But I wanted Amani's baby, and at the same time, I wanted to be cautious. I wanted to wait just to make sure, before announcing it to Amani or anyone else.

The first three months went smoothly, and with each passing day, I became increasingly confident. I decided to tell Amani at the end of the thirteenth week upon his return from a long business trip. I had planned the day well in advance, wanting to make it memorable.

It was.

The day started like any other day. I was planning to make a big dinner and surprise Amani with my news, but at midday there was some spotting and I called my doctor and he told me it was nothing, but I should see him in a day or two. So, I delayed telling Amani and went to see the doctor the very next day. He poked and prodded for a while and then told me it was nothing and I should expect a normal pregnancy. It was Wednesday, so I thought I would wait until the following Friday to tell Amani, just to be safe. Almost a week passed without an incident, and I felt emboldened again but decided to do it differently this time, as not to jinx it. I thought I would do a simple meal, nothing big. I went to the little store next to my work and bought little bunny socks, one with a pink bunny and the other with a blue one. I thought I'd put them on the center of the table and then let the night go as it would. But, as soon as I purchased the pair of socks, the spotting returned and then pain, and by Friday at 1:30 in the afternoon, the whole thing ended.

I should have called him when I was in the hospital, but it seemed every moment that things got worse, the doctors told me that it would be fine, and they kept telling me that until it was not. By then, I was no longer pregnant, and there was no reason to tell him anything.

When I went home that night, tired, heartbroken, and frustrated, Amani greeted me with such joy and love, holding the little socks in his hands that all I could do was burst into tears and have a meltdown on our front landing. He cried with me and loved me and cared for me, and then promised me that the next pregnancy would be fine. But when the doctors told me that a hysterectomy was the only option, I couldn't bring myself to tell him. So, I slowly drove him away instead. When I had the procedure, Amani did not know about it, nor my real reason for ending our relationship. It all made sense at the time, even if it makes no sense now.

*   *   *

Perhaps it never made sense. But, as I sat under the table with a man who was no longer mine, I knew it was too late.

"I'd have loved you no matter what," Amani said, after allowing me to cry for a long time.

I was thinking at least this revelation, no matter how he found out, had allowed Amani a sense of sanity, and it made me happy that some past tragedy might bring him back.

"I should've told you," I said.

"Yes, you should have trusted me. You lied to me and in the end betrayed us."

"That's not fair," I cried out.

"I know."

"How did you learn about it?"

"I just know," said Amani, and as if the words invoked the curse, he became silent and distant again.

"Not again. Just tell me, please. If you love me, if you ever loved me, you would tell me."

I tried the love angle, hoping it would work for the second time. He looked back at me again, and this time he focused on me and I saw a flicker of anger in his eyes. He shook his head as if dispelling it, but that action only replaced the ire with pain.

"You wouldn't ask if you knew."

"I'm scared, Amani. Just tell me."

"You'll be more terrified if I did tell you."

"Tell me *something*."

"You should go home. You should leave and never come back. If you love me, you will leave now. Can't you see I'm trying to save you . . . to forgive you."

At that moment, I was too distracted trying to save him to consider what he meant by that—I've never thought I needed forgiving. Yes, I kept the hysterectomy from him, but it was my choice to endure the trauma alone and not burden him.

But at the time, I was just focused on helping him.

"I cannot leave, Amani. You know I can't. I can't leave you because I love you. Or at least let me take you to a doctor, maybe—"

He chuckled sadly. "No doctor could fix this." Then he kissed me, lightly. I felt his chapped lips and warm breath, and I knew I loved him and would do anything for him. I was sure he felt something too. He put his hand on his mouth as if keeping himself from crying.

Wouldn't you step in front of a bullet for your child, for your spouse, for the person you loved the most? Wouldn't you consider your own life trivial if it would save your love? I would. But what if your action, the armor you provide to stop that bullet, does not protect them? Do you still make the conscious decision and step in front of them, knowing that nothing could save them?

"How could anything you say or do hurt me?" I demanded. "You can never hurt me, no matter what you say. You know that don't you? Our friendship withstood every obstacle that life could throw at us, so how could sharing a few words hurt us? You would tell me if you loved me."

"No! It's poison, and I can't infect you like I've been infected. It wants you and it's urging me to do its bidding."

"You're not serious. Goddamn it, Amani. Tell me, or I'll walk out of this house and leave you alone with your so-called poison."

"Leave. Then leave, for God's sake. That's what I want you to do. Please leave before it swallows the last of my resolve."

"Tell me."

"I've said enough."

"I need more," I shouted. "Tell me more!"

"Please don't tempt me," he begged. "Can't you see I'm losing control? It wants to infect you too. It's promising me solace if I whisper the poison into you. Leave now, or I will have no choice but to succumb to its wishes."

But I didn't understand, and I thought I was strong. I thought I could handle whatever he might throw at me. But it was too late, and I believe Amani knew that already.

A long time later, he leaned close, and I could see through his eyes, and I could smell his skin, and I could hear his heartbeat, and I knew he had made his decision.

Amani kissed me again and then put his lips against my ear and whispered. He spoke softly but deliberately, and I listened intently, waiting for the secret that was destroying him. Amani spoke for a few minutes, not long, and then withdrew. And I thought about what he had just said, and I was about to laugh at the simplicity of it, and ridicule him for scaring us so much over so little, when I noticed the change in him. He looked strong, and a sense of relief washed over him. The small black coals had transformed into two bright brown eyes and his cheeks, sullen and dark one minute, looked healthy and rosy.

"Amani?"

He leaned over and kissed me again, and his lips were soft and warm, and then as he had done earlier, he put his mouth against my ear, but this time he offered nothing but a simple sorrow: "Please forgive me, sweetheart," he said and then withdrew and crawled out from under the table and walked out of the kitchen.

I should have feared what would come next, but I was fearless. Ignorance makes one brave.

I felt nothing, neither good nor bad, for a moment. Dalia's remaining muffins sat in a row, all golden and beautiful as the evening sun cast the long shadow across the kitchen. I could hear Amani upstairs walking about, and I felt deep satisfaction. I sat down for a moment, but then I felt a strong need for a cup of espresso, in spite of the evening hour.

I left the house without saying goodbye to Amani, driven by the urge for coffee. I started the car and started backing out just as Dalia pulled up.

"Are you okay, Jackie?" Dalia shouted through her car window.

"Everything's fine," I replied. I wasn't sure if she heard me, but I didn't care. I drove away not thinking about Amani or what he had told me, as he'd told me nothing, it seemed, completely focused instead on finding and drinking a strong coffee.

I drove east as fast as I could until I reached a café on the corner of Fillmore and California, and as if it were expected, there was a vacant space right in front of the store. I walked in compelled by an invisible force, ordered a double shot of espresso to go along with a bottle of water and a giant candy bar, even though I only wanted coffee. I went outside and sat in my car with the door open and inhaled the bitter liquid, letting it coat my insides like a primer. I finished my coffee, drank the water, and, when done, drove to my office.

*　　　*　　　*

I sat at my desk and started reading the first manuscript's synopsis prepared by one of the assistant editors. The book was a four-hundred-page behemoth, so the outline itself was about fifty pages long. It was a diatribe on the current state of the economy. It was a book designed for the general public, despite its volume. There was nothing of substance in it, and I thought some prosaic reading would be an excellent end to an eerie day.

I started reading where I had left off a day before, but I couldn't remember what I had reviewed, so I went back to the beginning. I read a few pages, but the words didn't sound familiar, like it was a different document.

I recalled Amani's lips brushing against my face, as if getting ready to whisper sweet nothings into my ears, but instead he'd uttered a string of words, meaningless individually and at the time. The same kind of empty words that darkened the pages of this manuscript. Most of us feel this desolation every day, as if there are forces directing us—managing us. We dismiss them as stress, a symptom of modern living, and we find solace in our routines, and by and by, we get distracted by reality shows and sports and binge watching on Netflix.

The words on the pages were another diversion, and what had looked logical and expected now read and felt different. The author had devoted more than half of the book on basic economic theory, the same ideas you find in every other text on the topic. But she thought she had found something new, a thread that might lead to a third way spun out of the battles between the Keynesian and laissez-faire economics. She had called this theory the "Spenta Economics," which she posited would expose the current orthodoxy.

I remember how the author's thesis had made so much sense only a few days earlier, but now it had no meaning; even the book's title had become meaningless. So-called facts about the dark side of capitalism or socialism or any other ism abound on the Internet, but her book meant to be different. It meant to be scholarly and revealing. I don't know how I had neglected to notice before, but there it was now: she, like any other, spouting the same nonsense as a random conspiracist. She had come so close to the truth and yet had missed it. She was standing on the edge of the Grand Canyon but was distracted by a pebble. The book was missing a massive piece, and not in the sense that someone had forgotten something, but the words were in wrong places and therefore missing the truth. It was all there, yet it wasn't complete.

Amani's words floated in front of me strung together, pulling at me, and like a feverish woman, I could see doors opening, and I could see beyond and yet was afraid to take the step and cross the threshold, sensing nothing good would come of that action.

Truth has unintended consequences, a voice echoed in my head, and that fact was my certainty. It wasn't enough to know; the key was what you might do with that knowledge. My heart was pressing against my chest, and my arm felt numb, and I thought I was about to have a heart attack. I took several deep breaths and tried to relax my body.

I still couldn't dispel the nagging urge, so I took a red pen and started to underline the *wrong* pieces on the document. Then it occurred to me, this was a synopsis, meant to help with the cover design. This was not the actual book. I went to the editor's room and took the giant manuscript to my cubicle. I started reading it in its entirety, but it was not right; it was not complete. The author, without knowing it, had touched on some key points, but she didn't have the whole picture. I knew the author did not know she had touched on these vital points because she referenced them in passing and not as part of her main topic.

I took out my red pen again and started underlining the sections needing correction, elaboration, and emphasis. By the time I reached the end of the book, it was three in the morning, and I had missed my date. I looked at my phone, and there were several calls from my date. I ignored them and looked at my marks across the book, a sea of red on every page. But I had only underlined what needed correction. I needed to actually correct them now.

I took my black pen to start to write what needed to be said, but then Amani's voice echoed in my head, and I remembered what he had told me.

Amani had spoken of the past and of gods and men, and of Spenta, and between each word there were other words, so unassuming and innocent, and yet combined together, and unbeknownst to me, they planted a seed in my brain, and as it slowly grew, it reconnected new synapses and opened my eyes and revealed all.

But even in the infancy of my rebirth, I had an inkling of the perils of what Amani had given me and the power of my utterance. What is the value of knowledge if it's not shared? And yet, what are the ethics of sharing if the intended doesn't have the capacity to understand and will be crushed under the weight of it? I felt I was being pulled in two different directions at the same time, a dismemberment of my brain by two powerful forces. Although I didn't fully understand the source of it then, there was a real fear that consumed me even on the first night.

Looking at the manuscript, I knew I couldn't say what needed to be said, at least not this way, not so crudely on the pages of a worthless book. My hands trembled above the page, and I wanted to tell the author what I knew to be right, to be transformative, but I couldn't. I tried and tried again, but the best I could do to inform the author, to tell her that there was a piece missing, was to write: *I know!*

*   *   *

I went home and despite all that had happened I slept soundly, as if my body and brain needed to shut down to accommodate for the remake of my constitution. I woke up late and felt more like myself than ever. I was still me, rested and full of energy, and the dread that had followed me the night before had all but dissipated. I told myself Amani had failed to infect me, as he had intended, or if he had succeeded, I was strong enough to disallow his madness to govern my life. But despite my own denial, I could feel something strange growing within me, like tiny discomforts we feel right before the onset of the flu. And like most sick people, I ignored it, hoping it would go away by itself. It never does.

It was Saturday morning, and I had the whole weekend to myself. I listened to messages from my date, starting with concern and ending with anger. And there were two calls from Dalia, thanking me for saving Amani and asking me to join them for dinner. There was nothing from Amani.

I dressed, left the house, and walked toward the BART station, not wanting to take the car downtown, but stopped at a coffee shop first to get a cup of coffee to go. As I was waiting in line, I heard a young couple arguing. They were both saying the same things but from different angles. It was a simple banter about the city's ongoing social woes, and only a day earlier I would have agreed with them both. But today, I could see how wrong they were and how wrong I was. It was like the topic of the manuscript, mere scratches on the surface, but they were even more on the boundaries, and like in the massive book, the argument was only a shadow of what was real. They went back and forth as we waited, and I wanted to tell them they were both wrong—that I knew the truth, and they could too. The world they thought they were living in was a big lie, and they were perpetuating this deceit. They were so proud of their comprehension and thought their arguments actually mattered.

Their hubris was pulling at my skin. It was like watching two flat earthers arguing about which side might have a steeper drop. I knew deep within that I should tell them, but I held my tongue. I still feared what lay behind the doors, and I didn't want to lead this young couple to a murky world. I got my coffee and started to leave, but they were still arguing, each doubling down. I pushed the door to get out, but at the last minute, and despite my fear, I couldn't control the urge and said or, rather, hollered, "I know!"

The couple stopped and looked at me as if I were crazy—just as I must have looked at Amani when he'd finally opened the bedroom door. But I knew I was right, and they were wrong. The couple went back to their argument as I left the shop.

I walked to the BART station, and the train arrived as I did. Naturally, I thought, *how lucky*, and stepped in; I didn't yet understand that luck no longer played a role in my life. I sat down and tried to clear my mind of the couple, the manuscript, and most of all, Amani, hoping that the process would clean my body of his poison that by then I was certain had anchored itself onto me, but it was not to be. The more I tried to purge it, the more it grew inside me, and my recognition of it only made it grow faster.

The man across from me was reading the *San Francisco Chronicle*, and I could see the headline: Global protests break out in 951 cities in 82 countries. I could read part of the article addressing the reasons and pointing to growing economic inequality, corporate influence over people's lives, and the lack of democratic institutions at all levels. This was a newspaper with tens of thousands of readers, and one would have thought they would know more, but they were even more oblivious than the couple in the coffee shop. They were just repeating what other news media said. How could this be? How could we be so ignorant of the truth that lay right in front of us?

"That is wrong." I shouted at the man, pointing at the headline. I put my hand on my mouth, trying to control the urge to cry out even more. The man looked over the paper and smiled, expecting another crazy person on the metro. I had dressed up to go downtown; I had done my hair and put on makeup. I looked fine, as my mother would say. I smelled of expensive perfume, so perhaps the smile was not to dismiss me but to agree with me—one professional to another.

I could see and understand what would have been invisible only a day earlier: without having ever met this man in my life, I knew that he was a lawyer, a corporate lawyer. But he was still as clueless as the headline. He took my comment as an invitation and started to shuffle the pages of the paper as he tried to build the courage to engage me.

"That's so wrong," I repeated, as if the urge to speak out, like the urge to drink coffee, was taking me over.

"What's wrong?" the man asked, and, now feeling encouraged, he stood up.

I was about to tell him. The words, the truth, all knotted in my body, and all I wanted to do was purge myself of it as one does with poison, but at the same time, my sane self knew the consequences of such deliverance. My old self wondered if Amani understood these consequences too.

A tinge of bitterness washed over me. He'd picked Dalia to marry and me to suffer. But I could no longer devote time to my own indignation.

I was about to say how misguided the article was, and I had the answer, the answer, but then I remembered the words whispered so delicately the day before, and I could feel Amani's warm breath on my skin, and so instead of saying what I knew to be the truth, I wailed, "I know!"

Why say it out loud? I asked myself, but despite everything, that simple answer eluded me. It was a sign of madness, shouting at strangers, but how could you not? Wouldn't you cry out too if you could save someone?

The man, I knew, had a deep well of empathy, took a step closer and asked with an inviting smile, "What is it that you know, Miss?" He thought he was being supportive, but this was no game.

"I know," I repeated. "I know!" I cried out and put my hands on my mouth to stop myself saying what I knew would come out. But I couldn't lie. I couldn't stop, so before he could respond, I added, "But I can't tell you."

He smiled, a weak, dawning smile, and he sat down.

I gained some control even though my brain was on fire. I kept my mouth shut the rest of the ride and got off at Powell station on Market Street. I left the station and told myself I would not let the day be ruined by headlines or arguments. I walked into a small boutique off Geary Street, and even though I couldn't afford anything in the shop, I thought I would buy something small anyway, as a way of treating myself—something to make me feel good about life.

The place was elegant, and the clothes were stylish, and the air smelled of something sweet and spicy, like Dalia's cupcakes. There were two young women at the counter, both tall and blond and thin, and one of them, the one who was hoping to be a lawyer and not the one who was worried she might be pregnant, walked over and asked if she could assist me with my selection. I dismissed her, and she went back to her colleague. I roamed the shop, looking at each article carefully with my endowed, discerning eyes. I could tell what was right and what was not. And nothing in this store was right.

The women at the counter, bored with my slow inspection, started talking about their dates from the night before, the restaurants and the wine, the incredible sex. They spoke without paying attention to me—playful talk between two young women. I heard them get excited about the men and their jobs, and what they did and did not do. Their conversation continued on and led to the topic of the men's politics and their own. One of them used the term "United for Global Democracy," the same slogan used by the protestors, and the other laughed and said, "Who would be against it?" And then continued on whining about the unfairness of it all.

Although they didn't know it, they would inevitably reach the same conclusion as the couple in the café. I could understand why: they all based their discussions on the same false set of premises. The corruption was at the source and thus no matter the angle of trajectory they would reach the wrong destination. The same way both political parties are inherently married to the idea of neoliberalism and thus all policies, conservative or liberal, flow from the same well, though cautiously colored by each party.

The ladies' conversation wasn't exactly on the same topic as the young couple's, and they were convivial, but what they said was not correct. It hinted at the facts, but it missed the essential ingredients, like eating a cupcake that looked like Dalia's, and smelled like Dalia's, but was missing the essence of what made it Dalia's cupcake.

"Ladies," I said.

They turned to look at me with disinterest. "Would you like to try something on?"

"You're both wrong about this."

"Wrong about what, ma'am?"

"You should free yourself," I said.

"Free? We're free," the woman who thought she may be pregnant said.

I bit my lip hard to keep myself in the sane world, trying hard to control the urge, knowing it would not end well. I laughed, hoping it would sound dismissive rather than crazy. "Free, you are not. That I know, ladies," I cried with a pained voice.

I knew I was right, and if you know something critical, wouldn't you want to reveal it, even if it might poison the world?

The young women didn't know, and if they did, they didn't care. "I'm sure," they offered in unison.

"I know," I insisted.

"Of course, you do. Then tell us," replied the one who seemed more reasonable, the future lawyer.

"I . . . I . . . I just know," I offered.

I wondered if all crazy people felt the same as what I was experiencing at that moment. I used to ignore the rants of the homeless man in my neighborhood, but now I wondered if he too had something vital to impart, or if I would become like him, living on the streets, and yelling at passersby. But then, I figured the fact that I acknowledged such a possibility should prove that I was rational. Of course, it may be that all insane people think they are lucid.

It didn't matter either way, because I shouted my new mantra a few more times, and in the end, they asked me to leave, politely, of course, and I left with tears in my eyes, frustrated and humiliated. I went straight back to the station with my head down, my ears blocked, and my mind focused on my feet as I took step after step toward the entrance.

I stepped inside the train and took a seat as if in a trance. The train jerked forward and picked up speed as I stared at the dark window. There was silence, and it felt good to be away from all those falsities. Then the train arrived at the next station, and a few people walked in. They were tourists. A family huddled by the door and started talking about the deYoung Museum they had visited a day before. The father was telling them about its history and its impact on the city.

He had little information about the place, as most tourists do. He was ignorant of the main facts but had most of it right and his teenage daughter, wanting to be helpful, searched the web on her phone and then gave it to her father so he could read the correct information. She was sweet, unlike most brooding teenagers, and the father thanked her for correcting him.

It was good to feel normal for a minute, but then the conversation turned. They kept talking about the same thing, but I knew they were going in the wrong direction again, and I felt bad for the daughter, who had been so helpful. She was now being misled, and she would grow up not knowing any more about it than what was told to her on a subway during an autumn outing. She would grow up feeling confident that she knew how the world worked, and yet she knew nothing—as if one could learn how a train engine works by merely looking at a picture of a railroad. The father continued with confidence, and the children listened, and I knew they were all wrong, and they would always be wrong, and it finally became clear what Amani meant when he whispered his poison into me.

The train stopped, and the conversation continued, and I shouted, "You're all wrong!"

The father pulled his daughter closer.

"I know," I cried out, but my knowledge meant nothing unless I whispered it in each person's ear. "How could you live in such ignorance?"

The family looked at each other but no one said anything.

"I know," I shouted again, because even in that state, it was clear that I would not poison the kind girl even if she was going to stay ignorant of the secret that would save her and destroy her at the same time. I cried out again, no longer in control of my vocal cords. "But I can't tell you." The words rushed out of my mouth.

It didn't matter what they said behind my back because the doors slid open, and I left and walked toward my apartment. I felt exhausted and feverish and went straight to bed but couldn't fall asleep no matter how much I tried.

*   *   *

That was almost a month ago.

Since that Saturday morning in October, I've sequestered my-self in my apartment when I realized that I could never contain the effect of Amani's poison. The urge to share the knowledge and save humanity was as unbearable as the certainty that such actions would only destroy them. Like Amani. That is the ulti-mate comedy of life, the irony of knowledge. I told myself the exile would be temporary and I would find the third way, a solu-tion to the unwinnable dilemma.

I had called in sick on Monday and then on Tuesday and then again on Wednesday, and then I stopped calling. And my gen-erous boss waited until Friday, and then she called me and left a message wishing me to get well. She called again on the second week, and I told her I needed to take some time off. She must have heard something in my voice because she showed up at my door on the third week, but I didn't let her in, though I tried to assure her that all was well. I hadn't convinced her as she came back today, insisting on coming inside the apartment.

She expected to see a sick woman lying in bed, but I looked healthy. And the apartment looked clean and organized, if dark.

She looked around the living room and said, "I'm so glad you're feeling better." And then she pointed to the windows, all covered with brown papers, and the computer that was smashed and the TV with all its wires pulled out. "What's going on, Jackie?"

"I'll survive. I know I will survive. I can't watch TV or listen to the radio. I disconnected them all. No Internet or smartphone either. The landline works, so there's my daily ration of Chinese food delivered to my front step."

"You should see a doctor, Jackie. You had a nervous breakdown. You're depressed." She diagnosed me as well as any doctor might.

"Look at my immaculate apartment. If I'm depressed, then my depression has been good for my apartment," I offered.

"But then why not come back to work? Why are you living like a hermit?"

"Because I'm strong."

"I don't understand."

"I'm strong enough not to let the poison destroy me."

"What poison?"

She asked, so I told her about Amani and about Dalia's cup-cakes and his soft kisses.

And then I told her that Amani was dead. He'd killed himself on that very Saturday after I'd last seen him. He poisoned me and then, free of the poison, committed suicide as if without it, he had lost the will to live.

Dalia had called to inform me I had killed her husband. I didn't pick up the phone, so she left me a message to add to the poison that her husband had bestowed upon me. I played the voicemail for my boss:

Amani . . . He is dead. . . . What did you say to him? It has always been about you. You never wanted us to be happy. . . . And now he's dead. You did it. You killed him.

"So, what are you doing now?" my darling boss asked.

"I am surviving."

"Didn't you learn anything from your own story? There's no poison. Your friend was depressed, and now you are. He took his own life, and you loved him. So, you're grieving, sweetheart, and that's okay. It's normal to get sick, but you need to see a doctor."

"No one can cure me."

"How do you know?"

"Because I know. Weren't you listening to me? I know—"

"What is it, you know, Jackie? Tell me, what's this secret, sweetheart, that has made you crazy?"

"You really want to know?"

"I'm dying to know."

"Then lean closer, and let me tell you more. . . ."

THE HUBRIS OF AN EMPTY HAND

Charles Stock stood away from the rear door of the bus, allowing passengers to get off as others rushed to get on through the front door. The number Eleven bus was packed with people, and to alight, a fair amount of pushing and shoving was needed. A man stepped on Stock's foot, and Stock moved back, even more, leaning tightly against the railing. Stock had a good spot and didn't want to move too far, as he needed to scrutinize as many faces as possible—even though the unusually cold New Orleans winter night made the passengers move quickly, with their faces hidden behind woolen shawls and their heads covered with hats and beanies. The Mardi Gras season's start had added an inordinate number of passengers to this usually deserted route.

The bus driver generously allowed as many passengers as the bus could manage, but she finally had to close the doors, leaving a few people waiting on the sidewalk for the next one. The bus groaned under the burden of its human cargo and lurched forward like an old, overweight man. Stock stood where he was and continued to observe the other passengers with his discerning eyes. He was a tall, muscular man with constant facial stubble as if he could never get a clean shave. He wore a woolen suit with a starched white shirt and a thick tie underneath his heavy coat.

The bus halted suddenly and heavily at the traffic light, and Stock was propelled forward, stopped only by the other passengers' bodies. He smiled apologetically and tried to hold onto a handle as an anchor. He continued his observation. His five years of searching had made him efficient in scanning the faces of strangers, and he did so as he leaned back in the now warm spot on the bus.

After a few minutes of a smooth ride, the bus stopped and then jerked forward a bit and then halted noisily at the next stop.

"Spenta Park," the bus driver announced, and the passengers commenced their struggle to leave as others struggled to get on.

Stock's eyes fell on a young man who was sitting on the bench outside the bus window. He tried to stand up, but as if something had pulled him down, he toppled and fell on the other side of the seat. It seemed no one had noticed him. The man raised himself up and took a couple of steps toward the bus, but his legs gave out, and he fell on his side and stayed there. Some passengers on the bus finally noticed and made audible sounds, but no one moved, and a few took photos with their phones. A woman outside inspected the man from afar but did not approach him nor call for help.

Drunken, diseased, drugged-out, psychotic, homeless, or just human, whatever the ailment did not matter as these people were part of urban living. There is no reason to panic, as someone will call 911. That thought was on everyone's mind.

Stock hated the people on the bus for their callousness. He stepped off the bus and leaned over the man, and the bus drove away with an audible sigh of relief.

"Are you all right?" he asked, and even to himself, his question sounded moronic.

The man opened his eyes and smiled and sat up straight, his legs stretched in front of him. He was wearing a light charcoal gray suit with a red and black tie and a pair of black-rimmed glasses. Stock could see the man was wearing mismatched socks, one bright yellow and the other bright red. Then there was recognition.

Stock's heart pressed against his chest in anticipation. It had been more than a year since he felt sure about someone. He desperately wanted the exultation that would come with a real discovery—and yet was fearful of the possibility of having to give away the *Gift* he had been nurturing for a long time.

Five years earlier, a stranger had presented Stock with a gift that at first felt like an abstraction, but it slowly grew into something of a wonder. Each of us have a varying capacity for empathy, but Stock was empowered to bestow a sense of solace and contentment on his fellow human beings. He had become a propagator of joy but even a gift from the gods has its own burden.

"I was on my way to see you, Stock," the man said as he stood up erect, and Stock followed him. "But then I saw you on the bus and thought it was best to meet here."

"You know me?" Stock asked.

"Of course."

"And you are Joseph?"

"So, we both know each other," Joseph said.

Stock nodded and then added, "Perhaps the Gift recognizes you?"

"It makes sense." Joseph then reached out and touched Stock's face with his index finger for a moment. "Your journey is ending, Stock. The creator of your Gift will seek you soon."

The person who had bestowed the so-called Gift on Stock had promised he had to only keep it for a brief time, but it had been five years, and Stock had not been able to relinquish his *custody* of it. At times, he felt he was addicted to it and purposely failing on his task. He was like a parent who wants to keep his child with him forever but knew there would be a time when the child would become an adult and need a new life. "How soon?" he asked.

"I do not know, but I hope very soon. You saw first-hand the deprivation of compassion tonight." The Gift needed to be passed from one person to another to thrive, and Stock could feel its deterioration the longer it stayed with him.

"Then take it from me now," Stock demanded though even as he said it, he felt a touch of loss.

"I cannot, and I do not want it. This is your journey. I had my time with this Gift, longer than you can imagine."

"Why? Why such cruelty?"

Joseph laughed. "I said the same thing long before you. But in the end, there is no malice. We each have a task, and yours is the burden of this Gift for now. Use it well while you hold it." He then pointed behind Stock and added, "The next bus is here."

Stock looked over his shoulder and saw his bus approaching. "I have more . . ." he started to say as he returned his gaze, but the man with the mismatched socks was gone.

*   *   *

Stock thought he had found the right person only six months after receiving the Gift, back when he was just learning to understand it. He was living in San Francisco at the time and, on a whim, took the BART—the city's aging but reliable metro system—to go downtown. He didn't expect to find the right person on that ride because when he received the Gift it was intimated that the next person who deserved it might be in another place— or at least, he felt that had been implied. He didn't actually recall being told that; in fact, his memories of the event were just a vague dream of words and faces. Yet, he was confident the next recipient would be a woman and felt very strongly about the instructions that had guided him thus far.

Stock sat on his seat, reading the newspaper, not paying full attention to the world around him, though from time to time he would examine the passengers as they came in, just in case. A young woman entered and sat across from him, and Stock quickly scanned her face. She had a heart-shaped face that her long, black hair was partially covering. She was wearing a full-length black jacket and looked tense with worried eyes. She was wearing a pair of round, thin-rimmed glasses that, at times, reflected the light from the ceiling. She looked at him and he at her, but there was no connection.

He tried again to penetrate beyond her brown eyes, but he couldn't read her. There was something special about her, but he was still inexperienced and could not ascertain anything more, though the certainty that she may be the right person was creeping in his mind.

The train stopped, and one passenger left, and no one else came on. It was still early for Saturday, and downtown stations would not get busy until closer to noontime. The train moved slowly and then picked up speed and rode noisily in a dark tunnel.

"That is wrong," the woman shouted suddenly, and Stock looked over his paper and smiled. The woman had a certain power though he couldn't determine its meaning.

The Gift gave him deep contentment, and when it was necessary, and when its tug within him urged him, Stock could, with some effort, give part of it to others. It was a natural act; a gentle touch or a kind word or two was all that was needed to bring a degree of ease and gratification to others. He'd had to learn to harness and conduct it, and he had done well; he was proud of the deliberate management of his new power.

Stock smiled at the woman, hoping to penetrate her defenses and understand her pain. He wanted to convey to her that he understood her, even if that was not yet the case, if she would just lower her guard.

Stock shuffled the paper nervously. He had never encountered such a person before. He knew they were not opposites; they were both good people, as people go, but she held onto something different; she possessed something dangerous. He was now afraid of her.

"That's so wrong," the woman repeated, and he could see she was losing control. Something was rushing at her and pushing on her.

"What's wrong?" Stock asked in a kind, gentle voice.

The woman looked at him, puzzled as if she could see more in him. She opened her mouth to say something, and he saw a moment of joy in her eyes, and she replied in a hushed voice, "I know. . . ."

Stock stood up and took a step toward her and asked with an inviting smile, "What is it that you know, Miss?"

"I know," she repeated, and he could feel the depth of her misery. "I know," she cried out, and for an instant, there was a connection. But before Stock could understand it, she added, "But I can't tell you." And with that, her armor became as impenetrable as before.

Stock gave a weak, dawning smile and then sat down, knowing that he could not help her. There is only so much one can do, he told himself. She might look innocent or kind, but she must have a mental illness. He lowered his gaze, and for the first time in months, felt despondent. He thought he was there to save everyone. The woman kept her mouth shut the rest of the ride and got off on Powell Street station.

*   *   *

Charles Stock awoke with a sharp jerk as if trying to keep from falling. He opened his eyes and stared at the popcorn ceiling of his San Francisco apartment for a moment, trying to solidify the images. In his dream, the woman from the BART slipped and as she was falling reached out to him, and he could see the dread deep in her eyes. Stock wanted to comfort her and ease her fear, but the only thing he could do was to reach out and grab her. She held him tight, and for an instant, everything stopped, and they saw each other for who they were, and she understood and tried to let go of him. Stock wanted to help her, to save her. But she was stronger and pushed him away, and Stock lost his balance and almost fell the other way, but still reached out for her, stretching his arms as far as they went. But there was nothing but thin air.

Stock closed his eyes and contemplated his dream. He recalled calling her name as she fell silent and disappeared in the darkness. She was frightened and lonely, crushed under the weight of her burden.

It had been almost a year since Stock had encountered the woman on the BART and had not thought of her since then. He wondered why now as there was no room for coincidence in his new life. Everything had a meaning, and the woman, coming back to him, even in a dream, was no accident.

He closed his eyes and tried to go back to sleep, but his mind was a jumble of ghostly memories and abstract feelings. He kept his eyes closed, trying to remember, and the Gift, pounding against him like a drumbeat, urged him to do his job without delay. He wasn't ready. The woman in his dream was fearful yet strong, and as she fell into oblivion, she whispered something to him. He wondered what she had said in that momentary connection.

The phone's alarm startled him back to the real world. He reached and turned off the alarm, and even though he was still sleepy, he opened his email. He had promised himself to get off this habit, but he and billions of other people were already addicted, and even the Gift didn't have enough power to cure him. He finally relented and got up and showered and dressed. Now, he was late for his downtown meeting—he still had a job to attend to, even if he was the guardian of the Gift, so he took his coffee to go as that had become his routine too. The bus arrived as he made it to the bus stop, and he was soon in the lobby of the Transamerica Pyramid Center with a few minutes to spare. The building was a beautifully designed skyscraper that glowed in a lazy blue hue, and in the mornings, it reflected the Bay and the city below it like a massive mirror.

The lobby was serene and looked like an indoor park with colorful plants, and as usual, it was packed. Stock had to wait for two different elevator cars to arrive before he was able to get on. He was standing next to the buttons, so he became the de facto operator as people called their floors. Stock's meeting was on the penthouse. After he had met everyone's demands, he reached out to press his floor, and at the same time, the woman next to him reached for the same button. Their hands touched, and Stock felt the Gift awakened.

By the twentieth floor, Stock and the woman were the only ones in the elevator. He didn't know what to do, so he stood in the back of the car as it climbed to higher floors. On the twenty-fifth floor, the elevator stopped with a jerk, and the light flickered for a second. For a moment Stock thought it was somehow his doing, though that was impossible. Then the lights came back strong, and the elevator resumed its ascent.

Stock looked over and smiled meekly at the woman, who smiled back. They rode on in silence, but then the elevator again shuddered and stopped on the forty-eighth floor. The lights flickered and then went off and with them the hum of the airconditioning.

Stock reached out blindly for the emergency button, but before he could do anything, the elevator fell a few feet and then stopped hard. The woman gave a short cry and he put his hand on the wall to steady himself. The emergency lights begrudgingly came back on, and they could hear the soft hiss of air flowing through the vents.

"We'll be all right," Stock assured her.

The woman didn't respond and, despite her involutary scream earlier, didn't look afraid. She reached out and opened the emergency panel and pulled out a red phone, but before she could say anything, the ceiling speaker came alive with the husky voice of a man.

"Folks, we're deeply sorry for the scare," he said and then added hurriedly, "These elevators are very safe, and there is absolutely no chance of a free fall."

"Didn't you just see us fall?" the woman asked.

"Please use the phone," said the disembodied voice.

"The elevator just fell a few feet," she said into the red phone while staring at the small camera embedded in the ceiling.

"Oh, Ms. Smart . . . Again, our apologies. It's scary, but it was just an automatic correction to align you with the external door. The mechanic is on his way. You'll be out in no time."

"Are you sure?"

"Yes, Ms. Smart."

She put the headset back in the box and closed the panel.

"Dalia Smart." She offered Stock her hand. "I guess we're going to be together for a while."

"Charles Stock," Stock replied. "Most people call me Stock," he added as he shook her hand. The Gift energized with the contact, and Stock felt a lingering sadness and betrayal beneath Dalia's calm exterior.

"Why?"

"I don't know, Ms. Smart," he replied, trying keep his voice even.

"Please call me Dalia."

"Of course."

"What do you do, Stock?"

"I'm a lawyer."

"Of course. In this building?"

"No," he replied. "And you?"

"Investment," she said.

Stock nodded though he was more focused on absorbing Dalia's sadness. *She loved him and missed him deeply but couldn't wash away the sense of perfidy.*

Dalia took off her shoes and leaned against the wall. She was tall, even with her shoes off.

There was nothing more to say, and she was content waiting for the end of their ordeal. Stock, too, leaned against the wall on the other side of the elevator. He had thought it would be easy and straightforward when the right person showed up, but now he wasn't sure. The Gift was urging him to offer her the final test, the choices that would define her path.

He took a half step, but then he paused. Now, he wasn't sure. What if he was wrong about the options? There was no manual, no guidance, and the Gift had turned truculent. The only certainty in that elevator was Dalia Smart. Yet, he hesitated. He could read the sadness in her, and he wasn't sure if he was prepared to take the crushing weight of it.

The Gift, however, had no such doubts. It needed to move on, and it needed to move on at that moment.

"Relax," Dalia said and Stock was startled, so focused on her inner feelings that he had missed the weight of Dalia's stare. "We'll be okay," she added.

He took a step back and leaned against the wall again. "I know. I just hate confined spaces," he lied.

"Me too but try to focus on something else. Imagine there is a large meadow right in front of us," Dalia said as she glided her hand across the small elevator as if pointing to the vastness of the space.

"I'm okay now, thank you."

"My husband . . ." she started to say but stopped and touched her naked ring finger for a moment and then recovering, "Well . . . anyway . . . he passed away some time ago. . . . He was a real claustrophobe. That's what I wanted to say."

Stock watched her and felt the turbulence of her feelings as they washed over her. "I am sorry," he said.

"Yes. Me too."

"You know what I wish I had now?" Stock asked, staring at Dalia. She shook her head. "I want a large Sundae with all the trimmings. I could kill for Swensen's ice cream."

"I love that place," Dalia said. "Especially the original store on the corner of Union and Hyde."

"My dad used to take me there and I always ordered a—"

"Banana Boat." They said it in unison and laughed.

"I could never finish mine," Stock confessed.

Dalia gave a faux surprise look and said brightly, "You're a lightweight, Stock. I finished the whole thing and then some." She gave a warm smile as if assuring Stock that she was just teasing him.

"It hasn't been the same since Mr. Swensen died, though," Stock said.

He regretted it as soon as the words came out of his mouth, because Dalia's response was a quiet "I know," and then their little connection was lost. Stock, panicky, thought he needed to take some action to reconnect and the Gift that had been observing their banter from the side pressed Stock to make the next move.

"Ms. Smart . . . Dalia?"

"Yes?"

"I can see . . ."

"Yes?"

He had waited too long: the elevator door partially opened, and a man with a thick mustache peered through with a big smile. "Our sincere apologies, Ms. Smart. I hope you were not too inconvenienced."

"I don't want this to happen again."

"Of course. And again, our apologies to you."

"Not just to me, but to Mr. Stock as well."

The man looked at him, surprised as if he had just noticed Stock in the elevator. "Yes, of course. Our apologies, Mr. Stock," he said, though Stock could tell he was still talking to Dalia.

The technician reached out to help Dalia out of the elevator, but she declined his hand and started to put on her shoes. She exited the car, and Stock followed.

"Dalia . . ."

"Yes?"

"Could we meet for a cup of coffee?"

She looked at him for a moment as if assessing him.

"Maybe an ice cream?"

She smiled. "Are you a good person?"

Stock didn't respond immediately. He could tell she wasn't asking this question in jest. If she had asked a year earlier, he would have automatically answered with a confident affirmative, but now his world had changed and he with it.

He gazed at his shoes (they needed polishing) and then looked up and said, "I think so. I know a lot about honesty and try hard to be good."

Dalia nodded and replied, "Okay. We can meet later this week." She then walked away without looking back.

They met at a small coffee shop near Dalia's building, and despite the Gift's urging, Stock refrained from probing her or offering her the choices. For the first time in a year, Stock was himself or at least tried to be himself, freed from constantly probing other people's thoughts and feelings now that he had found the right person to be the next custodian of the Gift. They talked about work and living in San Francisco. They found they had many things in common beyond Swensen's and were happy and surprised to discover both were at Ernie's the night when the city's iconic restaurant closed its doors forever and how much they loved the Black and White Ball though neither had attended the last one. They argued about who had the best salted crab in the city. Dalia insisted there could be no other place but Ton Kiang on Geary and Stock's choice was Wing Lee on Polk, though he had to admit that *his* restaurant had closed a while back.

Stock could tell Dalia enjoyed herself as she had initially insisted that she could only spare thirty minutes. However, after an hour, they were still talking while ignoring her insistent phone. But in the end, she couldn't stay any longer. She put her hand on his and said, "This was fun, Stock. It's been a long time since I laughed."

The touch woke the Gift again, and he felt Dalia's joy wash over like never before. Perhaps Dalia felt the change too as she slightly increased the pressure on his hand as if trying to extract more information through his skin and said, "I can't put my finger on it, but there is something about you."

"Can I see you again?"

She thought for a moment. "I think so," she said with a small smile and then stood up. "Dinner. This Friday."

The Gift stayed quiet for the rest of the week, and Stock was happy he could spend the time being himself. He didn't have to look for a candidate, as he had already found Dalia. He could transfer the Gift to her after dinner and move on with his life. He would be free. He spent the remaining days preparing for the weight of the transfer.

He was early on Friday, so he stood outside Cotogna on Pacific Avenue and waited for her. The sky was clear, and the lights from the buildings and cars shone across the streets. The cool breeze picked up and then died as quickly, and the air became still and warm. It was early summer, and the city was still busy with residents and tourists alike. He had made a reservation for eight, but in his eagerness, he had shown up half an hour early. They offered him a table, but he didn't want to sit at the table and wait. He hated sitting in restaurants, waiting for a date that may or may not show up. He wouldn't know what to do alone at a table anyway. Would he order a glass of wine or water, or just sit? He didn't want to have something in front of him when she showed up, and he didn't want to sit at an empty table either. It didn't come naturally to him, so he waited outside.

He had debated for hours about what to wear, but he settled on a light gray suit with a greenish tie in the end. He was probably overdressed for the restaurant.

At eight o'clock, a cab pulled up to the curb, and Dalia got out. She was wearing a casual linen dress and had her long brown hair loose around her shoulders. She wore minimal makeup and almost no jewelry.

"Have you been waiting long?" she asked as soon as she stepped onto the curb.

He shook his head and reached for her hand, and she grasped his lightly. They walked into the restaurant and sat at the small table by the window.

"Date number two," he said brightly.

"Don't get cocky, Stock."

The waiter showed up, and she asked for a dry martini, and he felt obligated to do the same. The waiter left, and for a moment, it seemed they had nothing to say to each other. They waited in silence, each pretending to review the menu. He looked up to spy on her, but she was already watching him. She gave a small smile.

"Okay, I admit, I'm nervous," Dalia said and then gave a forced laugh to confirm.

"It's been a long time for me too. So yeah, I'm nervous too."

"Then, let's try to be ourselves," she said in earnest.

He nodded, but he didn't know what that meant. He was no longer the original Charles Stock. He had changed, and he carried something that, in the real world, should not exist. Yet, it was as real as anything to him, unless he was dreaming. But if this was a dream, then it was the longest and most elaborate dream in human history.

"You're different, aren't you?" Dalia asked as she leaned closer.

"I am." He hoped he was showing some swagger. But then he wondered if he was too transparent. He looked into her eyes, and her pain was swimming on the surface, and she was trying hard to contain it.

"But is it a good different or bad?" asked Dalia.

"Neither."

"But you are different," she said again and looked at him. He held her eyes, and he could read more and braced himself for what was going to come after dinner. He felt strong and confident when he was standing outside of the restaurant, but now, he could feel the roots of doubt growing within him despite the Gift's effort to squash it.

"I was lost for a while," he confessed without wanting to, and then, "But I'm all right now."

"Tell me more."

He paused for a moment, finally catching up with what he said. He wondered if he was even allowed to have such a conversation. He needed to start the test even though the result was already known. The Gift was active again after days of hibernation and was pressing him to move on.

He made his decision.

"Okay. What do you want to know?"

"Everything."

"Are you sure? Can you handle *everything*?" He meant it as a tease but wasn't sure if she took it that way.

"Yes," she replied with the confidence of a person who did not know what she was asking.

He had no intention of telling her everything. He only wanted to share some of his grief, so she would be prepared for the test, even though this wasn't the way the test was administered. He didn't know why he knew that, but he did—the same way he was sure he wasn't even supposed to go on a date with the Gift's next host. But here they were. Stock liked Dalia and her strength. He liked her beautiful long hair and how her light brown eyes glittered, exposing her feelings. He loved how she gave tiny, fleeting smiles, even when she wanted to look stern. He wanted to know her, like how ordinary people learned about each other, not just by his ability to penetrate into her inner feelings.

"I was married once," he started, and she looked at him without blinking. "I was married for ten years." He paused again, but she didn't say anything, her eyes glued to his. "Two years ago, she left me," he said, not being able to manage his cryptic tone. He then looked down as the waiter approached their table with the drinks.

"I fell apart inside," Stock continued once the waiter had gone, "but from the outside, I was fine because I was strong. That's what they wanted me to be, so I was. I was about to become a partner, and I put all my energy into being just that."

"I know what you mean," Dalia offered.

"Yes. And then one after the other, my parents passed, and I didn't even make it to my father's funeral because I was too busy becoming a partner at my firm. I have two sisters and I could have provided some solace while they were grieving, but I rationalized my behavior, convincing myself that I was more in need than them."

"Cold."

"Yes. That's exactly what my ex-wife called me—a cold, soulless man who had let his ambition destroy his life. Do you want to hear more?"

"I'm not sure now."

"I'll tell you anyway. About a year ago, in fact, it was Friday, April Fools, when I was ready to sign a big contract that would have made me a full partner. The person on the other side gave me an offer—really two choices. . . ."

"Go on," Dalia urged.

"Yeah, she gave me two options: sign the contract and stay on the path that I was on—the path that would make me a partner and all the glory that went with it, or the second option."

"And the second option was?" Dalia asked.

"Nothing," Stocked offered.

"What do you mean?"

"Exactly that. The woman offered me nothing tangible. She gave me her empty hand. She held a pen in her right hand and nothing in her left hand. She presented both hands to me."

It wasn't the whole truth, but it was its essence, and Dalia would learn the details when he offered her similar options. She wasn't ready to know, at least not yet.

"I don't understand."

"I took the empty hand, Dalia. She saved me."

"What was the deal? Who was this woman?"

"It may sound odd, but I can't remember her anymore. I don't know why, but everything about her is very hazy now. But what I am certain of is that she saved me."

"How? How did she save you?" Dalia asked, leaning forward as if trying to force the information out of Stock.

"I can't tell you. But I can do the same for you," Stock offered without thinking.

"Me? I don't need saving."

He had reached a crossroads. He hadn't meant to get there so fast without preparing Dalia, but he'd become lost in his own story, and now he needed to confront her. The Gift was excited and ready, but he wasn't. He had made a mistake by rushing through his own story. He had made a mistake by even speaking about his own life. It was a disaster before it had started, and he needed to backtrack and start again.

"I didn't mean it that way, Dalia. I didn't mean that you needed saving."

Dalia was taken aback but didn't want to start on the wrong path either. He could tell she liked him, easily reading her feelings, and she even thought he was honest and brave. "I'm glad you're good now," she offered pleasantly. "But not everyone needs saving and even if they do, what worked for you may not work for them."

"I know."

She smiled, feeling relieved that he wasn't going to press her. He could feel her relief, and he was happy that he could make her feel comfortable by just speaking to her. He looked at her expectantly, inviting her to pick the next topic. The Gift fell silent; perhaps it too understood the need for patience.

Dalia took a sip of her martini and smiled. "I wasn't happy either, Stock, but I am now," she lied. "I'm glad we were stuck in the elevator," she added in earnest. "It's good that you told me about your family even though it's a sad story. I was a bit scared to see you tonight. It's been a long time since I've gone on a proper date."

"I'm sorry to have spoiled the night before it even started."

"You didn't, but let's not talk more about our pasts, okay?"

"Okay."

The waiter showed up, and after they ordered, they talked about work and movies and books and travel. The night moved fast, and when they were done, the restaurant was almost empty. He paid, and she accepted it without a fuss. They walked out of the restaurant, and she hailed the passing taxi before he could say anything.

"It was fun, Stock," Dalia said, as she held the cab door open.

"Could we meet again?"

"Date number three? That's rather serious, Stock."

"I'm a serious man."

"Then, yes. I'd love to see you again."

She leaned over and kissed him on his cheek, and in that momentary connection, the Gift, in its urgent desire, gave her a sense of solace without Stock's consent. She pulled back, surprised, and smiled, her eyes shining for the first time in a year, and she felt relaxed and sleepy, like the feeling one has after re-

ceiving a long, patient massage. Stock was taken aback by the
Gift's strong will. He needed to be more careful or he could lose
his control over the Gift. He wasn't ready to relinquish it—not
yet, not while he was still getting to know Dalia. He had always
thought it would be easy: he would transfer the Gift to a new
host and move on with his life, and the sooner the better. But his
relationship with the Gift was anything but *easy*. It endowed him
to understand and relish human emotions better than anyone,
while it relentlessly compelled him to seek out and deliver it to a
new host. He wasn't ready. He could already feel the burgeoning
connection with Dalia, a competition of sort with the Gift. So, at
the moment, the only thing he wanted was to spend more time
with her. The Gift could wait even as it pressed against him, willing him to fulfill his duty.

Unaware of Stock's inner turmoil or the Gift's intention, Dalia
leaned over for another connection as if she was in a daze, but
he stepped back.

"Goodnight, Dalia."

"Oh, yes. Goodnight," she replied and stepped into the taxi.

*   *   *

A week passed, and Stock seemed to be living in a state of eu-
phoria. He went to work every day, but he gave scant attention to
the people around him. He was with a new firm and no longer
striving to be a partner. He had a much smaller salary than before and had to move to a small, two-bedroom apartment. After
a year of searching for a new host, he had become like everyone else, busy with his own life and oblivious to others' banal
emotions. He was going on his third date with Dalia, a Saturday
morning trek, and all week he thought of nothing but their outing. He was not much of an outdoorsman, but it seemed a hike
was the most natural next step.

Dalia picked him up at his apartment, as he didn't own a car.
It had rained earlier, and the air felt light, the smell of summer

permeating all around them. Dalia was wearing khaki shorts and hiking boots. She had a sleeveless shirt over a white camisole. She had pulled her hair in a ponytail and was sporting Twenties style sunglasses.

"Are you ready for our adventure?" she asked as soon as he got in on the passenger side.

"Should I be scared?"

"Not with me," she replied and took off sharply from the curb.

She drove fast but efficiently through the city, and before long, they were in the country. It drizzled again for a moment, but then the sun peeked through the clouds, and water vapors rose from the warmed pavement. By the time they reached their destination, the sun was fully exposed, and the clouds were spread into translucent parchment.

Dalia had packed a wooden basket with ornate handles, and each held one handle as they started their trek. The hike was pleasant, and the path, though steep at times, was smooth and solid. The rain had brought out wildflowers in the meadow, and they blanketed the hills with their myriads of colors. A light wind rose from the other side of the field, and the flowers and the grass undulated in a steady wave. They walked in silence for a while, each thinking of the other.

When they reached a bend, Dalia pulled him away from the path, and they walked through the shrubbery and onto an old narrow pathway that seemed to have been forgotten. After five minutes, they reached a large crescent field, and the city and the ocean were below them shining under the bright sun.

There was only a solitary tree in the field, and they walked toward it and put the basket next to its thick trunk. In its full early summer bloom, the tree cast a thin shadow, and Dalia pulled out a red and black blanket and laid it on the ground. She took out a bottle of wine and two glasses, uncorked the bottle, and poured half a glass each. She handed Stock one, and they touched glasses and took a sip. The wine had a deep and rich flavor, and Stock took another sip, feeling its warmth in his body. The walk, the sun, and the wine had made them tired, and they sat next to each other and looked at the city below them feeling content.

"It's a beautiful place," Stock broke the silence after a while.

"Yes."

"Do you come here often?"

"I used to."

Dalia opened the basket again, took out two plates, put several small handmade sandwiches along with pieces of fruit on them, and handed one of the plates to Stock. She served him pleasantly and without the self-consciousness that obscures relationships in their infancy at times, and he welcomed it without reading more into it.

The sandwiches were delicious and subtle in flavor, with thin pieces of cured spiced meat and a mix of herbs and vegetables rolled in homemade bread. Dalia watched him eat and was pleased to see him enjoy her cooking.

"These are amazing, Dalia."

"They're good, aren't they?"

She said it in earnest and without any trace of bluster, and he was pleased that she hadn't demurred like most people would do.

"Delicious," Stock said.

"It's been a long time since I cooked, but I thought I should start again."

"I'm glad you did."

She took her plate and sat next to him, leaning against the tree, and they ate and talked about trivial things, happy to discover that they had so much in common. When they finished their meal, they sat back and stared at the sea below them. After a while, Stock felt the weight of her stare on him and turned to face her. She smiled, and he leaned closer, hesitant at first, but then emboldened, kissed her, warning the Gift to behave.

She kissed him back and Stock wanted the kiss to last forever but, scared of what the Gift might do, he pulled back.

Stock knew, without really understanding why, that he and Dalia could never be together if he passed the Gift to her. She would take the Gift, and she would have no room for him, and he would have no capacity for her. Although he couldn't remember the details surrounding the Gift's transfer, he was confident the same things had happened to the woman who gave him this Gift. Why else could he not remember the night and everything about it, except the woman?

"I'm sorry," he said though he was really sorry that he couldn't kiss her again without risking an accidental transfer.

Dalia nodded, accepting his hesitancy by pulling the basket toward her. She took out four small orange cupcakes, put them on the plate, and poured coffee into a pair of metal cups with wooden handles.

"I haven't made these cupcakes for more than a year. I thought I'd never make them again, but it's my mother's recipe and . . ." She trailed off, and he reached over and touched her hand, hoping to give her some solace.

She withdrew and folded her arms. "I've told you about my husband and how he died last year."

"Yes, and I am so sorry."

"It was awful, Stock. But even worse was how I changed. I was always driven, but his death made me cold and unsympathetic."

Stock again felt her deep sense of loss and betrayal as he had experienced it the first time they met. He was not surprised the Gift had selected her as her capacity for empathy ran deep, despite her own confession to the contrary. "It's natural. . . ."

"No, it is not. At first, I thought, it's not me; it's the world that was becoming cruel and punishing. I blamed my husband's death on my friend, even though she did nothing but help. I haven't seen her or talked to her all this time. How sad is that?"

Stock reached out and pulled her hand into his own and saw the calm in her eyes. "Reach out to her now."

"After our last date, I felt a sense of contentment. Maybe it was your story."

Stock nodded and to lighten the mood, offered, "Don't worry, I'll claim it. It was all me."

She laughed and then stopped sharply. "I called her, but she didn't pick up. I'm not surprised. I called and called again and left a dozen messages of apologies. She has all the right to never forgive me."

"I have learned we have a vast capacity for empathy and forgiveness."

"I hope you're right, Stock. I certainly will do my part."

Stock took another bite from the cupcake. "I'm glad you've decided to make these." He then offered his cupcake to her, and she took a bite from the same side. Stock could see that she was remembering and was both happy and sad.

She missed her husband but was angry still at the way he had ended his life. She wanted to move past it and live her life. Dalia didn't want to forget him, as he would always be part of her—but she also wanted her life back, and at that moment, she wanted Stock to kiss her again.

Stock wanted the same thing. He wanted to lock the Gift deep within himself so he could hold her and kiss her without the fear of what the Gift might do. He was learning to control the Gift more every day, and he was certain he could fully dominate it with time.

Stock put the cupcake down, and she waited, but nothing happened. Impatient with his diffidence, she kissed him. He tasted orange and ginger on her lips, subtle and yet profound, and she welcomed him kissing her back.

*   *   *

The third date led to the fourth and then the fifth, and without them noticing, summer ended, autumn air began to rise, and the leaves started to lose their grip on the branches, slowly falling on the sidewalks and the streets. By the time the rain began to wash them across the town, Stock and Dalia had been together for four months.

By then, Stock had a set of clothes at her house, and Dalia had some at his apartment. The Gift, so defiant in the beginning, had quieted to the point of hibernation, and Stock started to forget about his task and slowly became ordinary.

By their celebratory fiftieth date, Stock wanted to use the opportunity to ask if he could move in with her. He wondered if it was too soon, but he didn't want to overthink it. He loved her and he knew she loved him back. He had read it in her earlier and that had emboldened him despite the shame he felt for knowing her feelings toward him before she was ready to speak of it.

On the Thursday before their date, Stock stopped at Stanton wine shop on Kearny Street at Clay, close by his apartment. He had been going to the same store for many years, and he liked how the proprietor was attentive to his customers and knowledgeable about wine.

The days were getting shorter and colder, and by the time Stock left his office and made it to the shop, the sun was receding behind the tall buildings and an icy breeze had picked up. Dalia had given him a mid-length cashmere coat on their twenty-fifth date, and he was glad he was wearing it. He walked briskly toward the shop and entered it. The store was warm and dry. He walked toward the New Zealand section and stared at the dozens of bottles across the aisle.

"Mr. Stock," Mr. Stanton called from behind his desk, "looking for something special?"

"Something from New Zealand." Dalia and Stock had been talking about New Zealand as a possible destination for Christmas, as neither of them had been there, and he thought wine from there would be a good start.

Mr. Stanton stood up and walked toward Stock, and they both stared at the rows of wine.

"What are you going to eat with it?"

"I don't know, but I'm sure it's going to be something fine, so I need an equally fine wine."

"Then, let me suggest Pyramid Valley Angel Flower Pinot Noir and Squawking Magpie Reserve Marlborough Sauvignon Blanc," he offered and then added, "They are kind of pricey, but they're worth it."

He then took down two reds and one white, and Stock nodded with approval. Mr. Stanton then took the bottles to the register, and Stock followed him obediently. Another customer, a small man with wire-rimmed glasses and a long woolen scarf, was in front of him. Stock stood next to the little man while the clerk tallied his bottles. He was buying a lot of liquor, several large bottles of whiskey.

"Big party?" asked Stock.

The man nodded absentmindedly and continued to fiddle with a wallet full of hundred-dollar bills. He grabbed a few of the notes, and in the process, one of them fell and landed on Stock's shoe.

Stock bent over and took the bill. The man was focused on counting and didn't even see that Stock was waving the money at him. He finally noticed and turned around and grabbed the bill from Stock's hand. Their eyes met, and Stock felt the Gift come alive. He averted his eyes quickly and took a step back. He didn't want to know about the man. He didn't want to know if the man would have a joyful night with his bottles, or if he was going to drown himself in his sorrow. He didn't care, and he didn't want to care. No one else did, so why should he be the one who took on everyone's pain?

He could feel the delay in giving the Gift to Dalia was killing it, but he didn't care as long as he was with Dalia. Joy, pain, and suffering have been part of human experience from the beginning, and they would continue to be with them with or without his help. He didn't want this job, and he was willing to let the Gift die if necessary.

This would have been fine, if only the small man with the wire-rimmed glasses in the wine shop had not that same night drunk those bottles of whiskey and then killed his three young children and his wife before killing himself. It would have been just another sad story, if only Stock could have convinced himself that a little touch from him in the wine shop wouldn't have prevented the tragedy. But on Friday afternoon, on his way to Dalia's with the three bottles of expensive wine in hand, he saw the headline in the *San Francisco Chronicle*. The papers were stacked on an old-fashioned rack in Donut World's doorway on the corner of 9th and Judah. This was his favorite donut shop, and because he knew he had no willpower when it came to glazed donuts, he tried avoiding getting even close to the Donut World. But that afternoon, inexplicably, he found himself on that corner and as he started to cross the street, he saw the headlines, and he knew he had not only failed the man and his family but Dalia as well.

He was a good lawyer, and there were always loopholes in any transaction. Yet it seemed each pathway led to the conclusion that this was going to be his last night with Dalia. He looked at the paper and then the bottles of wine with their fancy labels and inviting colors, and he thought how sad that with the last drop of wine that night, he and Dalia would end too.

* * *

Stock paid the Yellow Cab that had dropped him in front of Dalia's house and walked to the front door. He had a key to the house, but instead of using it, he rang the bell and waited, wishing for a moment that she wouldn't answer, but the door opened, and Dalia stood at the door smiling.

"Did you forget your key again?" She was wearing a black knitted dress and had her hair hanging loose on her shoulders. She kissed him and then took his hand and guided him toward the kitchen.

The first time Stock went to Dalia's house for dinner, she had taken his hand, like she'd just done, and led him to the staircase where a dozen framed pictures of Dalia and her late husband, Amani Parker, were on prominent display. She had pointed to the strong, handsome man in the photo and, as if introducing them, told Stock about Amani, and told Amani about Stock. With the second photo, she talked about their marriage, and with the third, their lives, and at the top of the staircase, she told Stock about Amani's depression and his final act of desperation. And throughout the narrative, Stock had stayed silent but kept his connection with Dalia and given her comfort through his touch.

"Now you know," she had said, and he had kissed her in response.

The second time he went to her house, the framed pictures were taken down, except one, the dark traces of the frames still visible on the wall. They didn't speak of the photos or the man in them. And tonight, as he passed the staircase, Stock noticed that even the black traces of the old frames were gone.

He put the wine bottles on the kitchen table, and Dalia inspected them and nodded with approval.

"You've gone all out. . . . Let's open one of the Pinot."

She took out an ornate decanter from a large wooden cabinet and poured the wine far above it to aerate it. The red liquid made a loud splashing sound as it folded onto itself, and when the task was done, she licked the top of the bottle and smacked her lips.

"Nice," she said. "Open the other one, and we can drink that now."

She took out two crystal goblets and put them on the table as Stock uncorked the second bottle and filled them. They clinked their glasses, and the sweet melody of heavy crystal reverberated for a moment before quieting down. Dalia took a small sip, smiled, and then took a big gulp, holding the liquid in her mouth before swallowing.

"It's a damn good wine, Stock." He nodded, but she had noticed his trepidation. "Don't you like it?"

"I like it fine," he replied and took a sip. It tasted bitter to him.

"Do you like hanger steak?"

"Of course."

"It will go nicely with this Pinot."

"Yes," Stock replied, reaching out to touch the table as if he needed the anchor.

"Are you okay?"

"Yes, of course. This is a beautiful table."

She nodded and moved closer and ran her hand on top of it, feeling the heavy texture. "It was a gift for Amani. I was going to get rid of it, but it took me so long to make it."

Stock reached out and put his hand on top of hers, and at once, he could feel her and all the emotions that had been trapped in the table.

They stood in silence for a moment, but then Dalia asked, "Do you mind if we eat here in the kitchen? I've set the table in the dining room, but somehow I feel it's important to be here again."

He wanted to say no—this handmade table carried its own sad history, and he didn't want his last night with her to also end at this table—but he nodded, and she smiled and started setting the table for the two of them.

As he watched her work, Dalia proceeded to make the hanger steaks, and with every movement, she took a sip from the wine glass. By the time dinner was served, they had almost finished the first bottle.

She put the steaks on a long blue and white platter and alongside some yellow split pea puree in a blue bowl.

"I've been experimenting with Brussels sprouts. Do you want to try?" she asked. He nodded, and she took a small container from the fridge. "It's shaved Brussels sprouts with apples, Grana Padano and hazelnut." She looked at him, and he put some in his mouth.

"This is amazing."

"It turned out okay. I've also made some seared mushrooms and English peas with tomato reduction," Dalia offered as she brought the last of their dinner to the table.

Stock surveyed the table and said, "And I only brought you wine."

"Excellent wine, my dear sir. And that's the most important." She poured the last of the bottle in their glasses. "Though you're not in a drinking mood."

"I am. I will." He took a large sip that he knew would only make the end come sooner.

By the time, the meal was over, they had finished the red wine, and Dalia wasn't interested in the white. He wondered if that meant he could delay his task even further, as the promise of the last drop of wine had not been fulfilled. But even in his inebriated state, he knew he had no choice but to end it all tonight.

"Dalia."

"Yes."

He reached out and took her hands into his. "You know I love you."

"I do? You do?"

"Yes. I do love you."

Dalia smiled and leaned over and kissed him. "I love you too, Stock. I don't make this kind of meal for just anyone, you know."

"I do. And that's why I need to tell you something."

"I need to tell you something too," she said, and waited for Stock to respond but then, not being able to contain herself, said, "I think you should move in with me."

"Move in with you?"

"I know you are your own man and all that but giving up being a partner at your law firm says a lot about you. But this is a bigger place, and I think we are ready for the next step."

Stock wondered if there could be a world where Dalia's and his photos would adorn the staircase and he would be able to live with her like a *normal* person. Stock wanted to reach in and tear from his body the Gift that at the moment felt more like a heavy rock where his heart should be. But no matter his desire to abandon his task, Stock couldn't push away the images of the dead family.

He took a deep breath and emptied his mind, and the loophole he had been seeking all afternoon presented itself to him—*how simple*, he thought.

Yet, Stock was still afraid that he might be wrong, so he looked at Dalia and replied, "No," to buy time, more than anything else.

"What? Why? I thought you wanted the same thing."

"I do. I do, Dalia. But I need to ask you something first."

"What do you need? Just ask. You don't need to be coy about it."

"I . . . I want to offer you something," he said, and then he wasn't sure how the process worked. Would he follow what he thought was the right pattern and then force the loophole at the right moment? Was he supposed to offer the two choices, as had been presented to him? He could offer Dalia the option of going on with their normal life or taking the Gift, and unquestionably she would take what they had over what she would perceive as an abstraction. Would that mean he would have to keep the Gift forever, a Sisyphean task, though with the reward of keeping Dalia? Was this really the loophole he was looking for? But what if he was wrong? None of these thoughts were new to him, but they weren't real until now.

"Dalia," he said, struggling to get his words out, fearful of asking the wrong thing.

"What is it, Stock? You're acting strange."

He pulled back his right hand and formed a soft fist. "Dalia, in my left hand I hold you and a potential future for us together. And in my right hand," he opened his fist and put his hand palm up on the table, "I hold this. I need you to decide. Which hand do you want?"

"Are you totally bunkered, Stock? You want me to choose between an empty hand or us? What do you think I'd choose after we professed our love just now? Is this some silly game?"

"No. No. It's no game, sweetheart. This is important. Don't think, just react. Which hand would you take?"

"I remember you telling me about some woman offering you her empty hand, and you took it, and it saved you. But in reality, the *hand* was not empty, Stock. Was it? You may have attributed it to some fantasy woman who had freed you from the rat race of your life, but in reality, it was you. It was you who chose to become a better person. Do you think now it's me who needs saving?"

"No, Dalia. I'm not trying to save you. I am trying to save us."

"Save us? From what?"

"I don't know. Please. Just take one of the hands. Don't think. Don't analyze. Just do it. Could you do that for me?"

But what if she takes the empty hand as a tease? he thought. Would that commit him to the transfer? He held his breath while searching his mind for plan B.

"Then, of course, I take this hand." She grabbed his left hand and kissed it. "Of course, I take us over your empty hand, silly."

Stock gave a loud gasp and reached over and kissed her, and then kissed her again. "Thank you. Thank you."

"You are ridiculous. Did you have any doubts?"

"No, but the Gift . . ." He didn't mean to betray it, but the words had come out without his control.

"What gift? Did you buy me a gift?"

"No. Yes," Stock replied.

He was confused because nothing had happened. He was the same, the Gift was the same. It still wanted her, and he felt it was sneering at him and his incompetence. He had done the whole thing wrong. He was not done yet.

He wondered if there were other ways, another loophole. If the Gift had the power to wipe out memories, then why not use it to buy some time? He could try to make Dalia forget him until he found another host. But what if she rejected him when he came back for her? What if it didn't work? He could feel the Gift dying, and perhaps that was the solution—but that was more of the dream of his selfish side than a real option. The right solution was to give it to someone else, anyone. It didn't matter. He needed time, perhaps two weeks. That was it. Two weeks. That's all he needed.

Dalia was staring at him, and he needed to make his next move. He remembered their first kiss, when Dalia was drawn by the power of the touch. Then that must be it—a kiss, but a different type of kiss, one that would give her enough of the Gift to soothe her so that she could empathize with him, without his having to explain everything. Just like a short breakup, he thought, until he could be free to be with her.

"Dalia," he said. His voice came out breathless, as if he had been running.

"Yes? More games of options, or may I serve dessert now?"

"Just one more, please. It will be good. I want you to come over and kiss me."

"That I can do," she exclaimed.

She got up, walked over, and kissed him softly on his lips.

"I don't understand," Stock said but more to himself than her.

"What?"

"I don't understand what it wants from me," he cried out in frustration.

"Who? You're scaring me now." And then, as if talking to herself. "That's how it started before, too."

"I'm sorry, Dalia. Don't be frightened. Let's try again. Kiss me again but kiss me like it's our last."

"I hope not," she said.

But it was. And as Dalia complied, Stock was already sure he had picked the right path. He was doing the right thing. He had become a better person because of the Gift, and in return he had served it and humanity. But it was time for another to take the burden. The Gift wanted Dalia, but that was too high of a price for Stock. She didn't need saving like he did. His ex-wife was wrong. It was not always about him and his life. He had become more empathetic and selfless. He would do what was needed to protect Dalia *and* finish his task.

"Was that good enough?" Dalia asked after they kissed.

"It was perfect."

"Could we talk about the moving in together issue now?"

"No, not yet. I want to say how sorry I am, Dalia."

Dalia pressed her hands against her forehead and gave a big sigh. "Sorry about what?" she cried out. "You've gone mad, my man."

"No, darling. Just listen to me, please. I know it doesn't make sense now, but I just want to say: please forgive me for what I am about to say, and please try to understand."

"What are you saying? Are you drunk? I don't understand."

"I do love you, Dalia, but I must go now," he said.

"Now? Why? What's happening? Did I move too fast, Stock? We don't have to move in together if you're not ready. I thought you were . . ."

"Do you trust me?"

"I did, but now you're just scaring me."

"Don't be. Just try your best to remember how much I love you. But now, I need to leave."

"Will I see you tomorrow?" Dalia asked.

"No," he replied, trying hard to hold back his tears. "I . . . I just need a short break, Dalia. Just give me two weeks. That's all."

"Is it what you want?" she asked. She was angry and felt betrayed yet again by someone who she had loved and trusted.

"God, no. But we must. You will understand soon, Dalia."

"Are you breaking up with me after you confessed your love? What kind of a man are you?"

"No. No. I just need a bit of time to finish something. We must. It's what we must agree to do."

"I think you're scared. Let's just have some more wine. We can talk about it later, Stock."

"Yes," he replied. "But I must leave now. Just promise you will not contact me for two weeks. That's all. I will find you again, and I will come back to you. Will you wait for me?"

"I don't understand. We had a good night. We just confessed our love for each other, and now you want time off?"

"Just two weeks," he said again.

"Are you in trouble?" she asked, and when he shook his head, she added, "If you're not ready to move in together, we can just continue as before."

"Will you promise to wait?"

"Of course, Stock. If that's what you want. I can certainly give you two weeks. But I am here for you, too."

She reached out to kiss him again, but Stock ran out of the house, sure he had done the right thing. He had bought them some time, and he would do his best to find a new host. He was focused and determined akin to the time when he pursued the partnership of his law firm.

No plan is perfect.

*   *   *

Stock went back to his apartment and fell into a deep, dreamless sleep. Dalia called a day later and left a short message telling him that he'd forgotten his jacket at her house, and she could bring it to him later. He didn't call her back. He would get the coat back when he was done with his task.

On the second night, he tried to recall Dalia's lips as he fell asleep, her touch, her smell, and all of her being. It was hard to remember those feelings, as is often the case, but he had enough to hold him through the night.

He resumed his task, after four months of hiatus, searching deep into each person he met, looking for the man or woman the Gift was willing to join. On the fifth night, he found himself on California Street, close to where Dalia lived. The Gift had stayed quiet as it was getting sicker, and he knew the success of his mission had become even more urgent. The night was chilly, but he didn't feel cold. He felt strong and warm. He walked fast, repeating her name, and trying to continue to feel her touch and remember her taste even though it was now just a faint dream.

He passed a liquor store on the corner of Fillmore and California, and he walked in and grabbed a bottle of water, thirsty from the long walk. He wanted a cup of coffee, but the coffee machine was broken. The cashier was a middle-aged man with a balding head and thin mustache. He didn't smile when Stock handed him the bottle but held it in his hand for a moment as if weighing it. He scanned the bar, and the price appeared on the cash register.

Stock took out a five-dollar bill and gave it to the man, and the man took it and held it and then opened the cash register. Stock noticed his slow moves, and all of a sudden, he felt a strange sadness blanket over him. And then he knew, he was once again taking on another person's pain. Stock, without thinking, reached out and touch the man's hand, and the Gift woke up.

"Thank you," the man said with a broad smile.

Stock nodded and walked out of the store with his bottle of water, exhausted from his efforts with the cashier and yet feeling exhilarated for providing a little solace to another person. It occurred to him that he hadn't done that for a while, and he wondered why. Then there was a sense of panic when he remembered the man at Stanton, who had gone home and killed his family.

Stock could clearly see the man in front of him in the line but couldn't recall why he did nothing to help. He put his hand on his heart as if trying to connect even more with the Gift, and the Gift in return made him feel at ease. It wasn't his fault. He had been a devoted custodian and would continue in his quest to find the next host, even if it took decades.

He took another step and felt the chilly wind of San Francisco. He wondered where he had left his favorite coat. He hugged himself tight to keep warm, and it occurred to him that not only was he on the wrong street, but he was in the wrong city.

*   *   *

Three years later, Stock was sitting against a far wall of a large board room in New Orleans, hidden behind several other lawyers from his firm, deep in thought about the man with the mismatched socks whom he had encountered only days earlier at the bus stop.

The large room was filled with lawyers and investment bankers, and they all fell into a suspended stillness as a tall woman entered the room. She was ten minutes late, but she didn't rush in as one would when late for an important event; instead, she walked in deliberately. She wore a dark Chanel suit, and her black pumps made a rasping tap on the hardwood floor as she circled the large conference table and sat on the chair next to her boss.

"My apologies, Mr. Wilmore," she offered and nodded to the man in front of the room as if permitting him to continue.

The woman's entrance had brought the speaker back from his reverie, and he stared at her as did the rest of his team.

Mr. Wilmore, a senior partner from Stock's law firm, looked at her and offered in earnest, "No apologies necessary, Ms. Smart. We're glad you were able to join us all the way from San Francisco."

Dalia Smart nodded, and with that, the meeting commenced. She listened intently as the senior partner presented the case and took notes. She had positioned her pad slightly off center so her boss could easily see her notes. Throughout the session, she only spoke a few times, using her words economically but leaving no room for argument from Stock's side of the table. Her boss may have been sitting next to her, and the questions may have been directed at him, and the final decision would come from his lips, but there wasn't any doubt in anyone's mind that nothing would be achieved without her consent.

Two hours into the meeting, Ms. Smart looked up to say something but stopped mid-sentence, as if she had seen something awful. Stock had been staring at her throughout the meeting, and when their eyes finally met, he registered puzzlement, sadness, and anger all at the same time. Stock felt the Gift energizing and knew there was more to this Ms. Smart. She was different—not like the woman in the San Francisco BART, but more like the man with the mismatched socks, though he could not imagine Ms. Smart would ever commit such a wardrobe error.

She recovered quickly and continued with her interrogation of Mr. Wilmore. But she must have seen something in him as well because, at the lunch break, Ms. Smart walked to him directly, ignoring everyone else's bids for her attention.

"It's you!" She held him with her piercing eyes. She looked calm though Stock could read a sea of anger and surprise beneath the façade. Some in the room had turned and were looking at them as she towered over him. Ms. Smart's breathing became shallow, but she closed her eyes and managed to control herself enough so no one else could notice. "We need to talk," she commanded.

He looked at her for a moment, pretending he was considering her *request*. But it was clear who was in charge, so he got up sharply and followed her out of the conference room, and they were closely followed with envious eyes.

The Gift felt more energized than before, though in a different and yet remotely familiar sense.

Ms. Smart walked fast despite her thin high heels, and Stock had to hurry to catch up with her. The elevator doors opened as they arrived, and she held the door for him to walk in. He felt very obedient.

"What are you doing here?" she asked as soon as the elevator door closed.

Stock was confused and thought he had somehow misunderstood her invitation. "I thought . . ."

"You made a promise."

"Did I? Did I misunderstand you just now?"

"Me? It was your idea," she replied, stepping forward as if to touch him but then holding back. Before she could say or do anything else, the elevator door opened, and throngs of people crowded in.

They rode the rest of the way in silence, and when the elevator opened again, they stepped out and stood in the lobby of the massive Energy Centre on Poydras Street. Stock stared at her, feeling nonplussed, and she looked back, holding her own. Stock didn't know why a simple invitation had turned into a row, but it was too late to back down.

"Do you still want me to go?" he asked.

"It was never me. It was you who thought it impossible."

"I don't understand."

Ms. Smart shook her head, her eyes holding onto the anger. "That's what you said before."

"Before? Are you sure?"

"No. No, I'm not sure. How could I be? I was distraught, and nothing was ever clear then," she said.

"I'm sorry."

"That's what you said then, too."

"Ms. Smart, I don't know what to say."

"*Ms. Smart*," she scoffed. "Is that what I've become?"

Stock concentrated hard to make sense of her comments. She was implying that they had met before, but he had no inkling of such a meeting. He would know—he was sure the Gift made him remember every face and every moment. His task would have been impossible without it.

"I'm sorry. Have we met?" he asked.

Ms. Smart made a fist and took a deep breath. "Jesus! Did you have an accident? Did you lose your memory? Or are you playing another sick game?"

"No game. I can assure you of that," Stock offered, feeling desperate.

"You've changed."

"Have I?" he asked. Stock knew he had changed. He was a better man now and not the selfish money-driven man that he had been five years ago.

"Yes," Ms. Smart replied, looking down at her shoes.

He could feel her anger and frustration but couldn't understand its source.

"Ms. Smart, I wouldn't have forgotten someone like you."

"And yet you did," she offered.

"I don't know how, but I am sorry."

"Yes, you said that already."

"I don't know what else to say."

"Nor do I," she said and started to walk toward the elevator.

The Gift cried out, and he felt the pain. She was the one, and yet he had missed it all morning and throughout their conversation. After five years of looking, he wasn't sure how it was possible not to recognize her as the one. He wondered again if he had become addicted and had intentionally avoided any recognition.

"Ms. Smart . . . Dalia!"

She turned around and looked at him sharply. "Yes?"

"Please help me to remember. I want to know more about you . . . about us. Maybe I did have an accident, but I don't recall. I want to know more. Please tell me more."

She thought for a moment and then nodded. "I cannot tell you what you don't want to know."

"Could we at least go to lunch? Please. . . ."

She looked at him for a long time, weighing her anger against her curiosity. Then she nodded and started toward the exit.

He expected to go somewhere close, but as they walked out of the building, she took out her phone and dialed. "I'm ready," she said.

A car pulled up from the side street and stopped in front of them. Dalia got in, and Stock followed.

"Let's go to Rosedale," she told the driver and then added, "Don't go on the freeway, please."

They drove on Poydras and then left on O'Keefe before taking Orleans Avenue, going through the Tremé and Bayou St. John neighborhoods. They made a left on City Park Avenue and then rode over a couple of narrow, unpaved roads before reaching their destination, all in silence. New Orleans is small, and a trip across town is never more than fifteen minutes, and they'd made it way below the unofficial NOLA time limit.

Rosedale is housed in the former Third District Police Station, with bars on some windows as a reminder. The building is white and long, surrounded by homes and some empty fields. Only a chef like Susan Spicer could have a restaurant in this place and be successful, and only in New Orleans.

They walked inside and into a busy restaurant with white linen tablecloths and a well-dressed staff. They were seated immediately. Dalia asked for a dry martini, and he felt obligated to do the same.

"So, what's your story, *Stock*?" she asked when the drinks arrived. She emphasized his name as if she was still uncomfortable with it.

"Same as others," he replied without thinking.

"Huh," she mocked him. "Don't you remember us?"

"I wish I did."

"Did you have an accident?" Dalia asked again.

"No. At least I don't think so. But maybe I have forgotten that, too. I feel there may be some gaps in my memory."

She held his eyes as he spoke, as if trying to assess his honesty, or perhaps looking for a sign of an accident or a trauma. In return, he wanted to open himself up as much as possible.

"I will tell you, then. We were together for four months . . . four months, almost three years ago," Dalia said in one breath. "How could you forget us?"

He could not believe what Dalia just said. Over the past five years, Stock had constrained his conversations with strangers so that he would not intrude into their private thoughts and deeds— the idea of him having a relationship with someone like Ms. Smart for four months? Preposterous.

Dalia took a sip of martini and looked straight at him again. "How could you forget us?"

"It's not possible, Ms. Smart," Stock offered.

"Well," Dalia shook her head but didn't offer anything more.

He added, "So, now you're playing with me."

"No," she said sharply. "I am *not* playing with you. I'm done playing. I'm not even angry anymore. You left me while confessing your love. If you think it was a game, then it was a cruel and heartless game, Mr. Stock."

"But it's not possible," he said again, more to convince himself than her.

"And yet here we are."

Stock was about to respond when the waitress came back to take their orders.

"We are not ready yet," Dalia said.

"Okay, I'll come back in a few," the waitress said and left.

"Was it that horrible?" Dalia asked.

"I don't know what to say," he replied honestly.

"Well, it was. It was for me."

"It may sound strange, but may I touch your hand?" Stock asked.

"No."

"It'll help me remember."

"We tried this once before."

"No. It can't be true," Stock said. He knew it was impossible. He would have remembered, but she wasn't lying. He searched his mind and then tried to compel the Gift to help.

"So, you do remember?"

"It's foggy, but I can feel something."

"You may be feeling your own betrayal. Do you still want to touch my hand?"

"Yes, please," he replied with certainty.

Dalia tentatively put her right hand on the table, and he slowly reached across and put his index finger on the palm of her hand, and then, feeling emboldened, held her hand. He still couldn't remember her, but he could read her, and understand her and feel her, see her pain, know her joy.

She was the one. She was the one to receive the Gift, but there was more. It was more complicated. He knew Dalia was not lying to him, even if he couldn't remember her. He couldn't just bestow the Gift and walk away like the woman had done to him five years ago.

But the Gift wanted to move on. It was exhausted, and it needed a new person. It wanted her, but Stock wasn't ready. He needed to learn more about their past. He could feel there was more to their story, and definitely Dalia wasn't prepared. She claimed they were together three years ago, which meant he had the Gift at the time, and if she was the one, why hadn't he transferred the Gift then? He needed to know, and he needed the time to find out. But he could do something for her first. He could take away some of the deep pain that she had been carrying for such a long time.

"I can help you," Stock offered.

"Help me? How? You can't even remember me. You need to help yourself first."

"No. I can help you. I see your pain."

"I don't need your help, Stock. You've said that before, too. You wanted to help me then, but you abandoned me. Is that how you help?"

She was getting angry, and Stock knew he had erred in his approach. It had happened before, in the early days, when he had misjudged people. He'd learned from his previous mistakes, and he had become sure in his steps, at least until now. He was at a loss on how to calm this situation.

"I'm sorry, Dalia. I meant no offense. I didn't mean it the way you've construed. Maybe I was in an accident. I just need time."

"No," said Dalia, shaking her head, gathering her purse from the back of the chair.

"Just help me remember, please," Stock pleaded.

"You hadn't had an accident when you left me. You asked me to remember you and wait for you, and I did, fool that I was. You asked for a two-week hiatus, and I gave it to you, thinking you were simply scared of moving in with me."

Stock nodded, not sure what to say.

"I waited for you," Dalia said again. "I believed you and gave you the two weeks you wanted, but when I came to your apartment, you were gone—no forwarding address. No notes. No apologies. I thought . . ." she trailed off but then added, "I don't know what I thought. I blamed myself, but now I only blame you. So, no, I don't want your help."

She then stood up and left the restaurant without another word, leaving Stock with a half-empty martini glass, no lunch, and a newfound, unshakable fear.

*   *   *

Stock called an Uber from the restaurant and went back to the meeting, but Dalia had already canceled the afternoon session. Later that evening, he asked his boss if he could skip the next meetings and was told that the exact request was made from the other team.

"Did they say why?" Stock asked.

"No. They just thought there were too many people from our side in the room and thought only the principals should attend for the next few days."

"It makes sense," Stock offered.

"Does it now? It didn't make sense to me, and it seems you know Ms. Smart."

"We crossed paths in San Francisco, nothing more."

"And you would tell me if there was more, correct?"

"Yes, boss," Stock agreed and walked out of the room before he could be interrogated any further.

Stock didn't attend the meetings, but it didn't prevent him from spying on her as much as he could. The Gift was urging him. But nothing came of it, and Dalia went back to San Francisco after a few days.

At the Gift's bidding and against his judgment, Stock followed her back, went to her office, and asked to see her.

"She won't see you," her assistant told Stock. "Not after what you did."

"Do you know me?" Stock asked him.

"Of course, I know you. We met several times. I guess Ms. Smart is right, and you have lost your memory. But that doesn't excuse your past behavior, Mr. Stock."

"Please. Just tell Ms. Smart I am here."

"She knows."

He repeated this every day for a week, but Dalia never called security and that emboldened him. Finally, she relented and allowed for a meeting.

"Thank you for agreeing to see me," Stock said as he walked into her office.

"This will be the final time, Stock," Dalia said without getting up from her chair. "I agreed to see you so I can tell you in person: There is no us."

"Dalia . . ."

"Why are you pursuing me when you can't even remember me?"

"I am trying to remember. I know I was not in any accidents . . . so it can only be the Gift."

"What? What nonsense is that?" Dalia shouted and stood up. "It's time for you to leave."

"Just give me a few minutes, Dalia. Let me try and explain something, and if in the end you still want me to leave, then I will."

"You have five minutes."

"May I touch your hand again?" Stock asked.

"Definitely not. I'm tired of your games."

"It's not a game. It's just so you can see . . . no, so you can *feel* that I am telling you the truth."

She scoffed. "Through our hands?"

"Yes. Yes," Stock said and took a few steps toward her. "Please."

"Okay, if that will make you leave me be," Dalia said.

"Thank you," he said and put his hand on her desk, palm up. He took a deep breath and tried hard to put a wall around the Gift so it would not escape him. "Put your hand on my mine but don't press."

She did as she was told. "Now what?" she asked.

"Do you feel the energy between us?"

"No," she replied, and then, "Wait, there is something. What is it?"

"It's a Gift that I have been carrying for five years."

"Is it like an electric stimulator of some sort? Are you in some cult?"

He shook his head. "No cult. No device." He then looked up, stared into her eyes, and explained all he could while holding back the Gift, which pressed hard against him.

"It needs a new host. I have kept it longer than I should, and it needs to move on," Stock said at last.

Dalia pulled back her hand.

"And you must find it a host?" she asked. "Is it a parasite?"

"Yes and no. So, you believe me?"

"I don't know. I could feel something through your skin, a sense of calmness and contentment. Is that it?"

"I believe so. But this has been with me for so long that I don't recall how I used to feel."

"And this so-called Gift was the reason why you were acting strangely three years ago, and that's why you left so abruptly?"

"I think so, but I cannot remember. Will you tell me everything you recall from our last day in San Francisco?"

She closed her eyes for a moment and told him about their last date, the fiftieth. She told him about the food and the wine and then his strange request, the final kiss, and the promise of his return.

"Do you recall any of that?" she asked when she finished her story.

"The more I see you, and the more we touch, the less obscure the memories are becoming. It's still a thick fog, and my vision is blurred, but the memories of the feelings are strengthening with each passing moment.

"Do you want to hold my hand again?" Dalia offered generously.

"I do, but I am afraid I might not be able to hold this Gift back."

"It's a good story, Stock. But you must recognize deep within you that what you call a 'gift' is your own sense of guilt and empathy and normal human emotion."

"No, it is as real as you."

"Then I must also be a figment of your imagination. I can't lie. . . . I did feel something through your hands. But I once loved you, so it's natural to have some residual sensations. I'm not a psychologist, but if believing in this thing makes you think you are a better person, then fine. But now what?"

"I must return to New Orleans, because I'm certain the next host can be found in that city. But could I come back after to see you?"

Dalia thought for a moment. "I'm not sure, Stock. This is too much. I'm still digesting this fantastic story. I accept that you believe it, and that you thought you were protecting me by leaving. It was cowardly, and you should have told me then what you just shared. We could've solved this together."

"I'm sorry, Dalia. I recall my desperation now. You just don't know what it is to carry this burden, which can take hold of another person and take them away from your life forever," Stock said as tears crawled down his face. "I felt your love for me when we touched, and I must have loved you very much as well. I want to come back."

Dalia wiped the tears from his face and said, "Come back to me when you have freed yourself of this horrid thing."

*   *   *

A month passed since Stock had met Dalia in her San Francisco office. He had called her every day, and at times she would return his calls. She was kind, but he knew there was no hope until he could unburden himself of the Gift.

Stock was on his way home from work, and as usual, he got off the bus one stop short of his own and started the walk toward his small flat. He had been doing this since he'd moved to New Orleans, somehow believing this leisurely walk—a last-minute search before resting for the day—would increase his chances of finding the person. He passed by the small liquor store around the corner from his house but didn't go inside, as a quick scan informed him that there were no customers inside.

"Can you spare a dollar?"

The voice startled him, and he searched for the source. A homeless man was half lying next to a green and blue railing only a few feet away from the shop. He had never seen the man before, though his setup was evidence of his long residence at this location.

"Hey man, can you spare . . ."

Stock looked down and saw the man for the first time. He couldn't believe his eyes; could it be that simple? Life's a twisted cliché, he thought to himself. His breathing became shallow, and he told himself to slow down. In his eagerness to find a new host, he had been aggressive, and each time he had been wrong and disappointed. He'd spent a lot of energy on a woman only a day earlier to find that she was not the right person. His eagerness to return to Dalia had made him impulsive, and he couldn't handle another near miss.

Stock approached the man slowly and kneeled in front of him. He calmed himself as much as he could while piercing into the puzzled homeless man. The eyes don't lie.

"Look, man, I just need a dollar to eat," the man pleaded, adding the smell of fear to the other odors that surrounded him. Stock, still kneeling, cleared his mind, trying to contain the excitement. He had been waiting for this moment for a long time, and he wanted this to be perfect.

"Friend, I'm here to offer you something more than a few coins. I'd like to offer you a choice that might change your life," Stock said very slowly and quietly, though his desire was to shout out in joy. He waited for a reply, but none were forthcoming. Both men stared at each other, expectantly for a while.

"Can you spare some money?" the man asked again, more as a matter of routine than out of expectation of anything tangible.

"Yes, I can offer you money, but I can also offer you more."

"Okay, money!"

"Hear my offer first."

"Whatever you say, boss."

"I'm going to offer you two options," Stock began, "but before I do that, I'd like to reach out and touch your hand."

Oddly, the man wasn't surprised at the request and nodded in assent.

Stock reached over and touched his hand with his index finger lightly, and he knew immediately what options he would offer the man.

And when it was done, Stock looked at him, expecting to be repelled by him and forget about the Gift, as the woman had done—but Stock stayed the same as the man transformed and became whole. The man stood up, and he was clean and brash. Stock was reminded of the man with the mismatched socks.

"Oh," Stock uttered, "You're Joseph, aren't you?"

The man laughed and touched Stock with his hand, and Stock felt calm and warm. "No," the man replied. "I'm not Joseph, though I can see why you might think I am."

"Then who are you?"

"I am the creator of this Gift."

"Then why not just take it back from me? Why make me go through this silly game?"

"I wasn't sure you would agree to just give it to me, and I couldn't force it from you. You had to be ready."

"Am I truly free then?"

"Yes."

"And Dalia? Is she safe?"

"She was never in danger, Stock, but yes, rest assured that the Gift no longer wants her, even though she has a bit of it in her. You all do."

"Me? Still?"

"Yes."

Stock felt horrified and took a step back, shaking his head. "No. No. Please take it all back."

"Do not fear, Stock. It will not harm you or her. When I first made the Gift eons ago, its first owner shared small pieces of it with others, and then others shared their pieces, and so on. You have a bit more than others, but Dalia holds some, as does the person who gave you the Gift. But that's a topic for another time."

"What about everyone else?"

The man shook his head as pain brushed across his face. He gave a sad smile and replied, "Not everyone, Stock. That was our failure. . . ."

"The Gift made me forget Dalia. Why?"

"The Gift doesn't have a mind of its own, Stock. You tried to keep it and made yourself forget."

"Will you restore my memories of her?"

"No."

"No? Why such cruelty?"

"There is no cruelty, Stock. Your memories are yours to restore. You willed yourself to forget, so will yourself to remember."

"No, it was the Gift," Stock insisted.

"No. It was always you."

"Then, I will remember you," Stock deduced.

"No, you will not."

"Will I forget everything about the Gift, then?"

"Not all, but it will be hazy, like a nice dream that you can never truly understand."

"I gave years of my life to this and then nothing," Stock moaned.

"*Nothing?* Have you forgotten the power you held already? You're both free, so move on. And I am whole again, so I can move on with my duty."

"Perhaps Dalia is right, and all this is a figment of my imagination. Perhaps I am talking to myself now. But it doesn't matter, because I am free of this relentless leech. I can be a normal person now, for Dalia's sake."

"That is fine, too, Stock. But it's time for me to depart," the man said. And with that, he was gone, and Stock was standing alone in the street.

I will remember you, so I can keep myself sane, he told himself.

*　　*　　*

"Are you okay?" Dalia asked in a hushed tone and leaned over and put her head on his chest.

It was still early in the morning, but the sun was creeping in the horizon, threatening to wake the whole city of New Orleans with the flood of light. A slow breeze was dancing with the white muslin curtain, and a whiff of early morning spring drizzle made Stock sleepy again.

It was their first night together again, after four dates—after fifty dates three years earlier—and her shy act of tenderness convinced him that he was close and on the right path.

He tried to remember, but only vague images of a man appeared in his mind. He wondered where he had seen him. It was so clear a few weeks ago, but now it felt like a dream that was so real for a moment and then fleeting as soon as you wake up. Stock closed his eyes and tried to bring the man to life, but all he could see were his mismatched socks.

He and Dalia were still debating what had happened to him in the past three years and why he would be afflicted with this strange amnesia. As days passed, he recalled increasingly more of his time with Dalia in San Francisco, but after a while, even the past didn't matter as they tried to move on.

He looked down at Dalia, and she looked up and smiled.

"I'm fine. I'm happy," he said with the same tenderness, and lowered his head and kissed the top of her head. "Go back to sleep."

"Okay. You too."

"Okay."

They both fell into a deep, dreamless sleep as the breeze picked up across the town, and the sun rose higher, filling their room with a strange brightness.

THE GODS IN-BETWEEN

Three men sat around a table in a small tavern in the center of a city called Susa—a city of immense importance that would survive for over five thousand years. Today, however, marked the first year of its conquest by the Persian King, and there were crowds in the streets in anticipation of the King's visit. The weather had warmed, and the trees were showing the first signs of spring. It had drizzled earlier in the day, settling the dust, and making the air churn with the earthy smell.

The small tavern had withstood hundreds of years of Elamites and Assyrians, and the patrons would not be faulted for believing it would endure the Persians too. The inn was busy with men and a few women eating lamb stew and drinking the region's dark, rich wine.

The place was noisy, with many conversations in a multitude of languages, but the three sat silently around the table. The men appeared to belong to the same family as they looked similar— same eyes and nose with a round, symmetric face. They were wearing identical Elamite cavalry costumes that indicated their high rank in the Court. Two of them wore low leather sandals with bare toes, fastened by four straps, but the person at the end of the table had selected a Susa yellow shoe for his left foot and a Persian royal red for his right.

The barmaid who had served them their wine had spoken to them in what we now call Ancient Persian, and the three replied with the same fluency as if it were their mother tongue. She had put a clay jug of wine and four goblets on the table, as she had been instructed, but did not seek payment, even though it was essential on such a busy day.

The three sat and waited.

The tavern's door opened, though no one was there, and a light wind entered the room as if it had been waiting outside for an invitation. The barmaid had come by the men's table to ask if they wanted some of the stew, but as she opened her mouth, a shiver ran down her spine, and her body trembled in response. At the very same moment, a few other customers felt the same chill.

However, the feeling was not widespread. Those who were sitting next to the open window, where the warm sun was streaming in, thought the light had dimmed a bit, as if a cloud had passed in front of the sun. A few looked up, but the sky was clear and blue. A few others, especially those closest to the door, felt a sudden melancholy deep within them, remembering the loss of loved ones. And a few felt nothing at all. For a moment, there was an absolute pause, and silence blanketed the room, and then all was gone, vanishing with the same speed that it had materialized.

Death appeared as he always did and sat regally across from the three men. The black cloak draped around him made him look taller. He had a long, strong face with deep dark eyes. He looked neither old nor young, and if one had the will to look into his eyes long enough, one could see the immense power that resided behind them.

Death beamed and took a sip from the cup that had been waiting for him. The barmaid looked at him, and he nodded.

"Go on with your work, Spenta. You will be fine for many years to come." Spenta bowed and walked away.

Death followed her with his eyes for a moment and then turned around and faced the three, and as a way of explanation, offered, "I try to make myself as pleasant and ordinary to humans as possible when I show myself to them, but some still can sense my true self and need some reassurance of their longevity. That's why I try to stay hidden most of the time." He gave a small smile as if he found the human's fear of mortality amusing. The others nodded, as they knew Death and his odd sense of humor well. Death then turned serious and asked earnestly, "Have you heard of the tale that is being told in the Babylonian Talmud?"

The other men shook their heads slightly but did not speak.

Death looked ahead through the window and stared at the blossoms on the trees across the tavern. "It'll be said better later, two millennia from now, but the essence of it is:

One day Joseph noted that I was sad. 'Why art thou sad?' he asked me. I answered, pointing at the men sitting behind him, 'Because, I must have these men by tomorrow.' Joseph did not want to lose his companions, so he sent them to Susa to be safe. But when they reached the city of Susa, and after they slept a restful night, I took their lives before the new sun rose in the sky. Joseph saw me that night and observed that I was full of mirth. 'Why art thou joyful?'—'To Susa, you sent your companions, where they were to meet me.'"

"Am I Joseph?" the man with the mismatched shoes asked.

"You may be one day, but not today."

"We are in Susa, and I brought them here. Did I wrong them as Joseph did his companions?"

The man in the middle stirred, but Death avoided his eyes, still staring ahead. "True. But the parable is of men and not of our kind."

"I gave them the *knowledge*," the man at the other end of the table said. "I don't believe I've done them wrong. This was not a conspiracy against anyone."

"I am Death," Death replied. And then he turned around and looked at the three at once. "I don't take lives, as human beings erroneously believe, but rather I'm the conduit from life to death. I don't take pleasure in doing my job, but neither do I shirk from doing it as I should. I was born with humans, and I will cease my existence when they end. I am here and now, but I am also there and then. I can see what you cannot. I have a job, and so does each one of you."

Death paused and looked at each man with a focus that only he could possess. The man with the mismatched shoes was called Misery, though he had been called *Achlys*, *Oizys*, and many other names throughout history. Still, none described him as it should. He was almost as old as Death, and he had been present in as many places and times as Death. And the man next to him was Empathy, and he was much younger, generations younger. He, too, had many names such as *Eleos*, *Rashnu*, and *Vishnu*. And the last person was called k'Nowledge. Compared to the rest, he was a child, though he had become the most powerful, acquiring names such as *Mimir*, *Odin*, and *Anahita*. They were men for today, but they were also many other things at various times. And of course, they were not alone as there were others like them—Eros, Mithra, Zurvan, who held the infinite time, and Angra Mainyu, who hated the humans and sowed discord and chaos—some keeping companions and others staying aloof.

"We have been faithful to our tasks. We are here to help them, but we are no slaves," Misery said.

Death shook his head with sympathy. "We evolve like any other being, but we will always have to do our tasks. We can only be who we are in our core."

"I've tried to be who I am meant to be," spoke Empathy for the first time in his usual deep, warm voice.

Death smiled but shook his head. "We must disagree. You're young and impetuous."

"But we cannot die until the end," interjected k'Nowledge.

"I'm not sure if it's true for all of us," Death replied.

"How long?"

"Long enough that my story is told again, and again."

"My intention was good," said Empathy.

"Perhaps, but its consequences are unpredictable."

"We can take it back," offered k'Nowledge.

"It's too late. Your infection is spreading as we speak. Where do you think this parable came from?"

"I can still stop the spread. It was a tiny piece. I can take it away from the King, and it will die its natural death," said Empathy hurriedly and without much conviction.

"Compassion is not something you can take away. You know that well," Death said.

"How did it spread?"

"As soon as you gave it to the King, he felt it, and he liked it. Perhaps he was ready for it; perhaps it was inevitable. I do not know. You gave him a gift, and it grew within him, and he didn't have the knowledge to understand it or manage it. He did not recognize the feeling. He had no name for it. Yet, he used it to free the people he had conquered in Babylon. He, unintentionally, broke your gift into pieces and passed some of it to his people."

"Aren't they better for having it?" Misery asked.

"We don't know. We cannot know everything. The fear is that some will be immune to it, and in the end, it may not help them."

Empathy smiled and leaned forward to make his point. "Is that so bad?" he asked in a hushed tone. "I disagree that they were better off without it. How could they evolve without true compassion, and not what they have been espousing as such?"

"Human beings were doing fine before your interference," Death replied.

"Were they? They were uncivilized and brutish, and now they feel something for their fellow men," Empathy said.

"I do not have the answers you seek. I know that you changed many lives, and what was mine will not be mine for decades. And those lives will create more lives and then more and then more. In the end, it will all be balanced from my end, of course, but the lives that were not meant to be, will be."

k'Nowledge leaned forward too. "I believe we've disproved your parable."

"You're a child, yet you're the most culpable. You've infected these conquered people, and the infection will grow stronger in years. They will know more than others, and that will be both their blessing and their penance. And the few lives that were to be taken now will be taken in multiples and all at once then."

"You cannot see the future so clearly," k'Nowledge rejoined. "I did not *infect* them. I gave humans a gift like Empathy has, and with our combined gifts, they will be better for it."

"I know my occupation," Death said wistfully. "Most misunderstand the allegory. It is not about one or two, but about nature's balance. And for certain, this balance will not change. These people, too, have a destiny, and they must keep their appointment. And they will do so in the most horrific way."

Death leaned closer to k'Nowledge and Empathy and proclaimed, "And for what you have done, you will be banished from the earthly realm for two thousand years."

"Why you? Why you as our judge and jury?"

"I am neither. Each of us has a job, and mine is to guide you from life to death."

"We are gods," k'Nowledge declared.

"Yes, in your ways, you are. It's the cruel irony that by infecting the humans, you have condemned the gods to slow oblivion."

"Who will do our jobs then? Who will guide them through time?" Empathy asked. He looked sad and worried and looked at each of his companions for support.

"Misery will absorb both empathy and knowledge. He brought you here, and therefore, he will carry the burden."

Misery stood up sharply. "It's both cruel and impossible. I cannot be all three at once. My job is to be there when the wretchedness of the world is upon the people. One cannot have a gift that gives when one requires selfishness. Despair does not want to empathize with another. I reject the Gift, but I'm willing to be the guardian of this infection that k'Nowledge has brought on them. I am certain it will need me when it has grown beyond human capacity."

Death stood up too. "You and I have been comrades in our tasks from almost the beginning, but we are nothing but simple servants. You have no choice in this matter, my friend."

He reached over and touched the two, and then there was only Misery, with his mismatched shoes, standing alone with four empty wine goblets.

*   *   *

Two women sat around a small, round table in Taberna San Isidro on Calle de Toledo in the center of Madrid. The autumn was almost over, and the threat of winter had brought poor weather and frosty nights. The proprietor had all the windows shut as soon as the sun edged closer to the west, and then he ushered everyone inside from the sidewalk tables. The night was going to be cold.

The room was full of men and women who were sitting around narrow wooden tables having their *merienda*. The talk of the town was about the return of King Phillip III back to Madrid after abandoning the city as the capital of the Empire five years earlier in 1601. The move had decimated the city's economy, with close to fifty percent of the residents moving from Madrid to Valladolid, following the king. But with the return of the Royal Court, the city was already feeling like its old self and with the prospect of even more greatness in the near future.

The two women at the round table were in their mid-forties but looked youthful, as though time had left no imprint on them. They were dressed fashionably, appropriate for their rank in the Court, each wearing an identical gold dress with wide red and black striped sleeves shaped with whalebone, intricately designed stomachers, kirtles, and collars. Their skirts were voluminous, while their bodices revealed significant décolletage. One was wearing a string of white pearls that shone in the light, and the other a simple gold necklace. They were sitting at one side of the table, as if leaving the rest of it for a larger guest. Each had a cup of what we later would come to call espresso in front of her, though at the time it was closer to a weak, unfiltered Turkish coffee, but neither had been touched. They looked almost identical in shape and size, tall and slender. A casual observer would be forgiven for thinking them if not twins, then siblings.

Empathy was sitting closer to the door and seemed to be content. She had pulled her long auburn hair back into a rolling ponytail and held a small smile on her face along with a definite sense of belonging. k'Nowledge, on the other hand, looked unsettled. She had cut her hair short, almost boyish, and her eyes appeared tired and unfocused, like when one is awakened suddenly from a deep siesta.

Empathy picked up her cup, more like a small, shallow "dish," and k'Nowledge followed tentatively, and they looked at each other before taking a small sip, then quickly drained the cup. They were sitting with their backs very straight as if at attention.

When the waiter came by, Empathy pointed to the cups and said, "Tres cafés, por favor."

The waiter nodded and collected the empty cups. He did not see anything strange about their behavior or look, or even the fact that they had ordered three coffees and not two. He only saw two elegant women having coffee. He was about to ask if they needed anything else, but as soon as he opened his mouth, he felt a chill run down his spine, his body shivering in response. The dark feeling cascaded across the room, affecting most customers, but not all, and their voices ceased, and the air felt tight.

Then the mood vanished with the same speed with which it had arrived. The waiter closed his mouth and walked away to get the coffees, and the rest of the customers went back to their conversations—the moment forgotten already.

The two women looked up and smiled shyly at Death, who had appeared a moment earlier, and now sat across from them.

"Did you order one for me as well?"

"Of course," replied Empathy with a soft assuring voice.

"I shouldn't, but I do love coffee," Death added solemnly, and the others nodded in agreement. He was wearing a long black cloak as he has done for millennia, but today he had decorated his long sleeves with red velveteen bands. His hands were hidden under the large sleeves, but when he stretched his arms, his long, manicured fingers peeked through. The large hood of his cloak rested on his back.

He looked at the women with a fatherly fondness. "Welcome back."

"Thank you," they replied in unison.

"It's been a long time, hasn't it?"

"Yes," k'Nowledge replied, slumping back a bit in her chair.

"Was it difficult?"

Empathy replied in a rehearsed tone, "We were in the Swedish Prison with its putrid yellow cinderblock houses, and time lost its meaning, and we were there but not there. We lost who we were and why we were there. And reality became fluid. But then we learned to focus, and it became like a theater, watching the past and the present and seeing the humans grow and the gods becoming a mere abstraction."

Death nodded with sympathy. "I've been there, though it was not always called by its current name."

"Perhaps the name is meant as a joke, even if I cannot see any humor in any of it," replied k'Nowledge.

Death leaned back a bit to see the women better. "In the end, your *gift* did truly little for humanity, and their vast *knowledge* made them efficient in their cruelty. One only has to consider the Crusades, just to name one amongst so many other untold brutalities."

k'Nowledge shook her head vehemently and retorted, "It's not fair to blame us for their cruelty. It's inherent in their design. We had no hand in that. And why not focus on their achievements for good? They're kinder and gentler. They care about each other, and if we're to be blamed for the bad, then we must get the credit for the good as well."

Death nodded, acquiescing to k'Nowledge's logic. "I see Empathy is coping better than you." He then looked about. "Where is Misery?"

"Misery has changed."

"Yes, he has become Joseph, hasn't he?" Death said.

The waiter came with their coffee but paused before reaching the table. He stood for a moment, confused about his strange hesitancy to take the last step.

"Step forward," Death commanded, and the waiter, as if released, advanced, and put the cups on the table with the utmost attention.

"May I get you anything else?" he asked, looking straight ahead.

"We are good, and you'll be fine, at least for the *moment*," Death replied without looking at him.

The waiter smiled and then, as if he couldn't contain himself, gave out a big laugh. He quickly covered his mouth and then offered, "My apologies."

"No need. Go about your business."

The waiter nodded and left quickly.

"They misunderstand us, don't they? That is why I try to stay away," Death said.

"We must be made whole again," Empathy demanded.

"You will never be that. You gave part of your beings to humans, and they took it, and it metamorphosed and spread amongst them. It no longer belongs to you."

k'Nowledge looked at Empathy as if for affirmation. "We understand, but our core beings are still with Joseph, and without them, we cannot exist in this world. I feel it more than Empathy, perhaps because I'm younger, but we're both hungry and empty, and we must be satiated again, or we will perish."

"I believe humans need us more than ever, even if they no longer believe in us," said Empathy.

"I agree. But we must ask Joseph to meet us," Death said.

*   *   *

A man sat at a small table in Caffé Greco in San Francisco's North Beach district. Spring was ending, and the air had grown cold, as is common in the city, and the intermittent rain kept the sidewalks shiny and slick. Then the sun came out in full force and dried the streets and warmed the air. The proprietor opened the large glass doors and put chairs and tables on the sidewalk.

The man took the opportunity to step outside with his espresso and sat at one of the small white round tables. He finished his coffee, and then when it was time, he went inside again and ordered two lattes and, on a whim, a full portion of tiramisù.

The man was wearing a light charcoal gray suit with a starched shirt and red and black striped tie. He sat down at the table, crossed his legs, showing his mismatched yellow and red socks. He was also sporting glasses with turtleshell frames. He sat and waited as the sun grew warmer, and more people came out of their apartments and flats to enjoy the day.

Then a small wind picked up, and the hum of customers that had been steady up to now died down for a moment, and a sense of foreboding permeated the café. And a few tourists who were checking out the restaurant next to Caffé Greco enthusiastically a moment earlier felt a sudden distaste for Italian food. Then, as quickly, the feeling disappeared, and the tourists walked in the restaurant still confused about the earlier feelings of misgiving.

Death sat at the white table across from the man and smiled at him.

"I see you have not changed your ways, but you've certainly changed yourself," said Death.

"You once told us that we could only be who we are," the man answered.

"Indeed. And are you?"

"Yes. I am Joseph now."

"Then why not give back what belongs to k'Nowledge?"

"I no longer possess what was never mine in the first place," Joseph replied.

"Empathy is whole again, but it is k'Nowledge that needs attention."

Joseph shook his head. "How?"

"Empathy felt the Gift's calling from a man called Charles Stock."

"So, Stock finally relinquished the Gift. I had given it to a woman, and she gave it to Stock. For a time, I was worried that Stock would not fulfill his duty. Once I confronted him and tried to guide him, but I wasn't sure if he understood. He offered the Gift to me instead, but I had had enough of that burden. And then I put him out of my mind."

"And why give away something that didn't belong to you in the first place?"

Joseph leaned forward and replied, "I was abandoned in this well of time for millennia, suffering the tug of three emotions. And you dare to ask me why?"

Death waved his hand as if dismissing Joseph's outburst. He grabbed his latte and took a small sip. "It's good. It's perfect actually," he said. He then took one of the forks and took a bite of the tiramisù. Death pursed his lips. "Not so good."

"Her name is Zuleika, the woman who had the Gift first," Joseph offered, and he too took a sip of his coffee. "You met her earlier, or will meet her depending on your current timeline, at a dinner party with her friends."

Death nodded in agreement. "Interesting coincidence."

"I thought so as well. Her married name was Poitifer, though she pronounced it the way Potiphar's wife did. Or perhaps I imagined it."

Death laughed. "Joseph sat in that deep well for eons, and he resisted Potiphar's wife. So, it's rather ironic that you who became Joseph gave away empathy to a woman called *Zuleika Poitifer.*"

"I see no irony or mirth in this affair. For over two thousand years, I waited. The tug of the burdens you bestowed upon me transformed me as I influenced them. You did not foresee the consequences of intertwining our essences in one home so closely."

"The result is rather surprising," Death replied.

"Oh, yes. And only you could describe this cataclysmic event as merely *surprising.*"

Death nodded but didn't say anything, so Joseph continued. "Well, empathy and knowledge did not belong to me, and they felt like prisoners constantly looking for weakness in my defenses to escape. Yet, I performed my duties diligently and kept them at bay. But time and the impact of these so-called gifts changed me too. I became Joseph, and because of that, their urge to flee me and seek their true home increased. I welcomed it."

"Indeed," Death replied.

"I feel no regrets. *Love* interceded, and she gave me Zuleika. It was not my intention for Zuleika to have the Gift, but she took it, nevertheless."

"And she promptly lost it."

"No. Zuleika saw me as who I was and rejected me. So, no, it was I who lost her." Joseph took a deep breath and closed his eyes for a moment. "She felt too much, and she could not handle humans' misery. She passed the Gift to Charles Stock, and he took it willingly, and he was a good steward of it. He helped countless people."

"It's all fascinating, but he has it back now. Empathy connected with Stock in New Orleans, of all places, and he gave it back willingly, as was his duty. Empathy is whole again. But I worry about k'Nowledge. She surely dies, if we cannot succeed, and with her humanity."

"Oh, yes, the *knowledge*. It was too soon for them. They used it well for both good and evil, but I only saw and felt their wickedness. I stayed the course for a long time. However, when the Gift left, I could no longer keep k'Nowledge's core at bay. It had become ravenous and poison to those who touched it."

"I had suspected as much but had hoped it would stay safe with you," Death confessed.

Joseph shook his head and replied, "I did my duty, but then it was taken away from me as if by the sheer will of humanity. A man, a kind man in his core, a man who should not have ever met me, took it away. But in the end, he was not strong enough. He was not brave enough. It was too much for him. It became a disease, and he could not cure himself. You know him, of course."

Death nodded. "Amani Parker."

"Yes."

"When I met him, he was free of the disease, but he'd been left empty. There was nothing there. He was no longer a human," Death said. "I do not often participate in their deaths, but for him, there was no choice."

"That is why I was not there with you, then. Amani gave it away to his best friend. A woman called Jackie Goodwin. Do you remember her?" Death nodded. "She was so sweet. He gave it to her, and she took it willingly to protect him. He didn't deserve her. I wondered if she knew the consequences of her bravado. No matter, as she is now lost."

"Tell me more," Death said.

"I don't know more about Jackie. She has vanished."

"She is still alive, or she would have visited me."

"That much is true," Joseph confirmed.

"Tell me about Zuleika then."

"Oh, I will. Lean closer and I will tell you all. You may need another cup of coffee for this."

*   *   *

A woman was sitting one of the wooden tables in Saint Frank Coffee on Polk Street, her head slightly tilted down, when I walked in. A newspaper was spread on the table, and she had her hand resting on the newspaper with her fingers arched like a dome on top of a column. Even from afar, I could see her gaze was on the paper as if at that moment, she was mesmerized not by the whole article but by a single word.

Saint Frank Coffee has a clean, modern feel to it, with a long, curved white countertop, hardwood floors, and pine chairs and tables. The sun was beaming through the large windows and cast a wide pathway into the café. Despite the brightness of the day, there were small lamps on the walls, aligned on top of each table, shining warm white light on them. The lamp on her table was turned off, or it had a burnt out bulb. Most of the café's clientele were young, there with their laptops. But at a glance, it seemed the woman was the only person that didn't have an electronic gadget.

I was pulled into Saint Frank Coffee by a deep sense of melancholy that had been engendered by her. And now I could see the gloom as it slowly oozed out of her and fell around her, but more like waves than a smooth river. The massive waves would fall on top of the slower, smaller ones, and they would engulf them in a slow-motion dance. The dark gloom made its way to the table and flew on the edges but didn't hit the floor as it hovered like light clouds, then evaporated as it hit the sunlight.

I sat at a table, the only one available, away from her, hesitant to intrude. I had been carrying these conflicting sentiments, these forced tasks, with me for more than two millennia, and I was weary and weak. It had taken everything I had to keep these essences within me separate and stay true to my original being.

I sat at the table looking at her. She had long black hair with an oval face. She had a Roman nose that added intrigue and nobility to her face. She looked up, sensing the weight of my intrusion, and I saw her chestnut brown eyes. I glanced in another direction immediately, and she went back to her newspaper. But I remembered her, or if not her, then the essence that made her, which had come and gone many times in hundreds of years. And the old feelings of love and passion exploded within me, and I became more confused.

The woman was dressed in a smart suit, and her hair was pulled back tightly to keep it from her face. At first, it appeared as though she was reading the paper in a leisurely fashion like one does on a Sunday morning—though that is going out of style even before it had time to mature. I noticed she wasn't reading but rather staring at the paper.

It was her melancholy that had called me in, but it was the Gift inside of me, which had grown in strength, that allowed me to feel her pain. I had nourished the Gift (though it had not been a gift but a curse to me) with my energy, but it had grown to depend on humans, and it wanted out. I must confess the Gift had changed me, too, for I could feel what humans felt, and I was at a loss. Yet the Gift had become bold and was urging me to act.

I had never been hesitant in my existence, but I couldn't find the courage to do my task that day. She looked up from her newspaper again, and our eyes met, and I mustered all my courage and held her eyes with mine. I could feel her profound misery, and I felt ashamed that I had a role in it. We no longer interact with human beings as we once did, but I needed to speak with her. I searched and tried hard to find the strength, though, in truth, it was the Gift that was giving me the enterprise. I stood up and walked toward her, all the while anchored by a strange new feeling. She was an ordinary human being, without any extraordinary powers, and yet she held me with something else, perhaps as Potiphar's wife had hoped to do. One must never forget history.

I reached her table and sat across from her, and she, without words, spread the newspaper on the table. It was the obituary page, and she pointed to a small section. "My father," she said, putting her finger on his name. And then to the column next to it. "And my husband." She then pointed to the next name. "And my mother."

She looked up. "I miss them so much."

She looked down at the paper again and gently circled her family's obituary with her finger, as if trying to reach out to them. She permeated such sorrow that I could see a thick fog hovering around her. I could see that she was trying desperately to escape and find solace in her memories, but she was failing.

She looked at me again through the haze. "There was a delay with the paper, and the announcement came out two weeks late. And then I didn't want to look at it and waited longer. I thought I had it under control. I kept myself sane for two months. It was just like a bad dream, you know. But now that I see the words on the paper, I know it's real. My father is dead; my mother is dead, and my husband is dead, and yet I'm alive. I will never be able to speak with them again. I will never see them or touch them again. Touch him."

She looked away and stared straight ahead. "Why such cruelty?"

"There's no cruelty in this, even though it might appear otherwise."

"I've never felt such desolation in my life as I do now. Death is cruel," she declared.

"I am not," Death rejoined.

"I know, and you know. Let me tell the story," Joseph said.

"Okay. Fine. Go on, then."

I replied, "Misery is part of being human. If you need to have love, then you must have misery, too."

"That's not true. . . . And even if it was, it's not fair. Why did he take them so soon? Answer me this. Why them?" she insisted.

"I don't know. Death is but a servant, as am I."

"Exactly," Death confirmed.

"Please," Joseph begged.

"Fine. I won't say another word."

The woman looked at me sharply and stared into my eyes, searching for more answers. "Are you real? Or am I talking to myself?" She looked around to see if others were noticing her, but everybody was consumed by their gadgets.

"I assure you I'm as real as you need me to be."

She gave a short laugh. "That's exactly the kind of answer that proves I've gone insane."

I stretched my hand toward her. "Touch me if you don't believe me."

"It won't tell me anything."

"Touch my hand anyway."

She looked at me for a moment, and I could see that she had found some modicum of comfort in our simple conversation. I was enthralled by the magic of it. I had lived amongst humans for these many years, but I could never have imagined that I could have such an effect without the use of my powers.

She continued to stare into my eyes, and I was worried that she might discover me, and I felt anxious and strangely ashamed. I wondered if I had become more like them by living with them and carrying Empathy and k'Nowledge's burdens.

"I don't want to touch you," said the woman solemnly, and then before I could respond, she added, "Don't get me wrong. I'm afraid that you might disappear if I touch you."

I laughed out loud and felt the presence of Joy around me, and she joined in my moment of bliss before disappearing. "I am real. I can assure you, but I understand if you think I was too forward with my request."

The Gift, which had been quiet all this time, woke up suddenly and pressured me to touch her. But I wanted or perhaps needed to talk to her more. I wanted to know more about her, but I was afraid the Gift might try to escape me, as it had tried repeatedly. I stood up, threatening to leave, and that silenced the Gift. But I knew the urge for defection had become part of the Gift's characteristic.

"Stay," she commanded.

"I will if I could buy you a cup of coffee."

"Yes," she replied and started to close the newspaper.

"No, leave it open. Let's drink to your family."

"Yes."

I walked to the counter and ordered and went back to the table. Zuleika was still staring at the newspaper like she had done before. She looked up and said, "If the coffees come, then you are real."

"Unless you are the one who made the order."

She thought for a moment. "True. But wouldn't the person think it's weird ordering two cups of coffee, and there is only one of me?"

"Your date is coming later."

"Then, you talk to him when he comes and proves me wrong."

"I cannot."

"Why not? So, you are not real. . . . But I don't care."

A few minutes later, a young man with long hair approached with our coffee, but as he came closer, he felt anxious, so he quickly put the cups down and left without a word, not letting her test the hypothesis.

"You scared him," she said.

"It can happen sometimes," I replied in earnest.

"What's your name, my mystery man? Or should I know it, since you are merely a figment of my imagination?"

"What do you think?"

"I don't know. For some reason, I want to say something biblical."

"I'm called Joseph now."

She looked at me sideways for a moment and then gave a brief smile. She had heard my choice of words. I smiled back, meekly. I didn't want to confuse her more, but I couldn't lie either.

She let it go and asked, "Do you know my name?"

"I do not."

"I suppose it's expected."

"Is it?"

"Yes. I would want to pretend that you don't know me because I want to prove to myself you are real. Just a stranger who happened to pass by and sit by me and make me feel good. Make me forget."

"I should know your name, but I can't see it."

"So, your powers are limited, after all."

"Of course."

She smiled again and leaned back on the chair. And then picked up her cup and took a small sip. I mimicked her actions and then closed my eyes as the hot, potent liquid found its way through my body.

She stared at me for a moment and said, "You love coffee. I do too, but that would be expected as well, right?"

"Yes. No. It's strange, but we all love coffee."

"You mean all the imaginary people? Even those conjured up by a five-year-old child? That's not being a good imaginary friend, is it now?"

"I am real."

"It doesn't matter, Joseph. I was miserable, and you have made me smile. I don't care if you are real or not."

"What is your name?"

"Zuleika. Zuleika Poitifer."

"No! It's not possible."

She was taken aback. "It's an unusual name, I admit it, but this is the first time I heard such a negative reaction to it."

"I meant no offense, and my reaction was of surprise. It was the name of a person I knew long ago."

"Yes?"

"It's a biblical story. Potiphar's wife tried to seduce Joseph, but she failed."

"Hah! I was once Poitifer's wife, but I am no longer. He is no longer with us. He died in a car crash, and I survived," replied Zuleika.

"I am sorry."

She dismissed me with a wave of her hand. "No matter. I don't want to think about the dead for a few minutes. Could we do that?"

"Of course."

"So, she tried to seduce Joseph? And you are Joseph. But how could I seduce an imaginary person, even if he is handsome?"

You can understand, she meant it as a jest. She felt broken, and I could tell she genuinely didn't care if I was real or not. She needed this respite, and I had offered it to her. But her words made me feel warm and tender. I had never felt that way, not even with the real Potiphar's wife, and she was not called Zuleika anyway, despite the history books. But this Zuleika was different. She conjured a visit by Joy, and even though I've seen her many times, I had never *felt her touch like I felt it that day with Zuleika. It may sound strange, but I wanted to be seduced by this Zuleika.*

I felt tongue-tied, and she must have noticed it. "What? No one ever told you how handsome you look, Joseph? Are there no mirrors in your world?"

"I don't know what to say, Zuleika. I cannot see myself as you might see me, but you are kind to say that."

"I needed it, Joseph. I needed the distraction, and you gave that to me. I brought the paper thinking the obituary would bring closure, but it only made it real. And for some reason, I took refuge in this coffee shop. I needed to sit down, and then you appeared."

"I didn't do anything. I wanted to share your grief to help you, but we got distracted."

"You can't share sadness, Joseph. You must know that. It's a lonely journey. I needed the distraction, and now I'll go home. I'm sure I will cry myself to sleep, but that's good, isn't it?"

"Yes."

"Yes, it is. Sometimes, we all need a good cry, especially when we lose our whole family, and I haven't done it yet. I thought if I didn't cry, it wouldn't be real, but it doesn't make any difference. They are gone. Regrets, pain, and despair are all in me, and all of them are bursting to get out, but so are my love and tenderness for them and, of course, my memories. No one can take that away, can they?"

"No one can. I can assure you that no one would. And keep remembering your family because not even Death can take that away from you."

She stood up and gave a sad smile. "I really hope you are real, but then again, maybe it's better if you are not, so I can conjure you up whenever I need you."

"I can be there anytime you need me," I assured her.

She nodded and then walked away from the coffee shop, without looking back, pulling a trail of sadness behind her.

"That's it? You are done?" Death asked.

"There is more if you want to hear it," Joseph said.

"Indeed. But first another cup of this wonderful coffee. Make mine an Americano, please."

*   *   *

A man and a woman sat across from each other at Le Colonial on Cosmos Place.

The main dining room downstairs was full, and a glance at the reservation screen showed no tables were available for the whole night. The upstairs lounge bar was also busy, but there were still a few empty tables. I took the one in the least inconspicuous position and sat down. The woman looked up in midsentence and stared across the room toward me, but she quickly lowered her gaze without acknowledging my existence.

Zuleika no longer knew me, and therefore could no longer see me as Joseph. That simple fact, like nothing else, ripped my heart out of my body, and for a moment, I expected the end, and I'd have welcomed it.

Almost a year had passed since I first met Zuleika at Saint Frank Coffee, and those months had been the best and, in the end, the worst of my many lives.

I had gone to her apartment later that first night and, like ordinary people, rang the doorbell and allowed her to invite me in.

"Were you expecting me?" I asked as she opened the door.

"Yes. . . . No. I kind of expected you to appear like you did this morning."

"I didn't want to scare you."

"I'm glad you decided to visit me again. Come in."

She stepped away from the door and allowed me to enter. I felt her misery as I brushed past her. Once again, I was taken aback by this new feeling. I had been an observer for millennia, and now I had become an active participant.

She noticed something in me and asked as she closed the door behind us, "Are you okay, my imaginary friend?"

I thought about her question for a moment and then looked at her as a man would see a woman. "I do not know, Zuleika. It's all new to me."

She led me to her living room where a bottle of wine, with four half-full glasses, was sitting on the coffee table. She looked at the table and then at me, and without another word, went to the kitchen and came back with a new wine glass. She poured what was left in the bottle into it and handed it to me.

"To my family."

I understood the ritual, as I had seen it a million times before, but I had never participated in one. I raised my glass and drained the little wine that was in it. It tasted naked, like cherry and wood and cinnamon, and I could taste the bitterness of her despair in the last drop. She drank hers and then took one of the other glasses from the table and handed it to me. She took the other two and held them close to her chest.

"To love, and memories, and times we had but shall never have again," she pronounced.

I took a sip from my new glass, and the wine tasted full, like strawberry and oak and vanilla and the sweetness of her love for her family.

We had been standing all this while, so she sat down on the couch when she finished her wine and patted the cushion next to her for me to sit. I sat down, and she opened a new bottle but only poured two glasses.

"To my new friend."

I took a sip of the new wine, and this time it tasted like ripe blackberry and vanilla spice. It was a touch hot upfront, causing a slight sting, but mellowed out after the second sip. It was warm and potent like Zuleika.

She topped our glasses and took a large sip. "This was a gift from my husband." She reached over and touched the bottle gingerly, and I could see the label, Calera Pinot Noir from the Central Coast. It didn't matter where it was from; it only mattered that it was hers.

"I miss him."

"I know," I said.

She turned and faced me. "Will I ever stop missing my husband?" I held her eyes for a moment, but before I could respond, she added, "Don't answer. I don't want to know."

I nodded and took a sip from the glass. Its taste hadn't changed. I could still feel Zuleika's warmth through the wine. She leaned back and laid her head on my shoulder. "Will you stay?"

"As long as you need me."

She closed her eyes and cried softly, and the Gift came alive again. And the melancholy that had engulfed her would not relent, as if I had lost all powers over it.

Time moves so fast for them. Humans have such short lives, and before they have a chance to recognize who they are, they must make their appointment. But time slowed for us, and I loved her as I have never loved a human being.

Is it wrong to have love and joy while the object of your affection is in agony? I had a decision to make.

My presence did not allow Joy to stay with her but in ephemeral moments. Yet, I could not find the power to step away from her. Zuleika wanted me to be with her, not knowing, or understanding, that my presence was the cause of her unrelenting wretchedness. And the Gift, with all its vile trickery, encouraged me to stay.

Three months passed, and my love for her grew more profound, and I became more human. We kissed for the first time, and I could taste her like I had tasted the wine. The kisses grew, and after a while, we made love for the first time, and Joy and Love lived with us for days.

But then in a moment of ecstasy—when my guard was down and I had been more human than anything else—the Gift escaped me and joined with her. The transaction was painful but quick. She was not ready for what Empathy had created, and she was overwhelmed. She believed I was not real, and that gave her the new reality of the Gift. I was banished from her presence. I was expelled by the Gift that I had nourished for millennia, and what was left in its place was misery. Do you see the irony of this? It took months, but I managed to become more of myself, though the abyss the Gift had created will never be filled. That is certain.

So, when I walked into Le Colonial, six months had passed since I was rejected. Though in that time, I had not stayed away. I had watched over her from afar, hoping to get her back. Zuleika had somewhat managed to control the Gift, but she could not contain it forever and was getting ready to give it to another.

The man's name was Charles Stock, and when she offered the Gift to him, he thought about it for a long time, but it seemed he understood what was given to him. I saw the shock of its power on his face, but he seemed to accept it. Zuleika, on the other hand, wasn't ready for the pain of her memories and felt despondent. But her feeling of misery resurrected her for me. I became real to her again. She saw me and she left Stock, slowly forgetting him and the Gift, and walked over to me.

"You're back?"

"I never left you, Zuleika. I told you I will be with you as long as you need me. Do you need me now?"

"Yes."

She came and sat next to me and then reached out and touched my face. "You are real?"

"Yes."

"I feel like I've woken up from a dream."

"You were sad. The loss of your family was too much, but I am here for you, if you'll have me. It will take more time, but you can overcome the sadness."

"I want to try." *She reached over and touched me again and then leaned closer and kissed me. She tasted warm and strong like the wine she had served on our first night.* "What will happen to us?"

"We can grow old together."

"Is it possible?"

"Anything is possible, if you believe it, Zuleika. You've been part of my life for a long time through myth and reality, and you are part of it again."

She kissed me, and I kissed her back. Her life is short, but to me, it is an eternity of joy.

*   *   *

Two men sat at a small table in Caffé Greco in San Francisco's North Beach district. One had been listening intently to the other, and now that Joseph had finished his story, Death looked at his coffee cup and then touched the side of it.

"You had me rapt by your story, and now my coffee is cold."

Joseph nodded and stood up and then walked inside. A few minutes later, he returned with two new cups of coffee and put them on the table.

"Should we try a different piece of tiramisu? A middle piece?"

Joseph nodded again and went back inside and came back with a new piece.

"Did you ask for the middle piece?"

"Yes," Joseph replied.

"Let's hope this is better than the last." Death grabbed his cup and held it between his hands. "I must drink my coffee while it's still hot, but what will happen to you when Zuleika meets with me for her appointment?"

"I will be there if you allow me, and I will mourn her. But I'm sure I'll see her again, and then again."

"You're very certain," Death said.

"I have to be, or all will be for naught."

"I hope you're right. Believe it or not, this is all new to me too. What of Amani Parker, then? Why did you give the knowledge to him?"

"I kept it for six months after Zuleika passed the Gift to Stock. But I was worried that it would infect her, and I would lose her forever."

"Why Amani then? He was an ordinary person, and he had done nothing to hurt you."

"It's true. He didn't deserve it."

"You sacrificed Amani for her," Death declared.

Joseph stared into Death's eyes. "Yes," he replied.

"And you told her about what you were holding even though her memory of the Gift had completely dissipated."

Joseph took a sip of his coffee and breathed in its aroma before responding. "I didn't tell her about her role, but she needed to know."

Death too held the cup close to his nose. "It's intoxicating," he said and then, "Why?"

"The Gift was forceful, but at the end, it was no threat to her. But k'Nowledge's essence can be poison to them. I couldn't risk it, and I was right, as we've seen in Amani's case."

"You could have kept it as it was asked of you."

Joseph pushed his empty cup to the side. "I was never asked. I never consented. I was given this task, and I faithfully performed it. I guarded these cargos to the best of my abilities. But I could not lose Zuleika again. Can you understand that?"

"No," replied Death. "I cannot see what you see, and I cannot feel what you feel." He reached out and touched Joseph's hand softly. "So, no. Sadly, my friend, I cannot understand it. We all have a job to do, and this is not the one for me. Nevertheless, tell me more. Tell me Amani's story."

"That story doesn't belong to me. I'm sure it will be told, but perhaps not for a while."

"I understand. We are patient, you, and me. But there is another story that needs to be told."

"Yes, the story of the woman who loved him so much that she took on this curse without regard to herself. That too doesn't belong to me. I can only say that my intentions were good. I was hoping to give it to him and then take it back quickly."

"It seems not quick enough," Death replied.

"When I met Amani, I thought he had all the characteristics of a person who could bear this burden. But I was wrong. What I attributed to him was the projection of what his friend, Jackie Goodwin, saw in him. She is an extraordinary woman but perhaps confused by her love for Amani. Although I sensed something in her at our first encounter, I didn't understand its significance. She was the strong one."

"You are probably right because, as you know, he gave it to her almost immediately."

"He lasted a mere four days. And yet Jackie has lasted five years."

"She had an opportunity to relinquish it after mere days. And yet . . ."

Joseph nodded. "She's had many opportunities to unburden herself of it, but she is too kind."

Death gave a slight smile. "It should be impossible, but it's true."

Joseph nodded again. "Yes. She would have been a god if not for the times we live in."

"You should have given it to her in the first place," Death said. "You could have guided her through the process."

"That's clear now, and it's easy for you to say. You were there at that fateful dinner party when I first met Amani, but you didn't follow up days later when he took it from me."

"True and it's all in the past anyway," Death replied. "Where is Jackie now?"

"I don't know. Amani infected her and killed himself before I could reach him. I could not sense Jackie after that because she had shielded herself with the power of knowledge."

"She is powerful, perhaps stronger than the both of us," Death offered.

"Yes. And that's why I cannot tell her story. It belongs to her and perhaps to you."

"I doubt it. When I met Amani, he was no longer a human. So here we are." Death sipped the last of the hot aromatic liquid and closed his eyes for a moment. "I cannot ever stop drinking this. I will be sad when its consumption ends."

"I hope it will last a long time, but then again, human beings are clever, and they will think of something else."

"Will they?" Death asked, staring at his empty cup.

"That's the question. Will they survive without knowledge? We must find Jackie."

"Yes, *we* must. Though I cannot feel her presence or see her essence."

Joseph was about to answer when he stopped and extended his hand, drops of rain falling on it. It was a short drizzle, but the air shifted with a smell of spring. He took a deep breath.

"After coffee, my favorite thing in this world is the smell of rain in the spring." He took another deep breath, but the sky had cleared. He looked at Death and said, "But Jackie must be here somewhere, amongst the billions of other souls."

"I don't know. She is lost to me, and I no longer know her appointment time."

"Has that happened before?"

"Never."

"And what will happen to humanity if we cannot take back the knowledge?"

"That is the eternal question," Death replied and picked up his cup to drink, but he had already finished it. He put the cup back on the table looking disappointed. "It could be the end of us, and the end of them," he said before disappearing.

Joseph sat there for a few more minutes hoping for more rain, but nothing happened. He stood up and walked away from the café.

The tiramisù sat untouched.

JOSEPH

A small café on Polk Street: that's where I thought I should go to face my misery, which had been kept at bay for two months. Misery did show up, but it was not what I had expected. But before then, there was the accident.

It felt as if time had stopped, or at least that's how I remember the accident, with every detail so vividly pronounced.

I saw the massive truck inches away from the driver's side with its shiny chrome bulldog sitting keenly on the top of the hood, looking straight through the window. I saw the smoke from the tires rise in the air in a circular fashion, creating dirty dust devils, and the cabin bending forward under the weight of its haul as it tried to slow down faster than its designers had intended. I saw fear in the driver's eyes and knew the inevitability of the collision.

My husband's body was relaxed, his hands casual around the steering wheel. At that moment, he was smiling at my mother through the rearview mirror. She had been charming all night long, happy to have spent her birthday with us. Earlier, she had moved to the middle seat to be closer, so she could hear better as we chatted about the food and the wine we had an hour earlier in San Francisco. She wanted to go back to the same restaurant for my father's birthday. My parents had gone to the original restaurant, Spenta, on Mira Road in Mumbai, years earlier, and this one had reminded them of their trip to India. My father, who'd several glasses of the fine wine, was leaning his head against the window behind the driver's seat, snoring softly, oblivious to our conversation. Their birthdays were a week apart, so we had to make a reservation as soon as possible if we wanted to have a good table.

I looked over at the headlights of the Mack truck, and the bull-dog smiled mischievously. Then time started again, and I saw Death.

Then, there was silence, as if the pulverization of our small car by a 60-ton truck had deafened all the noises around us. Nothing moved, and there was a strange calm in the air. I could taste its metallic flavor. The full moon cast a gray light over the road and the long shadows draping across the hills of Marin Headlands. From my vantage point, I could see across the San Francisco Bay, the thousands of lights twinkling in the night. My mother's stomach and the airbag that was still inflated held me in place, the blood from her body dripping to the floor. The left side of the car had been pressed to a sliver, and my husband had merged into my mother. My father was no longer in the car. The truck had come to a full stop on the other side of the road, its red taillights blinking unsteadily, as if unsure of their new role.

I felt warm and calm against the softness of my mother's stomach, and I sat there, not sure what was to be done next. And then, the airbag deflated with a loud hiss, and I was free though I couldn't gather my strength to move. I knew there was nothing for me to do but wait.

*   *   *

I saw the red lights reflected on the darkened hills before I heard the siren. The fire truck pulled next to our car, followed by an ambulance. I wondered who had called them and how much time had passed since the accident. I was still leaning against the warm body of my mother. I turned my head to have a better view of the new arrivals.

A young man came out of the ambulance and ambled toward me, and I could see his face under the moonlight. He was so young and looked fearless. He took out a flashlight from his bag and shined the light on our car and then on my face. I felt as if God was looking at me.

"Try and stay calm," he ordered through a shattered window. He now looked frantic despite his words. He moved his head to see me better and then said, "Don't try to move. We're going to get you out."

I was calm, nestling against my mother, and had no intention of moving. I didn't say anything. I didn't think I had to respond to his command.

"Are you hurt?"

He was now shouting, and I wondered why, given he was standing so close to me. I looked at him as he shined the light over my body and inspected me through the window.

He put the light on my face and stared at me, and I stared back in silence. He asked again, "Are you hurt, Ma'am?"

I wasn't sure. I was getting cold. Would that count? I wanted to ask him but thought better of it.

"What's your name? Are you hurt?"

I still didn't respond, and he gave up and looked at his partner, a woman who looked even younger than him. I thought I was being rescued by children. And then two firemen showed up with a Hurst Jaws of Life. Odd how I remembered the brand, having only dated a fireman for under a year. I looked at their brand new looking Hurst and smiled.

The man who was holding the saw was older with a full beard. He saw me and nodded. "We're going to get you out in a jiffy," he assured me.

I shook my head and then closed my eyes.

When I opened them again, I was lying on a hospital bed and Dalia Smart was sitting next to me. She was holding my hand while staring at something beyond the room. I moved my fingers, and she turned around, and I saw the quick change of demeanor.

"You're awake, Zolie," Dalia said. She leaned over and kissed me on my forehead.

I squeezed her hand and she returned the gesture. "Where am I?" I asked. My voice was raspy as the air struggled to leave my throat.

"We're at UCSF, darling. You were in an accident. Do you remember?"

But before I could answer, another voice intruded. "Mrs. Poitifer, my name is Dr. Ash. You gave us a bit of a scare. How are you feeling?"

How am I feeling? I thought. I've seen Death. That's how I am feeling. I stared at the new person.

"Can you hear me?" Dr. Ash asked.

"Yes, she can hear you. Give her a minute," Dalia ordered.

"I'm fine," I finally replied and looked outside, and I could see the sun rising above the hills. "How long?"

"A few hours, Mrs. Poitifer. You were in an accident. Do you remember?"

I nodded and tried to turn my head, but the pain was too much. I gave an involuntary cry.

"Best not to move. You're lucky, Mrs. Poitifer. Nothing is broken, but the left side of your body is bruised," Dr. Ash offered in a slow sensible tone. "You passed out as you were taken out of the car, but overall, you are okay. You were lucky," he added and then, after a pause, said again, "Very lucky," as if it was hard for him to believe as well.

"My family?" I asked, but one should never ask a question when the answer is known already.

"I am so sorry, Zolie," Dalia offered and then leaned over and hugged me. The touch was painful, but I welcomed it. You want the physical pain. It's a reminder that what you have experienced is real and not just a bad dream.

"I want to go home," I said.

"Mrs. Poitifer, it would be best if you stay until this afternoon," Dr. Ash said in an authoritative way that doctors use when they know they are in control. "I will discharge you then," he offered as consolation.

"I want to go home now," I said again and started to move, but even the slightest move brought a deep pain on my side.

"Mrs. Poitifer . . ."

"Are you ordering her to stay?" Dalia demanded.

"Of course not. She is free to leave, but it's best if she is monitored."

I had become an object to be talked about by the two adults in the room.

"I'll monitor her," Dalia said in a tone that she often used with her staff when there was no room for argument. She understood my need to leave, and I felt safe knowing she would be with me.

"Of course. Let me call an orderly to help you," the doctor said, and then looking at Dalia, said, "I'd also suggest a grief counselor. She may look okay to you now, but the gravity of this accident will dawn on her soon."

"Yes," Dalia responded and then stroked my face as assurance. "I'll go get the car."

I sat on the passenger side as Dalia drove on Parnassus Avenue and then turned left on Stanyan Street. It was late morning, but the air was cold. I lowered the window and let the breeze envelop my face. I closed my eyes and fell asleep for a few minutes, because when I opened my eyes again, we were already on Geary Street going east.

"You passed my house."

"I thought you might want to stay with me for a few days," Dalia offered and turned around to look at me.

"Thank you, but I want to go home. I need to be at home."

"Are you sure, Zolie? Can you handle it?"

"Yes," I replied with a bravado that I should not have possessed.

She thought for a moment and then turned the car around and drove toward Richmond District.

"Thank you."

"I will check on you later, okay?" Dalia said and then reached out to squeeze my hand.

"Of course."

"In a couple of hours."

"I'll be fine, Dalia. But check on me as often as you like."

We drove the rest of the way in silence, and I fell back to sleep and opened my eyes when we arrived in front of my house.

We managed to get me to the house without incident, and Dalia guided me to my bedroom, and all the while, I ignored every little remanence of my husband. He would be home soon, and I needed to rest. I made it to the bedroom and laid on my side of the bed. Dalia sat with me for a while, and I closed my eyes.

When I opened them again, it was early in the afternoon and I was alone, but a tray of Chinese food was sitting next to my bed. I took a single noodle from the plate and I put it in my mouth; it felt warm, but I could not taste anything even though Dalia had ordered it the way I liked, with lots of the black bean sauce.

"Oh, you're awake," Dalia said as she walked into the room, carrying a pitcher of water. "I was hoping you were up, so you could eat." She helped me sit up, and then served me a bowl of noodles and handed me two silver chopsticks.

I took another single noodle and chewed it carefully. It tasted good, but I didn't want to taste anything.

"Eat," said Dalia. "You need your strength."

"Come and sit next to me, please." She was wearing her work clothes, and I knew she wouldn't want to get them wrinkled. "You can put on my house clothes."

She nodded and took a shirt and a pair of sweatpants from the drawer and went to the bathroom to change. She came back, hung her clothes on wooden hangers in her meticulous way, and came and sat next to me on the bed.

I ate my food in silence, Dalia watching me eat like my mother used to do. I looked up. "Aren't you hungry?"

She shook her head, and I ate a bit more before putting my plate on the nightstand.

"You should eat more."

"No. I can't. I just want to sit here with you."

"Okay."

I leaned against her, and she held my hand. It felt good to have her next to me. We didn't talk. There was no point to it. And we sat there and stared at the wall in front of us for a long time.

I must have fallen asleep again because when I opened my eyes, the room looked darker. Dalia was standing in front of the bed.

"I should go," she said and came over to kiss me.

"Can you stay the night?"

She didn't hesitate. "Sure. Let me call Amani and tell him."

"He doesn't mind?"

"Of course not, don't be silly," she offered with a laugh, but I wasn't convinced. It wasn't like Amani would have objected, given that I had lost my whole family, but he would find a way to fuss about it later. He saw Dalia's relationship with me as equal to his relationship with our friend Jackie Goodwin, who had been a close friend of his since college. And since Dalia didn't like Jackie, he felt he had to dislike me to balance the equation, at least from *his* point of view. It wasn't fair, but relationships are complex and life itself is even more complicated.

I needed Dalia then so that I wouldn't crash and burn, as she would need me less than two years later, when she'd lose her husband. Being there for each other. That's the test of real friendship, is it not? But there was more to our circle of friends. I didn't know then how our lives would intertwine in a tight knot that only gods could untangle. On that night, I just needed my friend.

Dalia walked to the other room to call her husband. It only lasted a few minutes, and she came back in. "Do you want to go back to sleep?" I nodded, so she added, "Do you want me to brush your teeth for you?"

I laughed. "No, I can make it to the bathroom. I need to pee anyway," I replied, even though I didn't want to move. But Dalia was a stickler about a proper nightly brushing.

She helped me get up and then escorted me to the bathroom. I rummaged through the medicine cabinet and produced a brand-new toothbrush for her. She smiled appreciatively, and we both stood in front of the mirror and brushed our teeth like we used to when we shared an apartment during our college years. She then helped me sit on the toilet and waited for me on the threshold. I sauntered to the sink and washed my hands, and she dried them for me.

She helped me back into the bed and then crawled next to me, and we talked a bit about her work and a new Yum Cha (dim sum) place that had opened on Geary and 23rd.

Then I asked, "How did you know?"

"I got a call from the sheriff's office," she replied, as if it was the most common thing. But she wouldn't look me in the eyes.

"Oh."

She then wanted to talk about the accident, but I shook my head, and she respected it and didn't mention it again. I started talking about the book I was reading and went on for a while, desperately wanting to avoid any conversation about the accident. When I looked over, she was fast asleep.

Dalia worked hard, harder than anyone should, but she was driven and successful. I knew she would work even harder to make up for the hours spent taking care of me. Dalia was always exhausted, even though she tried awfully hard not to show it. She was in a deep sleep and looked beautiful with her soft skin and thick long hair. I felt sleepy too, but we had left the light on, and though it didn't bother me, I knew it would disturb her sleep.

I got up and turned off the light but left the bathroom light on so I could find my way back to the bed. Dalia had not even stirred, lying in the exact same position that I had left her in.

I crawled next to her and laid on my good side. As soon as I touched her, she turned as if instinctively, and I held her from behind like my husband had held me, and she held on to my hand as if afraid that I might let go.

I fell asleep and dreamt of my husband holding me and kissing me and then turning away from me and allowing me to have him for a while. I reached out and touched his chest and his arms and his stomach, moving my hands up and down his body as he leaned against me harder. I could feel his warm buttocks nuzzling my body, and I started to breathe harder, and, like most dreams when you are ready to reach the peak, I woke up.

The room was dark, except for the stream of light from the bathroom. For a mere second, I thought I was next to my husband, but then I remembered, and a deep melancholy descended over me. I wanted to sob, but I felt paralyzed and catatonic all night long.

*   *   *

Hours turned to days and days to weeks, and like everything else, life after seeing death became routine. I called my husband's family, as I had none left of my own, and notified them of his death. I arranged for the cremation of my parents and my husband, ignoring his parents' protestation, and set a date for their funerals. Called his office—done. Called a few of his friends—done. Called some of my parents' friends—check.

Each phone call was like reliving the accident and all the pain associated with it. The pain of the death of your loved ones doesn't go away even with time. Time mutes it a bit and may even provide some respite from it, but the ache you feel in your heart is always there, and when it decides to reappear, it covers you like a cold, dark void. The retelling of the accident over and over again should have desensitized me, but it only created a hardened façade, burying my grief deep within me until I met Joseph.

I bought three different placements in the obituary section of the *San Francisco Chronicle*. My husband and I liked reading the obituaries, so I thought he would get a kick out of having one of his own. I added my parents to be fair. The *Chronicle* promised that it would take two days before the notices would appear, but it didn't happen. I called, and they promised it would happen in three days. So, more phone calls and more having to relive the life I had but could never have again.

My parents were gone, and so was my husband. I was a widow and an orphan all at the same instant.

My husband! I keep saying "my husband" and not using his name. I wonder why? It doesn't make any difference what name he held. He could have been Joe Poitifer, Don Poitifer, Graham or Chin or Pierre, or Mohammad. It doesn't matter anymore. It makes no difference what his name was. He is not a name to me.

When she died, my mother was battling late-stage breast cancer with insurance that did not cover all the costs. I used to worry about her health, but no need anymore. Her medical costs had put tremendous stress on our finances, too, as my parents needed help from us. Only weeks earlier, I was worrying about whether we could keep up with our ballooning debt. But, no more. My husband had excellent life insurance, as did my father. So, their deaths brought financial security. I now have no need for money. Money for their lives. Was it a fair tradeoff? What do you think?

I want them back. I want those hours of not knowing the outcome of my mother's illness, and the fights with my father for drinking too much, and my arguments with my husband, whatever his name, over silly things that initially were endearing but later in the marriage became annoying and an excuse for unfounded fights. I'd exchange all that misery with the one I hold now and will forever.

*   *   *

The funeral went well, even if the notices didn't appear in the paper. I called again and they apologized profusely, refunding my money, and promising to post the pieces for free. Did they think it's the money? My in-laws, I guess former in-laws, haven't forgiven me for cremating their son. But that's what he had wanted, not that they cared. His brother and sister were more understanding. I liked them, and they liked me, but I wondered if we would see each other after the initial shock dissipated.

The obituaries were finally printed, two weeks after they were promised. But I couldn't look at them. I was too busy with the insurance companies, banks, and my husband's family and parents' affairs. I kept myself active, so I didn't have to feel. I stayed strong for myself. My husband's brother and sister were supportive and helped me stay sane. Dalia was fantastic. She helped me live.

So, I stayed sane and calm, and I managed to settle everyone's affairs. I was a good manager. And then, it was time. It was time to read the obituaries that I had written, and it was time to feel again.

I had bought three copies of the *Chronicle* when the notices finally came out. I don't know why I bought three, perhaps one for each of the dead. I wasn't thinking of it that way then; it just felt natural to pick up three. I brought the crisp newspapers home and put them on the kitchen counter, not daring to open them.

After a few minutes of looking at the stack, I thought it was disrespectful to have them on the counter, like junkmail or pieces of fruit. So, I took them to our bedroom, well, my bedroom now. But I couldn't decide where to put them. First, I tried the bed, and then his dresser, which was a mistake, because I opened one of his drawers and took out his undershirt, and then I was paralyzed for a long time. Finally, I managed to step away and redraw the shield that had been protecting me these many days. I took the papers and put them on my dresser after clearing every single piece of junk that had gathered on the top with one big sweep of the hand, ignoring the fallen dusty articles.

Like identical triplets, the newspapers sat there silently and alone for a while. Then on the third day, I felt they looked ugly and imposing, so I tied them with a large red ribbon. Two days later, I added a green ribbon, and they finally looked happy and presentable.

Now, I had no reason to disturb them, so they sat there like a present to be opened on Christmas day. But of course, it was not the kind of present that anyone wants to be opened. It was more like that inkling one has with a boyfriend when you both know it's time to end it, and you each hope the other would start the *conversation*, but no one dares, and days pass. I'd walk by the stack of newspapers, pretend to ignore them, though I secretly observed their silence, and the papers did the same by slowly changing colors after many days of sitting in the sunlight. It was more difficult at night, when the only light in the room came from a faint streetlight that made everything awful. Why should nights be any different than days? Why would the newspapers cry louder at night? I had started keeping the bathroom light on to quiet down the noises. It partly worked since, after almost a month, even the ribbons were losing their luster.

But one day, after our long, passive-aggressive relationship, we decided it was time, time for them to reveal themselves and for me to be bold. But I couldn't bring myself to do it in the bedroom, where my husband's ghost was still present. I carefully untied the ribbons and grabbed the middle newspaper—it was the freshest, protected by the others for a month. I put the paper in my bag and left the house without thinking about a destination. I turned on Turk Street and walked on the north side. It was a lovely day with a bright sky, and the cool breeze from the ocean nudged me forward. I walked through Western Addition and thought about reading the paper in Jefferson Square, but the grass was still wet from the night's drizzle, despite the sun. I continued my stroll, and when I reached Polk Street, I turned left and walked into Saint Frank Coffee.

A sunbeam followed me through the large windows and cast a pathway. I took the last table and sat there for a moment. There was a small lamp on the wall, but it wouldn't turn on when I

pushed the button. No matter, the light from the outside had giv-
en the place a warm, cozy feeling.

I opened the newspaper to the obituary section and read the
words that I had written several weeks earlier. Three short pieces, each describing the people I had loved, and yet the words
sounded foreign to me. They were not really who these obituaries
proclaimed. They were not the two-dimensional beings spread in
the newspaper by me and then read by me.

They were real, and now they were gone, and then in the depth
of my desolation, I conjured him. He was not there, and then he
was—beautiful and strong. I needed someone to be there for me
and to understand me and to share my pain. I wished for him,
and he appeared. Dalia had been worrying about my mental
health and insisted that I should see a grief counselor, but I had
assured her of my sanity, and this proved it. What could be more
rational than conjuring a beautiful man to listen to you and give
you solace?

I saw him, and he saw me, and he walked over and sat by me.
I imagined him, and he was created and then appeared precisely
as I wanted him. Unlike my husband, this imaginary being had
a name.

"I'm called Joseph now," he had offered after much prodding.
He told me he had been Joseph for a long time, hundreds of
years, but not as long as he had been others. At the time, it made
perfect sense to me. I have always prided myself on my imagination, so why would I conjure an ordinary man with an ordinary
life? No, I summoned a beautiful creature that mesmerized me.

He spoke strangely but kindly, and each word felt like the velvety cool texture of aloe vera on burnt skin. When I questioned
him further, he added more peculiarities to our already strange
conversation. After a while, I wondered why I would create such
complexity when simple solace was what I needed. But I welcomed it and invited more.

He asked for my name as if he didn't know, and it felt good to
be unknown to my own mind. I told him, and he reacted oddly,

as if he hadn't realized my unusual name before that day. I knew Zuleika and Joseph's biblical story, so it was not too surprising for him to invoke it after hearing my name. It didn't matter. Nothing mattered at the time. I just wanted to learn more about him. I needed him to speak to me, so I looked into his eyes, and wished him to be real.

"Tell me more. Just talk to me as if you were real."

He agreed and offered a soliloquy as one might expect of an expressive, imaginary man named Joseph. "I had sat in the well of time, not knowing, and then I knew, and the dreams of the sun and the moon and the stars became clear because I had the knowledge. And then I felt what they felt, and then I was truly Joseph. The stories of Joseph, false or true, have been told, but they all missed my feelings for my true love."

"Who is this love?" I asked, and for a moment, I forgot my own lost love.

"It was Zuleika, and it is Zuleika, and it will be Zuleika."

"Me?" I laughed. "You didn't even know my name a few minutes ago, my imaginary friend, but no matter. Since I conjured you, it's not surprising that you would love me."

"I am as real as you want me to be," he said, as he had done earlier.

I laughed again and then realized that it was my first laughter in more than two months. "Thank you."

He shook his head as if trying to make himself less opaque and more real. I looked at him and said, "I needed it, Joseph. I needed the distraction, and you gave that to me. I brought the paper thinking the obituary would bring closure, but it only made it real. And for some reason, I took refuge in this coffee shop. I needed to sit down, and then you appeared."

"I didn't do anything. I wanted to share your grief to help you, but we got distracted."

"You can't share sadness, Joseph. You must know that. It's a lonely journey. I needed the distraction, and now I'll go home. I'm sure I will cry myself to sleep, but that's good, isn't it?"

"Yes."

"Yes, it is. Sometimes, we all need a good cry, especially when we lose our whole family, and I haven't done it yet. I thought if I didn't cry, it wouldn't be real, but it doesn't make any difference. They are gone. Regrets, pain, and despair are all in me, and all of them are bursting to get out, but so are my love and tenderness for them and, of course, my memories. No one can take that away, can they?"

"No one can. I can assure you that no one would. And keep remembering your family because not even Death can take that away from you."

I was done. I didn't think I would need Joseph again, but at the same, I was hoping he would be there anyway. I don't know what a real Faustian deal is, but I think if this was not exactly it, it was close.

*   *   *

I took a taxi home. I felt neither happy nor sad. There was a sense of contentment that stayed with me throughout the ride home. I sat in the back of the cab and looked outside and saw the city as one might consider an old friend. There were so many good memories of my own childhood in San Francisco and my adult life with my husband. Every intersection that we passed was a marker of my own life. I smiled, thinking of the ridiculousness of talking to an imaginary person. But he was so beautiful, I thought. I felt proud that I could conjure such imagery in the depth of my own grief.

Before long, the taxi pulled up next to my house, and I paid and went in. I was ready. I was prepared to mourn them all and then hold on to their memories. I was ready to accept.

I took out the old photo albums, wanting to touch something real rather than quickly going through hundreds of digital photos. I walked through my parents' life and then my own childhood and then my husband's, and finally our life together. Photos in albums give you a different sense of life, as we tend to keep those rare few that we consider precious at times. Hence each snapshot requires your own storytelling. One of the photos had my parents, my husband, Dalia, Amani, Jackie, and me sitting at a round table at Sam Wo Restaurant on Washington Street. We were staring at the camera, none of us smiling, except my husband, who held a large, silly grin. The restaurant was somewhat famous (infamous) for having rude waiters, particularly Edsel Ford Fung, who was known locally as the "world's rudest waiter." My dad had been going there for forty years and had known Edsel. He even went to Edsel's funereal when he died in 1984. He loved that place and had wanted to show it off to Dalia's new boyfriend.

It didn't go well. Amani started arguing with one of the waiters, which made my dad angry, thereby making my mom mad at him for being angry, and Dalia mad at Amani, and then at Jackie, who had tried to calm Amani. My husband, the consummate peacemaker, thought a group photo would do us good, so he asked a woman at the next table to take the shot. He had put the picture all by itself because he thought the whole event *amusing*.

After a while, I realized that I hadn't eaten all day, so I went to the kitchen thinking I'd have a simple sandwich, but then it occurred to me that I hadn't cooked for a long time, and I started preparing a meal for my dead family. One might think of this as morbid but not me. It gave me solace and joy.

When I was done with all the plates on the kitchen counter, I ate from each dish voraciously until I was satiated and tired. I went back to the living room and lay on the couch, where I fell into a deep, dreamless sleep.

When I woke up it was dark outside, but I was not done with my process. I went to the kitchen, opened a bottle of Bordeaux, and poured a small amount into a crystal goblet. I put the glass to my nose, and the aroma reminded me of my husband. It was intense and kind. I drank the wine slowly and tasted bitterness and loss. I cried as I had promised Joseph I would, a slow, steady, muffled cry that I thought would cleanse me. After I finished the first glass, I took out three more wine glasses and took them, along with the open bottle, to the living room. I poured a tiny bit of wine in the four glasses and sipped from each in order, each drop, a conversation with my parents and husband. I had drunk half of the bottle, but I was not finished. I needed to drink and taste memories as much as my body could take. I opened two new bottles from my husband's collection, a Calera Pinot Noir from the Central Coast that he was saving for our anniversary. I rinsed the glasses, dried them, and then filled each with the new wine. I put them on the coffee table, and I was ready to repeat the ritual when the doorbell rang.

I thought it was Dalia as part of her constant vigil. I opened the door but instead of my best friend, there stood my new friend, Joseph.

"Were you expecting me?" he asked, teasing.

"Yes. . . . No. I kind of expected you to merely appear like you did this morning."

"I didn't want to scare you."

"I'm glad you decided to visit me again. Come in."

He walked in but, unlike most people who would look around the place to observe the new surroundings, he went ahead as if he knew the layout of the house. He noticed my bottles and the glasses and then looked at me and smiled. I didn't want to give him any of those, so I went to the kitchen and brought a new wine glass.

I poured what was left in the bottle and handed it to him, then took my glass and said, "To my family."

Joseph nodded, not saying anything, but following my every movement with his own. I drained my glass quickly and could taste nothing of the wine.

I should share one of the glasses with him, I thought, but I wasn't sure which one would be appropriate. I gave him my mother's, and he took it without a word. I took the other two glasses and held them close to my chest.

"To love and memories, and times we had but shall never have again," I offered.

I took a sip from my husband's glass, and the wine tasted like a lustful dream that one might have in the middle of the night—like the one I had, that night. I sat down on the couch and drank from my father's glass, and this time, the wine tasted of patience and strength, like a massive oak in the middle of a meadow. Joseph was still standing, so I patted the cushion next to me for him to sit.

I filled his glass from the Pinot then grabbed my own and did the same. He took the wine glass but didn't drink and I sat with mine next to him. We sat there in silence for a long time and then I offered, "To my new friend."

He nodded and took a small drink. I took a sip as well and this time, the wine tasted mellow, like the feeling one has on a sunny lazy Sunday morning. I looked at the bottles—the wine that was to have been part of my gift to my husband for our upcoming anniversary.

"I miss him," I confessed.

"I know," Joseph replied, and I believed him. Somehow, I knew he could feel what I felt as if he was in my mind—silly me. Of course, he was.

But that didn't stop me from asking the obvious. "Will I ever stop missing my husband?" I looked into his eyes and I knew what he was going to say. "Don't answer. I don't want to know."

Another pause and then I asked, "Will you stay?"

"As long as you need me."

I closed my eyes and cried softly, and I fell into a deep asleep.

*   *   *

I woke up late and I was alone on the couch. My head felt heavy and was pulsating, and I expected it to explode any minute. I turned to see if I was truly alone; I was. There were only four glasses and two empty wine bottles on the coffee table.

A week passed and Joseph did not return. I told Dalia all about him and we had a good laugh at my vivid imagination.

"But he felt so real," I insisted.

"Yes, but where is the fifth glass?"

"I don't know. That's the part that has put doubt in my mind. I looked for it, you know. I thought he had put it back. Then I thought maybe he took it with him?"

"Why would anyone do that? That's crazy, Zolie. You had three bottles of wine."

"Not three, he had some as well," I corrected her, but she gave me a usual Dalia look, telling me to get over myself. But before she could press her point, I added, "But what about seeing him in the café? I was sober then."

"Were you? Are you sure? You've been drinking a lot lately."

True, I thought, but I wasn't going to give in that easily. "That's not fair, Dalia."

"I know."

"But where is the fifth glass?" I asked again, hoping my insistence would make it real.

"I don't know. But I think you know he is not real."

"Maybe you're right."

"I know I am. He won't be back now that you've acknowledged it," Dalia replied with a certainty that she alone could possess.

But she was wrong.

Joseph came back a week later when I felt incredibly lonely in the night, when not even the light from the bathroom could keep me safe. He walked into the room as if he lived there and sat next to me on the bed. He held me and I cried and then I fell asleep. And once again, when I woke up, he was gone.

I smelled the pillow next to me to see if it would recall him, but it did not. He came back several days later, again with the same routine, me feeling lonely and naked and he, appearing and keeping me warm and safe.

Dalia started to worry even more than before and felt that my *attitude* did not allow for the healing process to begin. She wanted me to feel happy and start thinking about the future. But there was no happiness, and I knew I could have Joseph anytime I felt the desolation of my losses.

Three months passed, and my feelings for him grew, and then I knew with a certainty that I had never possessed before that I loved him. Perhaps it was heartless of me to love a man so soon after losing my husband. Maybe so, but I felt it deep within me, and no amount of shame would diminish those feelings. For three months, he was there any time I needed him, and he held me and protected me, and I felt whole again, even though I never gained real happiness, whatever that is. We had not even held hands, not really, but then one night, when I felt especially dark, it all changed.

"I can't do this anymore, Joseph," I said to myself more than to him as he held me in his arms. I was staring ahead but could see our reflections in the glass cabinet. "You're not real. Your presence is just proving that I have gone insane."

Joseph lowered his head and put his face in my hand as if proving a point. "I'm as real as you want me to be," he offered as he had done before.

"That's exactly what I'm saying. You don't give certainty. You give options. I don't want options, Joseph. I want you to be a real person. I want you to be there and to make me happy and let me move on."

He was staring at my reflection as well. He looked sad and helpless, and I felt sorry for him.

He closed his eyes and said, "I want all these for you, Zuleika. I want you to be happy."

"But I'm not. I'm dying. Can't you see I'm dying?" I felt it. I felt how part of me was disappearing as if consumed by a never-ending misery.

"I can leave and come back later," he offered. He sounded like a child and not an imaginary friend with thousands of years behind him.

I disentangled myself from his arms and sat straight, now facing him. He looked so real. I wanted to put my fingers on his face and feel his warm skin, but I was afraid any touch might make him disappear forever. Yet, I replied, "That's not what I want. I don't want you to leave and then come back. I want you to leave and never come back unless you are real."

Joseph looked at me and for the first time I saw a momentary doubt in his eyes. He shook his head slightly but didn't say anything.

I couldn't stop. Dalia may have been correct, and I needed help, real help from a real person. Yet, I still needed convincing.

"Could I truly be insane if I know I am imagining you?" I asked, but now I wasn't sure at whom this question was directed. "I know you're not here and I know I have conjured you so I can have someone to keep me company in these lonely nights. Wouldn't this be considered a sign of sanity? I am a no-nonsense woman, so why do I torture myself so much?"

"You are sane, Zuleika. I can assure you of it," Joseph said in his calm, warm way as he had done since our first encounter.

I laughed, the mirthless cackle of an insane woman who craves assurance from an empty room. But this time, he did not try to assure me with mere words. He leaned over and kissed me. I felt him, truly felt his physical presence, and I tasted him like I had savored the wine. He tasted like a never-ending vacation on a tropical beach. I kissed him back and his lips were warm and tasted of joy now. And then we kissed more, and I felt a deep sensation within me. I looked at him, and he was beautiful—no earthly person could ever possess such loveliness—and he looked at me, and I could see he was seeing me differently, as if for the first time.

We made love and when he entered me, I felt as if he had taken over my whole being with his own. He possessed me, and I possessed him. We were in sync like no other beings could have possibly achieved. He was in me and with me and not like what a mortal man could ever do through simple penetration. And it felt as if I was melding with him and each movement took me closer to a perpetual ecstasy.

Afterward, I fell into a deep, dreamless sleep, and I slept all night and all day long. I missed work, but they understood. When I woke up again, it was dark, and I felt ravenous. I ordered the whole menu from Ton Kiang, and when the food arrived, I ate boxes of noodles, rice, and vegetable until I could not move. Joseph did not come back that night, and I was fine. I did not need him to sleep soundly that night.

But he was back again, and again. We talked and we danced and we ate and then we made love, and each time I felt purer and more assured. But routines bring sensibility, and after a while it was not all about me. I could see that the act was a struggle for him, as if he could not truly let go. There was a barrier between us, and he fought hard to keep its integrity.

I questioned him, but in his usual fashion, he was guarded. And then one night when I was sure that I was in love—and even though, without knowing why, I knew it was risky to feel such love and even more perilous to say it out loud, I said it: "I love you," I cried out as he penetrated deeper, reaching my inner soul.

He looked at me, and I could see he loved me too, and as the guard that he had been holding for so long and so valiantly came down, I felt such an intense orgasm that I thought I might die. I closed my eyes for an instant to capture the feelings, but then when I opened them, he was gone. I was naked and alone with one hand on my breast and the other inside me.

He disappeared, and strangely I felt confident that he was gone forever. And therefore, the story should have ended there. I was crazy, induced by the grief of losing my family. That would be understandable, no? No one would fault me for wanting to have this beautiful person as my companion to fill the void that my loss had created. So, what if his lips, his touch, his body, his everything felt so real? So what? I banished this imaginary friend when he was no longer needed. Most children do as they grow up. I just did it differently than most.

The story should have ended here, and I should have moved on with my life. I didn't even miss him. And when I thought of him,

I felt no sadness and no fear of loss. He no longer mattered. But of course, this was not the end.

Because days later, when I touched my chest, I felt something growing within me, and I could feel its strength and with it, my own power. I could feel my neighbor's laughter, and I could sense the burgeoning love of a couple who had passed by my house. I felt everything around me but the melancholy that had been my companion for the past months. I know the whole thing sounds odd and unbelievable. I had my own doubts at first, another sign of my insanity. But it was real, and I sensed it within me and after a while, it felt as natural as any organ in my body, and I understood its power of pure empathy.

"My imaginary friend has impregnated me with something strange," I told Dalia when she came by after my distressful call to her.

"Don't be silly, Zolie. You look different, yes. You look happy and contented, and that's good, but I still think you should see someone."

I could feel her pain—she had had an awful day at work and yet was worried she wasn't working hard enough. She was concerned about Amani. She felt she wasn't taking care of him enough and that she might lose him one day.

I could read her feelings as if they were being shouted at me, and it was getting more challenging for me to think. I felt like crawling under the blanket and covering my ears with the pillows. I wanted to tell Dalia to stop feeling so loud, but that would be ridiculous, right? That would just prove her point. This zygote in me spoke to me, or at least I felt its thoughts, but that's not even an accurate description. There was something within me; I could feel it, and it *spoke* to me in its own way, as if they were all my own thoughts and feelings.

Dalia was still looking at me, and I sensed her worries for me getting added to her other piles. I reached out and touched her face. My little touch made her feel calm, and she sank down on the chair and closed her eyes. I could feel the sea of calmness surrounding her. At first, I was surprised by her reaction, but then I understood it, as if I had always had this calming effect on people. But before our connection was broken, I also felt my new, yet unborn progeny craving her. *But not yet*, it assured me, in its own way, *though one day*, it promised.

I admit, I was somewhat jealous that this thing wanted Dalia before I had a chance to even acquaint myself with it. But more importantly, my natural instinct was to protect Dalia from any unknown, as at the time, I had so many doubts about it and myself.

I spent the next six months nurturing the thing that was growing in me, and with every passing minute, it became more assertive and more willful. I went to work and came home and took care of what needed to be taken care of. I held no feelings of my own, as everyone I saw shouted their feelings at me. But it didn't take long for me to manage it, as I had my grief in those initial months. Then I was numb and going through life, feeling nothing.

After that day, I limited my interactions with Dalia, worried about her health and the promise of this parasite possessing her one day. I wasn't sure how it would impact Dalia. I was not afraid of it for me, because I was sure it was bestowed upon me by my own creation. In certain moments when I felt comforted, I thought of it as a gift and not a parasite that was flooding my senses with other people's emotions. The grief that was ever-present before had been replaced with a sense of contentment, and the imaginary friend had become just that, a distant reflection of imagination. He had become as nameless as my husband.

It was a gift that I'd come to cherish, but I was sure it would be a parasite to Dalia. Why? I don't know. Perhaps I was like some people who operated on the philosophy that what may be good for them was not good for others. I loved Dalia too much to allow that to happen.

The Gift, as I later learned its title, its name, bestowed the power of empathy to its hosts, but it also tasked, or rather compelled, them with using it to help others and, of course, seeking a new host.

What a gift, you might say. *Who wouldn't want that?* Before you answer, just imagine feeling everyone's feelings shouting at you, gnawing at your soul, and all the while you know that you can only do so much to help, as you are also driven to pass the Gift along. It's both an honor and a burden, and right or wrong, I didn't want it for Dalia. So, I was on a mission like a devout soldier and as single-minded about its success. I needed a new host, not Dalia, that was willing, and ironically, did not protest.

It didn't take long.

I had a meeting with one of my client's lawyers, Mr. Charles Stock. He was a handsome man in his early forties, tall and muscular, and he shaved his head even though his receding hairline was still in its infancy. The engagement with this man was not due to my genius or diligence, as I thought then. He had a role to play, as we all did, in a bigger game mystic in its design, one that had started hundreds of years before our time. Isn't it pretty to think that I made all the right choices then?

Stock and I had worked on a project for weeks, and the final signature would bring many rewards to both of us. We had agreed to meet at Le Colonial on Cosmo Place to sign and then celebrate. Le Colonial is a brilliant Vietnamese and French fusion restaurant, with a nice Tiki bar on its second floor.

He had arrived first and was sitting upstairs, making sure we would have a table to ourselves. We both ordered a Cosmo Place, a classic cosmo with guava and pineapple juice. It wasn't my usual drink, but the bartender had a way of making it irresistible.

"Here's to our success," he said, holding his cocktail glass.

We clanged the glasses and took a sip. When I looked up, the Gift churned as if it had recognized him for the first time even though I'd had many meetings with him. It made it clear that Stock was the one and he would be an attentive host, *unlike me*. I don't think the Gift actually conveyed the last part, but certainly that's how it felt at the time.

He may be the right host, I thought, but I wasn't sure how to transfer it. I had received it during sex, even if Joseph had felt ethereal at the moment. I was ready to fuck Mr. Stock if it would get rid of this thing. I would fuck Mr. Stock a hundred times if I could be free of it. I could feel that if not Stock, then Dalia would be next, and I would never let that happen. But now, this man would be far enough away from her so that she would remain protected. They would never meet, I assumed, and I would be rid of this parasite, my Gift. I was certainly wrong there.

In the end, it did not require any sordid affair between Mr. Stock and me. The Gift, eager to leave its home and its insane parent, guided me, and I only had to offer a choice to Stock.

"Mr. Stock," I began.

"You don't have to be so formal all the time. My friends just call me Stock."

"By your last name?"

"I hate my first."

"Okay. I know you are ready to sign this contract, which you've worked so hard to bring to fruition. And you would be a fool to pass on it."

"I couldn't agree more. I've given up so much to be here," Mr. Stock said.

I looked at him and nodded. In the way that two strangers can sometimes share secrets more freely than two intimates, he had, in a moment of honesty, told me about his wife leaving him because his work always came first. After this deal, he would make partner at his firm, a quest that had taken everything else from him. I wondered if he would think of me as silly or laugh at me after he heard what I was about to offer him instead.

"I want to offer you something different," I began again.

"Something good, I'd hope," he teased.

We had been flirting a bit for a while, and I couldn't deny my attraction to him. We stayed professional throughout our transactions, but I was sure he would ask me out after signing the contract.

Not if he takes my deal, I thought, and I wasn't ready anyway. "I think it is good. I think it will be good for you," I said, still worried how I might present the options without sounding foolish.

"Then get on with it, Zolie," he said and smiled. He was too sure of himself.

There was no option but to blurt it out—at least that's what the Gift told me, or that's what I thought it told me. Everything was an abstraction, wrapped in vagueness.

I took a deep breath and closed my eyes for a second, like you do a moment before taking a dive from high above into the deep end of the pool. I held a pen in my right hand, made a fist around it, then put my left hand on the table, palm up.

"Take my pen to sign the contract or take my empty hand," I said.

"Are you serious?" Stock asked, somewhat bemused.

"Don't think, Stock. Just choose. I have a pen in one hand, which will lead you to all you have struggled to achieve. But in my other hand, I hold all the other possibilities."

Any sane person would have taken the pen and signed the contract immediately, but not Stock as I had hoped.

"It may sound weird, but my I touch your face?" I asked, knowing full well nothing else would sound as strange as my offer.

He nodded, still thinking of this as a strange game. I touched his face very gently with my fingers while still holding the pen in my right hand, making sure the options were clear to him. I could feel a tiny bit of the power of empathy flowing through my fingers and penetrating his body. I pulled back and displayed my hands as I had done earlier. He hadn't yet understood what was offered in my hand, but he had felt the energy from it.

It's preposterous to think there is anything hidden in an empty hand, or that a sane person would consider it in place of rich rewards simply gained by a signature with the pen in the other hand. Yet, there we were, two strangers who, through a momentary touch, connected on the deepest level. I could easily feel that at that moment, this proposal was exactly what he needed in his life: a purpose beyond himself.

He looked down at my hands and then at me. "Just take it and you will understand," I said.

He kept his eyes on me. I could feel he desperately wanted to believe my absurd offer, and yet his rational lawyer-self was trying to dissuade him. The inner struggle didn't last long; after a few more moments of hesitation, he took my empty hand, and with that touch, the Gift left me and joined Stock.

Oddly, I felt betrayed by the parasite that I had nourished above everything else. I looked at Stock and I hated him for becoming such a gentle host. I hated him for taking it voluntarily, and then I felt empty and sad, and I wanted to cry because I remembered my husband and father and mother. And I felt ashamed for forgetting so quickly.

Is that how it is? When we die, we become another memory and nothing else? Dalia had insisted that we were energy, a force that travels from place to place, and we never die. "If we are made of energy, then we are neither created nor destroyed," she would say often. But it's not right, or at least it's not my truth: my family is dead and gone, and I can barely hold on to their memories. My mother's hug, my father's wise eyes, and my husband's touch are all gone. I tried to remember them but even then, the Gift gone from me, I could no longer feel them. There was only the man named Charles Stock, who at that moment was so enthralled by his newly found power that he could not even see me.

I got up from the table intent on leaving, but then I saw my imaginary friend, Joseph, sitting only a few feet away from me. I wondered where he had been in the past few months though even then I knew deep down that he had always been there, even if I had denied it to myself.

I walked over to him. "You're back?"

"I never left you, Zuleika. I told you I will be with you as long as you need me."

I reached out and touched his face. "You are real," I said.

"Yes."

I started to cry, and Joseph held me and tried to console me, and I kissed him. I needed to be sure. "Are you real?" I asked. I needed to *know*, even though I already knew.

"I am as real as you want me to be."

"No," I said. "That's not enough. I need you to be as real as *you* can be. Can you do that for me?"

"Yes. I can and I will."

I kissed him and he kissed me back and it felt real as real an ordinary kiss might feel. "What will happen to us?" I asked.

"We can grow old together."

"Is it possible?" I wasn't sure if I could believe him.

"Anything is possible, if you believe it, Zuleika. You've been part of my life for a long time through myth and reality, and you are part of it again."

I looked around and asked, "Why are you here?"

"I was waiting for you."

"Here? In this bar?"

"Yes. I was waiting for you. . . ." Joseph paused, thinking about what to say and then, "I was waiting for you to want me."

"Oh, you've been gone such a long time, I almost forgot about you," I said. "I was sure you were as imaginary as Dalia has been telling me."

"We will prove her wrong," he replied.

I looked over where Stock was still sitting. "Will I forget him?"

"I believe you will, though even I cannot be sure. The Gift may have a different lingering impact on different people." And then: "I think you can forget him if you want."

"I do," I replied, because I only wanted to look forward to my life with Joseph. But that's a folly of being involved with gods. Given the choice now, I would ask to preserve every detail of the memories of those past three months, but at that moment, I had no hint of Stock's future role in Dalia's life. Even though it is all clear now, at the time, I felt muzzy and unsure. It was like I was waking up from a long entailed dream only to find out that dreams and reality have intertwined, and my old life, the life before Joseph, was the one that was dishonest in its denial of the existence of gods in between us.

We kissed again. He was real and I believed in him, even though he held yet another secret. I could feel it within him as he touched me. There was yet another obstacle.

"What are you still holding back?"

"I'm not surprised you can feel it. That's why it scares me."

"What is it? Tell me."

"It's my burden and not yours, Zuleika, but, like the Gift, this one also needs a new host."

"Oh, the *Gift*," I said. "You should have warned me about it when you impregnated me with it. It felt more like a parasite for the longest time."

"The Gift made you push me away," Joseph said.

"Did it now? That's a fine excuse, Joseph."

"I am sorry. It was never meant for you. It was my fault. I lost control but never again. I will protect you."

I shook my head. "It became like a gift after a while, and it helped me cope with the loss of my family. But now that's gone, the misery is back and so are you." I smiled and he smiled back, clearly understanding how I was feeling.

I reached out and held his hand. "I am so miserable and yet so happy. Does that make sense?"

"It does, Zuleika. I will help you with your sadness and I can bring you joy. I can be Joseph to you, and for you and forever."

"I want to know more about you and the Gift and what you still hold within."

Joseph took a deep breath and then exhaled sharply. "I will try, but I don't have all the answers, Zuleika. One of my oldest comrades once told us that we are all nothing but simple servants. But I have tried to be more. I am Joseph now, and I will be Joseph for our sake."

"I still don't understand. I should be outraged. I should be in a state of disbelief. This is not normal. People don't have powers like this. How's that possible?"

"I don't know, Zuleika, and it won't matter anyway."

"It matters to me," I insisted, never liking to be dismissed.

"It won't matter because the Gift will be a distant dream to you, though I believe I can try to keep some of your memories of its power. If we are lucky, perhaps one day you will remember it all."

"No," I cried out. "No. I won't let that happen. I need to remember it now, so I can keep protecting Dalia."

Joseph shook his head. "I'll try to help. The fact that you have not forgotten it already is a good sign that perhaps some of the residues of the Gift will stay with you. But I cannot be sure. Your body may reject the remanence of it."

"What? No."

Joseph smiled and said, "You do not need to fear this change, Zuleika. I promise I will tell you about what I hold within, and I will try to make you believe me even if you forget all about the Gift. And I will ask you to accompany me as I find a new home for it."

I still didn't understand what Joseph was trying to tell me; I was focused on holding on to the memories of the Gift, telling myself that I was smart enough to manage this simple task. I was in denial then, but now I can admit that I did feel the clarity of emotions that had been part of me slowly seeping away. It felt like when you have the answer on the tip of your tongue, but the harder you try to remember it, the further you get from it.

"I will *not* forget the Gift," I said, hoping my forceful tone would settle the matter.

"But you may, Zuleika because you are only a human."

I wanted to cry in frustration, but my rational self told me I should listen to Joseph. Oddly, more than anything else, it was the term "human" that jolted me. Perhaps it was the way he said it, like a superior alien visiting the Earth.

"What are you?" I asked softly.

"I have been many things. I am Joseph now, but my essence is of misery. I am also a host, and I hope for not much longer, to the seed of knowledge."

"What does that mean, Joseph? It makes no sense."

"Did it make sense when you were holding the Gift and could truly empathize and feel other people's joy?"

"No, not really," I replied. "I was sad, and my sadness made me insane."

"You don't honestly believe that, even if the Gift *is* leaving you."

"I don't know what to believe. It's all too much for one person. It's too much to have myths enter our real world. It's miserable, Joseph."

"I understand. I have shared human misery since the beginning."

"How awful."

"No. . . . Please don't hate me. . . ."

"You misunderstood, Joseph. I meant how awful *for* you. It must be so painful to carry everyone's burden."

He leaned over and kissed me. "We all have a duty, and this is mine. I cherish it, but for now, I cherish being with you for the time we have together."

"I still remember the Gift." I felt like a proud student reporting to her teacher. But I had to add, "Though I don't remember how it really felt when it was with me."

"That's a good sign, Zuleika. But do you recall what you did with it?"

'Yes," I said, and then, "No. I think I gave it to a man."

"When?"

"Today?" I replied. "Well, recently. I am certain of that." Then added quickly, "And I still remember the Gift." I thought that if I kept saying, I would remember it more, but, of course, what I remembered then was a vague concept of what the gift of empathy could do.

"And this bar?"

"To be honest, I don't know why I came to this bar. It's a tiki bar, for God's sake."

Joseph laughed. "You came here to pass on the Gift to its next host."

"Oh, I guess it makes sense. But why a tiki bar? That's insane."

"You are as sane as any human."

"Stop saying, *human.*"

"Of course. I am sorry, Zuleika. I forget sometimes. 'Person.'"

The conversation felt good, like two ordinary people talking despite the strangeness of the topic. But I was still worried—though I had begun to forget why—and he had not really answered my first question. "Why did you disappear when you gave me the Gift? "

"I didn't *disappear.* You forgot about me, as the new host has started to forget about you. Don't be angry, but that is the effect of the Gift on humans."

"I still don't understand. . . . But you know, I started to feel sure that I had imagined you, as Dalia has been insisting."

"I am sorry. Now we will prove her wrong," he said.

I laughed. "Definitely. Dalia has to see you so we can put that notion to rest."

"We will, and we will prove to her that I am as real as you."

"You are," I said and kissed him. "And your kisses are real and normal. But there is more to you and your story."

"Yes, and I will tell you everything if you allow me."

"What will happen to us?" I asked.

"We can grow old together if you still want me."

"Oh, I do want you, Joseph, but is it possible?" I wasn't sure if I could believe him.

"Everything is possible if you believe it, Zuleika."

I blinked a few times and shook my ahead.

"What is it?" Joseph asked. "Wow. I just had a massive déja vue . . . as if we have had this conversation before," I said.

"Me too," Joseph replied. "But it's good to repeat some conversations."

A LONG, ORNATE DINNER TABLE

You must pay close attention, as this is an important story.

You will be observing a dinner party that is about to begin, and like most parties, it will start slow and clumsy, but in time it will solidify and take shape and steadily will find its path. It will reach a climax when most, though not all, secrets are revealed, and finally, it will quiet down, and then it will die as most things do.

And in less than four years, the world will change, as you have doubtless observed.

None of the guests are here yet, and I can tell you're not ready anyway, so let's start with the room and its owners. It's a twenty-five by fifteen-foot dining room that, at this time, belongs to a married couple named Dalia Smart and Amani Parker. It's a Saturday in early October, and it's about 6:30 in the afternoon. Dalia and Amani have been married for more than two years by now. But their relationship will be addressed later as well.

But the room . . .

The walls are brushed azure with red flowers on the two doorways, hand-stenciled by Dalia. One path leads to the kitchen through the hallway and the other to the sitting room. The floor lamps give the room warmth, balanced by several massive flickering candles that cast long shadows on the wall. A long, ornate dinner table sits in the middle of the room that could accommodate fourteen people if everyone sits close to each other.

At the moment, there is only one person at the table, but as indicated, more people will come. Amani Parker is sitting at the end of the table, the one closest to the kitchen. Amani is not forty yet, but his hair has been salt and pepper for several years now—more salt than pepper, I would say. He has intense eyes and two large ears to balance his head. As he takes a sip of his coffee, Dalia enters the room. She is tall, and with her heels on, she is even taller than Amani. She has a gray full bistro apron on, covering most of her black dress.

"Do you want more coffee?" she asks. Amani shakes his head in response. Dalia nods. "Aren't you going to change? I think the blue linen shirt."

"It's too early, but I will soon," Amani replies without turning around. "Do you need help?" he asks, though he knows the answer.

"No. But change before the guests arrive." She pauses for a second and Amani turns around to look at her. She tilts her head and arches an eyebrow, knowing what she will say might start a row. "You know Jackie always comes early."

"So what? She's not a guest, anyway."

Dalia frowns and replies, "I'm not sure why you had to invite her. This dinner was supposed to be for Zuleika and now you have not only invited Jackie, but others too."

"It's better this way," he tries to reassure.

"For you, yes—"

"Jesus, Dalia. I know you don't like Jackie. We all know. The entire world knows it. But Jackie is my oldest friend and she is staying put. If I can tolerate Zolie, then you can tolerate Jackie."

"Huh—"

"Don't be a bitch."

"Don't say that. You know how much I hate that sexist word."

"Well, if you don't act like one, I won't say it."

"You can be so heartless sometimes."

"Me? You're the one who started it. Why don't we call off this stupid party? Zolie and you, and whoever this new boyfriend of hers is, could all get together and have fun. That's how you like it anyway."

"Oh, yes. That's how I like it. That's why I've spent hours preparing food for your guests."

"My guests?"

She ignores him. He wouldn't get it anyway. "Right . . . go and get dressed before Jackie shows up."

"Sometimes I feel you think I work for you—one of your many minions. Open your mouth and we all snap to attention."

"I see. It's so easy to dismiss what I do and what I have done. I wonder what your response would be if I were a man?"

"The same."

She scoffs. "Of course. But we'll never know." She then turns around and leaves the room.

But wait, because a moment later, she comes back with a French press and tops off Amani's cup. She knows him well.

"Thank you," Amani says.

"Would you like anything else?"

"I am good, thank you." Amani takes a sip.

Dalia nods and goes back to the kitchen. Amani takes another sip but then gets up and leaves the room to change.

Now we are alone but stay put. Close your eyes, take a deep breath, and enjoy the lingering aroma of the freshly brewed coffee while we wait for the guests to arrive. Can you smell its dark, rich fragrance? Can you taste it? Keep your eyes closed and wait. Try and hold it with all your being . Coffee has a power all its own.

*   *   *

Open your eyes.

The doorbell has been ringing for a while, and Dalia will be wrong with her prediction, the first of many. The door chimes again with its long, singsong tone. Dalia is studiously ignoring it.

Amani finally comes down and walks toward the front entrance. He is wearing a blue linen shirt.

Let's follow him.

He opens the door and a look of surprise washes over him. He too expected Jackie to be first.

"John! Ashley! I'm so glad you guys made it."

"We thought you weren't home," John moans.

"Nah. Just upstairs, changing. Come on in," Amani says and walks away from the doorway to let them in. Ashley kisses him, and the men shake hands and then hug.

Ashley is short and has curly blond hair, but her eyes are hazel brown. She has a round face with a small, pointed nose. John is tall and big with brown hair and eyes. He has a long face that his short haircut has made look even longer. You don't have to memorize their faces as they are very distinct, and you won't miss them throughout the dinner.

"It's been a long time, Amani," Ashley says.

"Come on in," Amani offers again.

John shivers a bit and shakes his head as if dispelling an unwanted feeling. "Wow. That was strange. I felt a cold finger running up my spine." He rubs his hands and gives a shy a smile, as if he was caught doing something naughty.

That was my fault. I stood too close to him without guarding my presence. People sometimes get chills or shivers down their spine, and although most often it is normal frisson (and I love how you call it *musical chills*), occasionally it's because of me. I will be more careful, and they will dismiss my little faux pas anyway.

Amani laughs. "This is a haunted house," he says and John nods, as the feeling was not lasting (what did I tell you?). Amani escorts them to the dining room and before they can sit down, Dalia walks in.

"Dalia, John Archer and Ashley Negussie," Amani offers with an extended arm and then adds, "They are *Jackie's* and my good friends from college."

Dalia shakes hands with John first and then reaches over to Ashley but pauses. "You look so familiar," she says. "Have we met before?"

"I don't think so. We've been away for a long time now."

"Oh! You know how you get that feeling," Dalia says. "Never mind. I'm glad you both made it," she says and reaches to hug Ashley.

"Is Jackie coming too?" John asks.

"Of course, she is," Dalia replies. "It's nice meeting you both. I need to finish up in the kitchen," she adds, and then, looking at Amani, "Please offer them some wine, and pour me a glass too."

"Do you need help?" John asks.

"No, I'm good. Please enjoy yourselves and I'll be back soon," Dalia says as she leaves the room.

Amani takes out the decanter from the side table, pours some wine and hands each guest a glass without asking. He takes one to the kitchen for Dalia and returns as quickly.

"Sit. Sit. Don't be so formal," Amani says and then sits back on the same chair as before. Ashley and John sit on the other side of the table.

The doorbell rings again, and before Amani can stand up, Dalia calls out from the kitchen, "I'll get it."

Let's follow Dalia this time.

She walks through the side door of the kitchen to the foyer and opens the door.

"Hi, Dalia," says the woman with a small smile as she hands Dalia a bottle of wine.

"Hello," replies Dalia. They stand there for a moment, and then as if remembering the occasion, Dalia says, "Come in, Jackie."

Jackie walks in and gives us a furtive glance.

Ignore that for now. She didn't really see us, but Jackie is a special person, isn't she?

"Amani is in the dining room," Dalia says and walks away.

Jackie goes straight in.

There are no faults here, nor are any of these women unkind. Dalia doesn't trust or like Jackie. But Jackie is her husband's friend—as Amani reminds her often—and she is going to tolerate her.

Jackie has been Amani's friend for more than a decade and isn't going to give up on her friendship with him because she doesn't like Dalia. It is a perfect relationship of mutually hateful patience.

There is a more sordid story to the trio, and more on that later. Keep in mind the fault wholly belongs to Amani.

Let's follow Jackie now.

As soon as Jackie enters the room, Amani stands and goes to her. They hug each other affectionately but then pull away. That will be their only sign of tenderness toward each other tonight. John and Ashley also stand up and hug and kiss Jackie. They stand around in a tight circle chatting for a while, but then they all settle down and Jackie sits next to Amani as he pours her some wine.

Now that Jackie is here, a bit about the four, since there won't be another chance: John was Amani's roommate in college and Ashley was Jackie's friend at the same university. John and Ashley never got along in the beginning and for a time, it seemed the four might not make it, but at the end of their senior year, when Amani and Jackie had been romantically involved for a while—yes, the source of the cleave between Jackie and Dalia—John and Ashley also became a couple.

Okay, let's pause again. No one can judge how others may or may not feel. Let's agree on that. Jackie and Amani were a couple for two years and that was almost a decade before Dalia met Amani. Yes, he never told Dalia about those two years, or how they were planning to have children together. Of course, that's bad by itself, but it wasn't Jackie's fault. Okay, yes, Jackie could have said something, and perhaps she should have, but she didn't think it was her place. There is a time and place for everything. It's all about delivery.

We all know that, except perhaps Amani. He blurted all the details out when he asked Dalia to marry him—his way of starting a new life with a clean slate. He didn't think about the consequences of his action, and ultimately that's his Achilles heel. I can tell you more, but that is a story by itself. It suffices to say, it didn't work out the way he had played it in his mind, but in the end, he was fine with the results. He was happy, and he thought the two women should get over themselves. It's worth mentioning again that Amani is the only one at fault here.

That is now, but at the commencement, Jackie, Amani, Ashley, and John were focused on their immediate future. They never said it, but each thought the four of them would stay together, and they would have children at the same time, and the kids would call each other cousin and the adults aunt and uncle. John and Ashley married a few years later, well on their way to fulfilling the unspoken promise, but nothing else came to fruition. Amani and Jackie were no longer a couple; John and Ashley moved to Boston and decided they didn't want any children.

Now, the four start reminiscing about their college years, and it's not that interesting. They will speak uninterrupted for a while—none of them offering to help Dalia, as Amani would tell them it was pointless to offer anyway. It's going to be a boring conversation, so while we wait for the last guests to arrive, we can see what Dalia is doing in the kitchen.

Let's go.

*   *   *

In the kitchen, Dalia is putting green olives on a small blue plate. She takes a white towel and wipes the side of the dish of any unwanted liquid. She then takes out the tortilla from the pan, flips it over, and puts it on a pedestal designed for this dish. The tortilla, like a thick, round pillow, lies heavily on the plate, releasing steam. Next, she arranges the sardines and slides the rectangular plate toward the other dishes, the porcelain echoing as it glides across the granite countertop. She slices the *jamón* paper-thin and lays it like flower petals on a wooden plate. She then starts on *gambas al ajillo* on a stone-plated pan. The shrimps turn light orange as they soak the garlic through their thin shells.

She is shuffling and turning and stirring, and each dish whistles and whines and sizzles. The metal spoon bangs against the clay pot, and the liquid inside makes a burping sound. The dishes push against each other on the counter and the stove, each competing for her attention. She slides the ones on the counter to one side to make more room for new arrivals, walks to the stove and checks the food inside the lower oven through its glass door. With an approving nod, she steps back and takes a long sip from her wine glass. She opened a new bottle when she started cooking, and now it is half empty. The culinary orchestra is close to its finale.

Dalia closes her eyes and takes in the aroma of the wine. She is not ready to return to Amani's friends yet. She lets out a deep sigh and starts decorating the desert, happy doing the intricate work.

Let's leave her.

We can explore the house or go back and listen to the four friends reminiscing about the years before and all the good days they had.

No, wait. Let's step outside of the house as two new guests are arriving.

We know them well. Joseph is the tall man with a remarkably youthful face that most would claim as very handsome. The other is Zuleika, a woman with luxuriant black hair and rather intense eyes. They are holding hands facing the front door but they have yet to ring the bell. They look good together, as if they were made for each other. Don't you agree?

Zuleika lets go of Joseph's hand and faces him. "I really want Dalia to like you."

"She will," Joseph assures her.

"I know she will, when she knows you better." She kisses him. "But you know . . . sometimes you sound strange to people, and there will be other guests tonight, and . . ."

"I will do my best to be as human as possible."

She gives a nervous laugh and kisses him again. "Thank you, but it works better if you don't say *human* every time you refer to us."

"Yes, I see. But, Zuleika, as you well know, I also have a task, and I will need to do what I must to complete it."

"I know. And I understand. I am just a bit nervous. I should have asked Dalia to meet you before this party.""I could go away."

She smiles. "'Go away'? Don't be silly. Dalia is expecting you. I'm sure it will be fine."

"It will be fine," Joseph assures her again. "I'll blend in."

"That's very doubtful, my darling."

"Oh," Joseph says.

"What?"

"Zuleika, don't be alarmed, but I feel the presence of another powerful entity nearby."

It may be us, so let's step back a bit.

"Should I be worried?" Zuleika asks and looks around.

Don't worry; she cannot see us.

"No. Forget it. It could just be an old friend," he says with a smile.

Zuleika takes a deep breath. "Joseph?"

"Yes?"

"Could you do me a favor, and if you feel another invisible presence tonight, keep it to yourself? Could you do that for me?"

"Of course," he says, but in order to be truthful, he quickly adds, "I'll do my best."

"I guess that's all I can ask. Now, let's go in before I change my mind," she says and presses the doorbell.

Inside the doorbell chimes, but this time Dalia doesn't offer to get it, still busy with the last touches. In the dining room, they are involved with their conversation as the doorbell rings again.

Finally, Jackie calls out, "I'll get it."

Let's go.

She walks to the entrance and opens the large door.

"Hey, Jackie," Zuleika says, and she reaches over the threshold and kisses Jackie affectionately.

"God, I'm so glad to see you, Zolie. I've missed you. You look so much better."

After the accident that caused the death of Zuleika's family, they were all concerned with her physical and later her mental health. They are relieved that she's up for the party tonight, even if they don't know what to expect of her date.

"Thank you. I feel much better," Zolie replies and then looks at the person next to her. "This is my friend, Joseph."

"Hi. Come on in," Jackie says, then raises her hand to shake Joseph's, but before she can reach him, Zolie intervenes and hugs her again.

"Thank you again for visiting me. I needed it," Zuleika offers.

Jackie smiles and replies, "Don't be silly. You know we were all heartbroken after the car accident . . . and . . ."

"You are sweet. It meant a lot to have you visit me while I was recovering, Jackie."

Jackie gives a shy smile but doesn't press the point.

Joseph has been standing back and has withdrawn his hand, as if he'd never offered it. He smiles and says, "I'm glad to meet you, Jackie. I've heard so much about you."

"You have?"

"Yes. I feel I know all of Zuleika's friends."

Dalia walks in from the kitchen and says with relief, "Great, Zolie, you made it." And she then stares at Joseph.

He gives a knowing smile but doesn't say anything. Zuleika nudges Dalia, and says, "This is Joseph."

Dalia blinks twice and laughs nervously. "I'm sorry, but I have to ask, has anyone told you how handsome you look?"

"Yes," replies Joseph.

Dalia composes herself quickly and adds, "Oh, yes, of course. I do apologize, Joseph, but for a moment, you looked rather angelic."

Zuleika laughs and Dalia joins in while Jackie watches the odd interaction.

"I don't know how to explain it, Dalia," Zuleika stammers. "I guess . . . I could say . . . Well, Joseph evokes a certain reaction from people. It's all good, you know, and it won't last long. He is just a regular guy, really."

For a while, you see, Zuleika had only thought of Joseph as a figment of a sad mind, a kind of anchor to help her through her misery. They had come a long way from those dark days and could now easily laugh, though at the moment Zuleika's laugh is more to cover her nervousness. Introducing a new boyfriend to friends is always tricky but more so when the partner happens to be a deity.

Yet Joseph's appearance at tonight's dinner is not a coincidence. That's why this is an important story, and you must pay attention.

Dalia nods and says, "I guess I shouldn't be surprised that Zolie would only *imagine* someone like you."

"Yes," Joseph replies. "She needed me and I was there for her and will be there as long as she wants me."

Graciously, Dalia ignores the odd response. "Again, my apologies, Joseph. It was rather forward of me. I'm so glad to have finally met you."

Well, that's finally settled.

Dalia grabs Zuleika's hand and gives a warm smile. "I've a bit more to do in the kitchen. Come with me so we can chat more."

Zuleika hesitates for a moment, clearly nervous about leaving Joseph alone. She looks at Joseph and then at Dalia. She squeezes Dalia's hand and says, "Yes, of course."

She cannot be with him every moment of the night and she trusts Jackie.

"Jackie, could you introduce Joseph to Amani?" "Of course."

Zuleika looks at Joseph and says, "Remember what we just talked about."

"Yes," he says.

Zuleika nods a few times, though it doesn't look like she is entirely convinced. Nevertheless, she grabs Dalia's hand and leads her to the kitchen, her odd remark hanging in the air.

Jackie leads Joseph to the dining room but before entering, she stops and asks, "What did Zolie mean?"

"Sometimes people have an odd reaction to me."

"Why?"

"I'm not sure I can explain. But I look normal to you?"

"Shouldn't you?"

"I should. I am. It'll be ok," Joseph says, and he then looks be-hind him, stares at us, and then smacks his lips.

You can smack your lips too or, better yet, ignore him for now. He thinks we are judging him. . . . Well, he is sort of right, but we are not here just for him. Let's follow them in.

They both walk in the room and Jackie announces, "Everyone, this is Joseph, Zolie's friend."

Joseph walks over and shakes hands with Amani, John, and then Ashley. The last handshake lingers for a moment as Ashley won't let go, and says in a singsong tone, "You're a handsome devil, aren't you?" They all stare at her and her face turns red. "So sorry, did I say that out loud?"

At the same moment, Dalia and Zuleika walk in with trays of tapas, little forks, and plates and lay the food on the table. It's somewhat surprising that they came back so quickly. You would think they would talk more about Joseph in private, but probably Zuleika wants to keep an eye on Joseph.

"Sit down, Joseph, before you annoy everyone," Zuleika says, and with that, everyone starts moving. Joseph walks over and sits obediently next to John, and Jackie sits next to him. Zuleika sits on the other side of the table, next to Amani.

There is a momentary hush, as if no one knows what to say next. Then Amani reaches over and takes a slice of tortilla with his little fork and puts it in his mouth. Others follow, taking pieces of *gambas al ajillo*, sardines, and tortilla.

The bowl of olives is next to Joseph, and John tries to take a few but drops them on the way to his plate, so there is a row of green olives on the table. Joseph takes one off the table, puts it in his mouth, and chews slowly as if tasting it for the first time.

"What do you do, Joseph?" John asks, perhaps to recover from his faux pas.

"I do nothing," he replies, still chewing the olive. He looks at Dalia and says, "These are different."

"Nothing!" Dalia says. "I thought you were a . . ." She trails off. "I'm sorry. I'm sure Zolie told me, but I can't remember."

"He's a consultant," Zuleika adds quickly.

"What type?" John asks.

"I'm not a consultant," he replies and takes another olive. "Dalia, how did you make them? They're so amazing."

"But, Zolie said . . ." John looks puzzled but then, remembering his manners, turns to Zuleika and says, "I'm sorry, may I call you Zolie?"

"Of course, everyone but Joseph does."

"Thank you. But you did say he is a consultant?"

"He likes to tease," offers Zuleika, and then turning to Joseph. "You like to tease, don't you? But stop it now. You are a consultant."

"Yes, I am a consultant," he replies automatically as he takes a third olive.

"I'm glad that's resolved," Amani says, "and not to push the point, but what kind?"

"The kind that consults," Joseph replies.

"He's joking again, and he should stop," Zuleika warns. "He's a boring business consultant."

"I am a boring consultant," he says and then, "But more importantly, I can tell there is a hint of coffee in these olives."

"There is, actually," Dalia says. "No one has ever noticed before."

"I can tell. These olives are amazing. I could eat a million of them."

"I'm so glad you like them. Have more," Dalia says.

"I will, but you should have one too," Joseph says, then takes one of the olives with his delicate fingers and puts it in Dalia's mouth.

Amani looks annoyed, but it doesn't matter. It is not about him, and clearly Dalia doesn't mind as she welcomes the little gift and chews slowly. She smiles, looking rather contented. "These are good," Dalia says after finishing eating her gift. She looks happy.

"Maybe you should go in the olive consulting business," Ashley offers, wanting to get into the game. "You clearly have a magical touch."

"I should."

"Now I'm intrigued. What is it you do?" John asks.

"I am a consultant, especially if your business is misery," Joseph offers and looks at us wickedly.

Try and ignore his bad etiquette.

"My business *is* misery," Ashley says. "I work with stupid students who are getting dumber every day."

"That's not fair, Ashley," rejoins John. "We love our students. We have the best job in the world."

Ashley shakes her head but doesn't respond.

"I sympathize," Dalia says. "I don't know about your campus, but if it's anything like the ones we have in this city, then we are all in trouble. I can't hire a decent person to work for me."

"Admit it, Dalia, you just have too high of a standard," Jackie says, and we can tell she regrets speaking out. "I mean . . ."

Amani leans forward a bit and says, "I agree. Dalia, you sometimes forget that things can be difficult for some people, especially when they're just starting."

He sits back, but Dalia is focused on Jackie. "I'm sorry, *Jackie*, but not all of us can work in the high art of book cover design," Dalia answers.

"It's not as easy as you always make it out to be. I have to read every manuscript to make sure the cover speaks the truth."

"The truth? Tell me about the truth when you manage millions of dollars, and every single piece of information can take the market up or down by billions. *That's* the truth."

"And that's why I am in the business of misery," Joseph says calmly, looking at Jackie with some interest.

"Where do you guys work?" Zuleika asks, looking at Ashley and John.

"At good old DSU," John offers. "I teach philosophy and Ashley is a physicist."

"Is it a public school? How's the campus doing?" Zuleika asks quickly, not allowing others to chime in.

"As desperate as ever," Ashley replies.

"It's not all that bad. In fact, it's great," John says. "I love my students. I do. I wish I could spend more time with them."

"And I think they need that kind of extra attention," Amani says, leaning forward again. "To be honest, the more I think about it, the more I agree that students nowadays need more handholding."

"So now you agree with Ashley and me," Dalia says.

"I don't think it's a binary thing. I am just trying to digest what everyone is saying. I think you all are making good points, but it's rather a complex subject. We need to have the right data and correctly analyze them to get the right answer." Amani bangs on the table to stress his point. "Then you have knowledge. Then you have the power of knowledge. And that's how we move forward."

Dalia shakes her head. "It's just simple dinner time banter."

Ashley reaches out and pats Amani on the head. "Well, you haven't changed a bit, darling. Still seeking that morsel of hidden knowledge, aren't you?"

"Well, you know, *the secret things belong to God, but the things that are revealed belong to us*," Amani offers.

Jackie laughs and says, "Lovely, now you, an atheist, is quoting from the bible. That's why we love him."

"And some more than others," Dalia adds and then not wanting to start another argument quickly adds, "It won't be a fun conversation without Amani taking all sides of an argument."

Joseph opens his mouth to say something, but Zuleika shakes her head to stop him, and says rather loudly, "So, John, you love your students."

And that puts all the attention back on John.

"Yes. If I could teach more classes, I would. It's a blessing to be able to educate these students. It's a joy to see them love philosophy and history. It's so nice to see them grow as human beings. Ashley is complaining because she is going to be the department chair next semester."

"Wow. Nice," Jackie says.

"It's all right. I'm tired of dealing with stupid students," Ashley replies. "I feel each class is getting dumber and dumber and dumber, and I've only been teaching graduate classes for several years now. I don't even know how bad it is at the undergrad level. But I'm sure I'll learn soon."

"That's not true," says John. "My students aren't dumb. They are so enthusiastic. Yes, they need help, but it's difficult to work full-time and take classes. It's tough out there, nowadays."

"Yeah, and it was *so* easy for us," Amani says.

"That's not the point. Yes, it was hard for us too," John retorts, "but it was different. At DSU, we have students whose parents haven't even finished high school."

"My parents didn't go to college, and Jackie and I had to work to put ourselves through school," Amani says.

John shakes his head but gives a smile to reassure Amani. "I know. I was there, remember? I know it was hard, but I am telling you, it's much harder now."

Amani taps his finger on the table as if thinking of a response but doesn't reply.

"I still say they are getting dumber," Ashley insists. "And I don't mean it figuratively. I'm not one of those people who think the past has always been golden."

"I don't know. I work with lots of brilliant writers and editors," Jackie says.

"Maybe not dumber, but less inquisitive. Kids are so entitled," Dalia says.

Amani nods a few times. "That, I agree with."

"No, seriously," Ashley insists. "I think there is a worldwide deficit of mental capacity."

Joseph leans closer to her and asks, "Have you seen tangible evidence of this decay? Something measurable and not just your perception."

Zuleika puts her arms on the table and shakes her head. "Haven't you been listening to Ashley? Not that I agree with her."

"I have, but . . ."

Ashley cries out. "Yes, I have ample evidence. That's what I have been trying to say."

Joseph looks at Zuleika and says in earnest, "I was afraid of this, Zuleika. This means the knowledge must be released, even if for a brief time. If *she* can see its absence, then others will, too."

Zuleika was about to say something but everybody laughs at Joseph's deadpan urgency, and she joins them, relieved.

"You don't have to believe me," Ashley says. "Even though it's the truth."

"Oh, I believe you," Joseph says.

"But you don't," Zuleika insists.

"But I do. I thought we had more time, but maybe not."

"More time for what? Are you being serious?" Jackie asks.

"No," says Zuleika.

"Yes," Joseph replies.

"I'm confused," declares John.

"He's joking. He likes to rile up people and he shouldn't, especially when he just met you all. He has no filter. He's from Europe."

"What?" Dalia asks. "Where?"

"Okay, he is not from Europe, but he has no filter."

"That's true," Joseph offers and smiles at Zuleika. When she doesn't respond in kind, he adds, "I love a good argument and love to be the contrarian of the group. So please pardon my insistence."

That extracted a small smile from Zuleika. "That's fine, Joseph, as long as you don't go too far." She looks around the table. "I want them to like you," she moans.

"We like him just fine, but I still want to hear what Ashley has to say," Amani says. "There is certainly something to it."

No one objects, so Ashley sits up straight and says, "I think when the world was created, or at least when the modern world was created, there was a mountain of knowledge, and each person was given a tiny bit of it when they were born."

"What? Are you talking metaphorically?" Jackie asks.

"Maybe, but maybe not. I think most people did nothing with it. They died and took it to the grave with them."

"Are you discounting all the scientists, mathematicians, philosophers, and everybody else who adds and has added to our knowledge? You are a scientist, Ashley. Are you discounting yourself?" John asks.

"I'm not. We certainly helped grow knowledge, at least to a degree, but there is never enough of us."

"Huh, so people like me are useless?" Jackie cries out.

"It isn't about you, Jackie, or John or Amani. All of you are great people, and I am lucky to have known you. Please let me make my point."

"Okay."

"I think . . . No! I believe there was a large but limited supply of knowledge, and then too many people took a piece of it and did nothing with it . . . and when they died, it died with them."

"You said that already," Amani offers. "But go on. I am truly fascinated."

"Yes. We didn't notice the loss of knowledge because the population wasn't large enough, and from the inside, it looked like we were growing our comprehension, and perhaps we were. We certainly advanced our technology, but strictly speaking, that's not the same thing as knowledge."

"Literature, philosophy, medicine, mathematics, and everything else in between—what about that?" Jackie asks.

"Let me finish, Jackie, and then you can shred it apart as you always do."

"I never . . ."

"Right," Ashley says and then, looking at Dalia. "I'm sure you know, but Amani and Jackie never let anything go unchallenged."

Dalia nods but doesn't reply. Jackie adds, "That's not fair. It was never me."

"How about we let her finish, for God's sake," Amani demands and then glances at Jackie quickly adding, "Please."

Ashley continues, "If you step back and observe without bias, then you'll see that humanity has plateaued, and in some cases, has even regressed." She takes a deep breath but doesn't want to let others in, so adds quickly, "And it's not only with our students, you know. Consider our politicians, business and military leaders, and the so-called scholars and others we rely on to advance knowledge. They are all failing us. Can't you see that? Not only do I feel it, but increasingly, I can see it."

"I still love my students. And I still think they are gaining something from their education. Maybe it's our generation that's dumb, and the next one is going to make our world better. At least they are more welcoming and more inclusive," John says.

"Are they? Are they more welcoming? Are they more inclusive? I think they don't know what those things are. I think they wouldn't know how to tie their shoelaces if we didn't bend down and remind them how," Dalia declares.

"But wait," Amani interjects. "Wouldn't it be nice if it were true, though? Imagine if that's how we distributed knowledge. If there was this mountain and each got a bit. What if someone took more than a bit? Is that how some people are smarter than the rest of us? Would that even be possible?"

"That makes no sense," Jackie says. "That's not how intelligence or even knowledge is imparted."

Amani ignores her. "Imagine if someone took more than a little. If someone took a whole bunch. Imagine the awesome power of it."

"It's silly, Amani," Dalia adds. "There is no awesome power in absolute knowledge, even if such a thing were possible."

"I agree with Dalia," Jackie says. "But what really exists is the *curse of knowledge*, you know."

"Bullshit," Amani replies.

"You can call it whatever you want, and I don't recall the name of the scientist who came up with this term, but apparently, there is a natural tendency to forget what it is like not to know something once you know it really well." Everyone is listening to Jackie. "So, it becomes almost impossible for you to share your deep knowledge with others since you no longer have the capability of recreating another's state of mind. Now take that to its natural end with absolute knowledge."

"Exactly right, Jackie," Ashely says. "You can't dumb yourself down enough to tell dumb people how to learn."

"Knowledge is power, and that's a fact," Amani says. "Plus, we are not talking about simple human learning, we are talking about knowledge in its absolute form. I have no doubt it exists."

Jackie throws her hands up and says, "Remember the Persian proverb, *doubt is the key to knowledge*."

"What? It makes no sense, Jackie."

Jackie doesn't respond and Joseph, who has been listening to their debate with fascination, uses the momentary lull and pushes his chair back a bit to give himself more room, as if opening a large arena for his audience. See how he ignores Zuleika's gesture to stay put?

"What would you do with all that knowledge, Amani, or as you put it, *power*? Would you think of it as a gift?" he asks, and his layered tone is not missed by many.

"Imagine the good we could do," says Amani.

Joseph seems disappointed almost. "Bullshit, to use your term."

"Don't be rude, Joseph," Zuleika warns.

"I apologize, but I've heard that shi—*argument* before. I've seen the results of your kind doing *good*."

"My kind?" Amani cries out. "What's my kind?"

"Your kind is the human kind, Mr. Parker. I thought you would have known that by now," Joseph replies in his meticulous fashion.

Amani laughs heartily but doesn't respond, much to Zuleika's relief.

Dalia stands up and says, "At any rate . . . it's time for dinner."

Dalia is in a good mood. You can tell, and she even shows some warmth toward Jackie when she offers to help. Dalia accepts others' offer of help too. She instructs Jackie to take out dishes and utensils from a red china cabinet. John and Zuleika accompany her to the kitchen to bring the food in.

There is a lot of movement now, so let's step back a bit and let them do their work.

*   *   *

After the table is set to her satisfaction, Dalia sits down next to Zuleika.

"Please help yourself before the food gets cold," she offers and then to Jackie, "Do you mind serving the wine?" She is still in a good mood.

Jackie opens two more bottles and serves everyone. The dinner consists of stewed rabbit and wild mushrooms, red rice, salt-baked redfish, braised tomatoes, grilled eggplant with pomegranate, tahini and preserved lime, whole endives with gorgonzola cheese and walnut, baby green salad, watermelon with feta, fresh mint, and sea salt. There is also a basket of homemade sourdough bread in the middle. Dalia has been using the descendent of the same mother dough that her grandmother used.

Food is like the spring rain; it calms everyone. It slows us down (yes, even those of us who don't require it) and allows us to concentrate. It demands all our attention if we want to take it in thoroughly. After the initial flurry of activity, there is stillness now.

It's time for us to join them as well.

Close your eyes. . . . Savor the food with them.

We are lucky tonight because most of the people present love food. Keep your eyes closed and ignore their banal conversation accompanying the dinner. Those words are like the silence between the notes of taste, texture, and aroma. They are the rhythm needed to keep the flow, but not for us to notice.

So, close your ears, too, and put your senses to a different use for now.

Let's walk by each person around the table.

*   *   *

Dalia is a great cook, and though she is self-critical, she can stand back and take pleasure from her production. She cuts a small piece of the eggplant with all its accompaniments and puts it in the middle of her square, white plate. The eggplant's tight purple skin has turned dark and wrinkly, rippling against the flesh of the fruit. She takes her fork and slices a piece with tahini, pomegranate seeds, and preserved lime as its passengers. She puts the whole package in her mouth and takes delight in puncturing the pomegranate seeds with her teeth, the sweet and sour juice mixing with the other content. She can smell the seared eggplant mixed with sesame, and her tongue explores the soft, though not too soft, meat of the eggplant. There is a party in her mouth. She takes another bite and is happy with her product.

Dalia then leans over and cracks open the fish's salt casing, exposing the redfish's dull eye beneath it. She then takes a large fish knife and expertly filets a chunk of the white meat from the bone. She divides it into two, puts a piece on her plate, and carefully places the other portion on Zuleika's plate, next to the braised tomatoes.

Zuleika follows by taking a heap of salad from the salad bowl and carefully arranges the green leaves next to the redfish. She then takes the bowl and passes it to Amani. She takes a sip from her wine glass and tastes the bitterness of her lost family. She still feels anguished even after these many months. She was never going to stop grieving, and as much as she doesn't want to talk about the car accident and the death of her husband and her parents, she is still dismayed that no one had broached the subject yet.

She takes another sip and tastes cherrywood and cinnamon. It reminds her of her father and the rainy afternoons she spent with him playing chess. She wants to cry but instead takes the fork and attacks the baby greens. The tines of the fork bruise the soft leaves, enriching their green. She takes a bite and feels their velvety texture in her mouth.

Joseph feels the change in her disposition, gets up and walks over to the other side of the table. He doesn't want to bring attention to Zuleika, so he takes the bottle from the table and fills Dalia's and Zuleika's glasses in turn, putting his hand on Zuleika's shoulder for a moment as he does. Zuleika smiles and pats his hand. She already feels better, takes a sip from the new wine, and remembers her family's happy moments before the accident and the time she's spent with Joseph. Joy and misery are never too far apart, as he had promised. He goes back to his seat.

Zuleika takes a bit of the redfish and remembers how her mother used to make the same meal—not as beautifully displayed as Dalia's, but as good of taste and texture. A drop of sea salt stuck on the flesh adds to the flavor. She chews leisurely and as the fish grinds in between her teeth, she can smell the sea breeze.

Amani asks for the fish, and Dalia cuts him a large piece, all intact, shimmering under the candlelight. Amani is spoiled. Dalia is an excellent cook, and he expects perfection. He cuts a large chunk of the fish and chews it quickly. It tastes decent but not as good as her almond- and macadamia-crusted fish, or her seared tuna. He takes another bite and wishes she had prepared some of her young potatoes and fennel too. He takes the final morsel and reaches over to take a scoop of the stewed rabbit. It's good. He is not a fan of rabbit meat, but he can't deny it's good. He takes a small bite of the white meat and chews carefully. He wants the main meal to be over. He wants some of the pastries and a large glass of Irish coffee. He wants to hear more from Ashley.

Ashley wants to hear more from Ashley. She has piled up salad, rabbit, and fish on her dish, and a spoonful of each of the side dishes along with two of the endives. We all know what Dalia is thinking: she wants to get up and get Ashley a child's plate so each food could have its cell with walls separating the tastes. She is watching Ashley eating but can't take it for too long, so she tries to focus on the beautiful table. Ashley is oblivious to our stares. She has her head down, taking mouthfuls of food.

She only stops to say something. It could be profound or shallow; it doesn't matter. At this point, the rest of us don't want to hear from anyone. Keep your eyes closed even though you may be tempted to observe Ashley's head in the trough. Keep them closed and stay with me. Try to enjoy the food, at least once we move away from Ashley.

John is next to her. He is a slow eater. John loves to cook, but he is not particularly apt at the job. The problem is he gets distracted quickly, and cooking requires patience. John pays attention to his eating. He starts with the rabbit and takes a bite of the white meat drenched in the sauce, tasting the green pepper, garlic, and the slight hint of vinegar. The flesh is soft and it oozes the warm liquid. The aroma of paprika teases his nostrils as he chews carefully, trying to identify each ingredient.

John tells Dalia how much he loves the dish and asks her how she prepared the rabbit, making mental notes. He asks for a piece of the fish and then puts some of the eggplant next to it, as Dalia directs. The fish, the eggplant, and the bread all come to an explosion of flavors in his mouth. He doesn't want it to stop.

Each person enjoys the food in their way, even Ashley. But no one can appreciate what the world has to offer as Joseph does. All his senses are alive. Presently, he is dancing with the salad in front of him. He, like John, takes small bites. He touches the food with his fingers. He doesn't want his sense of touch to be left out. Don't ever let anyone tell you how to eat. Eat and drink with your whole body.

Joseph caresses the crust of the warm bread and takes in the aroma before putting it in his mouth. He chews carefully as his saliva changes the chemistry of the dough. Joseph picks up one of the small leaves from his plate, and the texture reminds him of a lamb's ear, soft and velvety. He takes a bite of it and then follows it with a fork full of greens. It's like a meadow. He takes a piece of the rabbit meat without any extra sauce, even after Dalia insists.

Joseph's plate is empty now, and he considers what's on the table. He takes one of the endives with his fingers. It feels dry and cold, and there is a slight cracking sound as the fibers break under his bite, and with it, the pungent flavor of the cheese mixed with walnut is released. He has never had this combination of flavors before and needs a moment to register it all. He takes another and puts the whole thing in his mouth, chewing deliberately so he can understand its complexity better.

The conversation has slowed down as it does in mid-meal. Everyone is busy eating and drinking. For most, as you have noticed, it's all about the senses.

*   *   *

Open your eyes.

Jackie gets up and walks around the table, serving wine. She doesn't ask, just pours some in each glass. No one complains. By the time she reaches Joseph, the bottle is empty. She leans over the table to grab a new bottle and as she does, he puts his hand on hers and says, "Not too much."

Jackie smiles but fills the cup full anyway. She walks over and sits back on her chair. The touch has triggered something, not for Jackie but for Joseph.

He looks at us, puzzled. There is nothing we can say or do. We can only observe. Even if we would make ourselves available, we do not know what has happened anyway.

Joseph looks at Zuleika and says, "I can't be sure, but she may be the one."

Zuleika shakes her head and says, "Don't you dare." She was trying to whisper the command, but it was clear everyone heard it.

"I am serious," he says. "She has such power. I think that's who I sensed earlier. She is almost like me."

"What's going on?" Dalia asks.

"I don't care," Zuleika says, this time not worrying about anyone hearing her. "Stop this silly conversation. You hear me, Joseph? Stop it now, or we will leave."

"What is it?" Jackie asks. "Did I do something wrong?"

"Of course not, Jackie. Sometimes, Joseph doesn't know when to keep his mouth shut."

"I'm sorry. I was joking," says Joseph. "Just a little private banter between Zuleika and me, but clearly I went too far. I do that
sometimes."

John claps his hands and announces, "You're a remarkably interesting man, Mr. Joseph. I found your statements so intriguing.
A joke with no punch line. Now that's a good joke."

"No, it's not. It's really just bad manners," Zuleika rejoins, and
then she takes a spoonful of red rice into her mouth and turns to
Dalia and says, "This is lovely. How did you make it red?"

Dalia nods but says, "What's all that about?"

"Nothing. Joseph is being absurd," Zuleika says.

"Yes," Joseph says, but then adds with an infectious smile, "I'm
incredibly happy to meet everyone tonight. There is certainly
something special about Zuleika's friends." He looks from Dalia
to Amani and then stops at Jackie. "There is this power in this
room, and most of it comes from you."

Jackie looks puzzled and laughs nervously. That's the last thing
she needs—strange attention from a strange man.

Zuleika laughs too, a forced laugh to distract. "Don't be silly,
Joseph. He sometimes says pointless things like this. Just ignore
him."

And they do, at least those who know. They can tolerate a weird
boyfriend. Zuleika lost her husband and her parents in an accident; she could bring a strange man to dinner if she wants. She
can bring dozens of strange men if it gets out of her rut.

After a few more minutes of silent eating, two different sets of
conversations start. Amani is speaking to Ashley and John about
life in Boston. Zuleika and Dalia are chatting about Dalia's new
project. Jackie enters the discussion, Dalia is pleasant, and the
three women have a gentle conversation as they savor the wine.
Dalia doesn't know John and Ashley, and perhaps she has pulled
Jackie into the conversation to prevent her from joining the other
group. That doesn't sound like Dalia, but she is in a good mood.
Joseph sits silently throughout, though occasionally spying on
Jackie.

Jackie looks contented as if every moment of the evening has been as right as the moment before it. She is sipping her wine and stays quiet. The conversations are benign and forgettable, a typical banter between old and new friends. Life in Boston. Life in San Francisco. Zuleika and Dalia's time in college. Ashley tells a funny story about when she was in a pool with John and Amani, and somehow her top was pushed off by Amani's leg as he swam away, but neither noticed, and John had to tell her, in his awkward way. And that was back when she hated John. Funny now, but certainly not then. She doesn't mention that Jackie was in the pool, too, nor does anybody else. Including Jackie.

Let's take a break. . . .

*   *   *

An hour or so passes. By now most of the food has been eaten, a few bottles of wine have been consumed, and the table looks lazy with half-empty platters and plates. The conversation slows and a hush takes over, as it does often when people are satiated with food and feel the soft buzz of wine in their head.

Amani takes John's seat and starts a conversation with Joseph as the rest help clear the table and Dalia prepares the dessert tray. We can lean closer and listen to Amani's almost desperate plea, but it's a repetition of the earlier argument. He is trying to convince Joseph that there are hidden powers in nature, and that's why once in eons, we get unique individuals like Einstein or Galileo who do not fit the human norm. Amani believes he is destined to be one of them and has since he was a child. He knows it sounds foolish, but he has found an audience in Joseph and doesn't want to let it go.

It's boring, and Joseph is not going to be convinced (at least that's what we hope). So, let's move on and go to the kitchen.

Dalia has made little puff pastries with custard and berries, each in the shape of a swan. They are sitting on a tray, all facing the same direction like soldiers on a march.

"Zolie, could you help me get something from the pantry?" Dalia asks.

Zuleika nods and follows her into the large pantry on the other side of the kitchen. The other three were busy chatting while making tea and coffee and didn't even notice they were gone.

The choice is clear: The pantry.

"What do you think?" Zuleika asks as soon as Dalia closes the door behind them.

"He is nice, Zolie. He's very handsome."

"But odd, right?"

Dalia laughs. "Just a bit, but who's not? Look at Amani. My god, he is relentless tonight."

"Amani is definitely passionate."

Dalia grabs Zuleika's hand and says, "Look, Zolie, I'm really sorry for not believing you before. I was so worried about you."

"I know."

"It's just that you kept referring to Joseph as imaginary and you were so sad, and I felt so helpless. . . ."

"I know, Dalia. You wanted to protect me, and I love you for it. You are the best friend anyone could want."

"I should have done more," Dalia insists.

They are both teary, and if they don't stop, they will make us cry.

"No. . . . It was my fault. I pushed you away as I pushed Joseph away, but in retrospect, I needed those months to find myself."

"I was so afraid for you."

"No. I knew I could always go to you. I am whole now, and I have you, and I have Joseph. He may say strange things and can be a bit of an annoyance, but he loves me and I need him. Everything is as it should be."

They hold each other tightly for a moment, glad to have each other.

"I just wished Joseph and Ashley and Amani would shut up about the fucking mountain of knowledge," Zuleika says, and they both laugh.

"Look what you've done," Dalia says and wipes the side of her eyes. "Now I have to redo my makeup."

"You look fine."

"Not everyone could be pretty without makeup, Zolie. Some of us need some help. Now be a good girl and take the pastries to the dining room."

They hug again and Zuleika leaves first. She takes the little swans to the table while others are still chatting in the kitchen.

She sits across from Amani. "What are you guys talking about?"

"Nothing," Amani replies automatically.

"Life and death," Joseph says.

"Could we not? Could we talk about something less morbid?" Zuleika asks, though the tone is an explicit command.

"There is nothing morbid here, Zolie," Amani says. "Your friend believes there is a place where one is neither dead nor alive."

"Yes," Joseph says in earnest, shaking his head as if dismissing a child.

"How would it work anyway?" Amani asks. "If you are dead, you are dead, and if you are alive, you are alive."

"That's deep," Jackie declares as she walks in with a tray of cups and saucers. She puts them on the table and sits next to Zuleika and across from Joseph. Zuleika puts her arm around her and pulls her close.

"It is a fact, Jackie. You are either dead or alive," Amani says.

"Is it now? How do you know?" Jackie sits up straight.

"It's obvious," he replies, looking around the table for confirmation.

"I'm not getting into this," Zuleika says.

"How does this world work, anyway?" Amani asks, looking at Joseph.

"I don't know. But I know it exists," Joseph replies.

"Is it like heaven and hell? But even if you believe in those things, which I don't, then it's your soul that lives there and not you," Amani says.

"I just know. I don't know how to explain it more."

"Ok. Let's say I believe you. Is it a good place?"

"It depends. Some will find solace, but others get lost in it," Joseph explains.

"You sound so assured. Are you some religious zealot?" Amani asks.

"No. Not that."

Zuleika reaches over and touches Joseph on the shoulder and says, "Let's stop this pointless conversation. I think you're annoying everyone."

"I love it. I love it when Amani gets all worked up over nothing," Jackie says.

"I'm not agitated," Amani says. "I'm actually enjoying this. It's like a science fiction movie."

"I don't know the science of it, but it's not fiction. At least not for some," Joseph replies in earnest.

Amani looks at Jackie and Zuleika and says, "You don't believe this nonsense, do you?"

"Believe what? In heaven and hell and purgatory?" Jackie asks. "Of course, I don't."

"Those are mere names that certain religions have given to their notion of the afterlife. The real world is different," Joseph says.

"And how is the *real world*, and how would you know?" Jackie asks.

"He doesn't. Joseph loves to get metaphysical," Zuleika says.

"I know what I know and even though I should not speak of it, I feel the urgency tonight. It's maybe you, Jackie, but then again, I could be wrong. No matter, the urge to find a resolution tonight is oppressive."

"Wait, Joseph" Zuleika says. "What the fuck are you doing?"

"I'm sorry, but I can see Spenta, and I can see Jackie, and I should not see both at the same time."

"They won't understand. Why do you have to do this now?"

Jackie ignores Zuleika's outburst. "Should I know who or what Spenta is? It sounds familiar. Is it from the classics?"

"Some say Spenta is the personification of the Swedish Prison, but I am not sure if it's true," Joseph replies.

Zuleika is about to speak when others walk into the room.

"Coffee time," John announces in a singsong as he puts down a large French press and a bone china teapot on the table. He sits next to Amani, Ashley sits on the other side of the table across from him, Dalia at the head of the table.

"What are we talking about?" Dalia asks.

"A strange place called Spenta," replies Jackie. "But we could also be talking about prison in Sweden. We are sorting that out."

"I know what Spenta is," John says. "It's *Amesha Spenta,* which literally means "Immortals," who are a class of divine entities emanating from Ahura Mazda, the highest divinity of the Zoroastrian religion."

"That's not entirely true," Joseph says. "The Persians borrowed the concept. . . ."

John ignores him, as everyone is now in his class. "Spenta," he continues, "refers to the great seven divine entities emanating from Ahura Mazda. These are the first seven emanations of the uncreated creator, through whom all subsequent creation was accomplished."

"So, why would Spenta be a prison?" Jackie asks.

"It is not," John replies.

Joseph ignores John. "All good questions, Jackie. I cannot tell you in words. You have to feel it."

"Feel it? How?"

"I will show you. But I must have a cup of coffee first. The olives were good, but I need real coffee. The aroma is too distracting," Joseph says.

We can agree the aroma is too much, but if Joseph cannot wait, we must.

"Great idea," Dalia says and pushes the coffee plunger down without waiting.

"I love coffee," Joseph says. His attention is turned to the cup that Dalia has put in front of him. He takes a sip. "What a lovely coffee. It's the Devil's brew, but the gods love it more than anything."

He is right, of course. We don't know why, but there is a real love affair.

"Okay," says Dalia. "Do the gods love it with cream or black?"

"I like it black most times, but I could have it with milk if the coffee is rich and strong."

Dalia serves coffee and tea as demanded. Everyone has gone quiet watching the movements of the cups and saucers.

When everyone is settled, they all turn to Joseph. But he is focused on his cup of coffee. He takes the cup to his nose and breathes in the aroma before taking small sips, then holds the hot liquid in his mouth before swallowing. When he finishes the cup, he asks for another and repeats the ritual.

"Watching you makes me want to switch to coffee," John says, looking at his untouched cup of tea. "It's strange, but it feels like I am drinking coffee by simply watching you." He laughs and then takes a sip of his tea. He closes his eyes and tries to mimic Joseph, but immediately opens them. "Oh, it's just tea," he says. "Great tea, mind you," he adds quickly, looking at Dalia.

"It's not the same. Coffee is for gods," Joseph says.

"I liked you better when you were more circumspect," Zuleika says.

"Oh, Mr. Joseph is an extraordinary person, Zolie, as you are," John says warmly. "I'm so glad we have met you both tonight."

"Thanks, John. Yes, he is a silly man," Zuleika says, "but I like him." And then looking at Joseph, "And I'd like you even more if you would shut up about Spenta and the Gift and . . ."

"What gift?" Dalia asks. "Did he give you a big gift?"

"No. . . . Nothing. It was silly of me to say it. Let's try these great pastries," Zuleika says and takes a massive bite from one of the swans to demonstrate, getting as much of the cream on her nose as in her mouth in the process. Joseph leans over and wipes it off her face, and she shakes her head with a smile, unable to stay mad at Joseph for too long. In the end, he is who he is and she cannot change him. Dalia seemed to like him, and that's all that matters tonight.

Joseph then turns to Jackie and asks, "May I give you one?"

"Yes."

Joseph takes one of the swans and puts the plate in front of Jackie, turning it so the swan faces her. "And coffee?"

"I already have some."

"A fresh cup, if you would." He takes his cup and puts it in front of Jackie.

They are looking at him puzzled, and Zuleika screws her eyes as if trying to reach Joseph telepathically.

Dalia smiles at her reassuringly, and she sits back. You can tell she is intrigued too. At times, Joseph reveals his awkwardness amongst people, his otherworldliness leaking slowly like an old faucet, but when he opens the tap willingly, his immense power shows, and that's a sight to see.

"We have more coffee. I can pour a fresh one for Jackie," Dalia offers, holding the coffee pot up as proof.

"Yes, please pour a new cup for me," Joseph says.

Everyone is watching him, asking themselves, what is this strange man doing?

Jackie's the one to say it. "What's special about this cup?"

"Only one way to find out," Joseph says.

"Okay," Jackie says, and she takes a tentative sip.

They all wait.

"Good coffee," Jackie says.

"You didn't take enough. Take a mouthful and savor the taste," Joseph orders, and Jackie does. "Now, take a bite of Dalia's beautiful swan."

Jackie does as she is told.

"Well?" asks Ashley.

"It's an amazing pastry, Dalia. It's so light and velvety."

"That's it?" Ashley asks. "That was pointless."

Joseph ignores her and says to Jackie, "Do you feel it?"

"Should I?"

"Yes, you should. Just let go."

"Are you hypnotizing her?" Dalia asks.

"Hypnosis through food," John says with a smirk

Jackie closes her eyes for a moment, and everyone waits as if expecting something spectacular. She opens her eyes and looks at Joseph. "Oh," she says.

Joseph nods.

"What happened?" Zuleika asks. She didn't expect this.

"I get it," Jackie says.

"Get what?" Zuleika insists. "Did you two plan this while I was in the kitchen earlier?"

"No," Joseph replies

"I get it," Jackie says again. "I could be Spenta. I could be like her. But there is also a downside to it, isn't there?"

"Yes," Joseph says in earnest.

"What do you see?" Zuleika asks

"I want to try his coffee," Ashley says and reaches over and takes the cup from Jackie. She puts it to her mouth without looking. "Oh, it's empty," she moans. "Let's do it again. Dalia, pour Joseph another cup."

"It's not for you," Joseph tells her.

"Well, that was fun," Dalia says. "Now, who wants more coffee?"

Dalia fills their cups and they drink it down, each waiting for the magic they surely know cannot exist.

Joseph looks at Jackie expectantly, but she is deep in thought.

After a while, Jackie shakes her head as though trying to get back to the present. "What is it, anyway, and what would I do with it?"

"I don't have an answer, Jackie. Just try to keep the feeling alive," Joseph orders.

"No. . . . I don't want it."

"It won't last long," he warns her.

"Could someone explain to me what's going on here?" John asks.

Jackie sits up straight and takes a bite of the swan, ignoring him. "This is great, Dalia. Could I have my own cup of coffee, too, with a bit of milk, please?"

Joseph says, "Let's say someone comes to you, John, and offers you a gift of knowledge. Would you take this gift?"

"For damn sure."

"Not so fast. What if even though I called it a gift, it's really a curse?"

"A curse of knowledge? Sure, I'd take that too," John replies in his professorial tone.

"I'm not talking about just knowing but *knowing*. Not some simple knowledge of facts, but rather the power of knowing—if not omniscience, then something close to it," Joseph explains.

"What would we do with such power?" Ashley asks.

Joseph ignores Ashley and stares at Jackie. "Will you use it for good, John?" He has kept his voice even and light, but no one missed the melancholy.

"For good, of course," John replies in earnest.

"And you, Jackie?" Joseph shakes his head, waiting.

It is getting somewhat awkward now, so Dalia leans forward to say something, but Jackie says, "I don't want it."

"Okay, that's enough, Joseph," Zuleika orders. "You heard Jackie's response."

But now, Amani, who has been conspicuously quiet, becomes animated and offers, "I don't believe anyone in the world would use it for anything but good."

Joseph shakes his head again and says, "You'll be surprised what horrible things people have done with the smallest kernel of knowledge."

"I get it," John says with a big laugh. "Very clever, Mr. Joseph. You took Ashley's earlier mountain of knowledge comment, and you made it into this gift of knowledge. You had us for a moment. Very clever."

"You're partially right, as was Ashley."

"I was hypothesizing," Ashley replies. "It was a metaphor for how our society is getting stupid. I didn't mean it literally," Ashley says. "And I'm sorry to say, you are taking this too seriously, which just proves my point."

"Perhaps," Joseph says.

"You're talking as if it exists. Knowledge is good, but you must earn it. You can't just give it away," Dalia says.

"I know Joseph is fooling around, but imagine if such a gift existed, Dalia," Amani interjects. "Imagine the good we could do. We would help people out of poverty, out of hunger. Imagine what we could do."

Joseph looks at Amani with a newfound interest but doesn't say anything.

"You're serious, aren't you?" Ashley says, her incredulous tone an echo of everyone's thoughts.

"No, he is not," Zuleika assures her. "Joseph doesn't know when to stop."

"I'll stop now. Sorry, everyone. Zuleika is right. I sometimes push silly points without thinking. I am sorry."

"So, you don't have this gift?" Amani asks, looking disappointed.

"Of course, he doesn't. Did you think he did?" Dalia says.

"No. . . . But he was so sincere. . . ."

"I'm sorry. I wish I had more," says Joseph, and then he adds as if talking to himself, "For an instant, I thought I did. I'm sorry, Jackie."

"That's okay. It was fun to think about it," Jackie replies and then, "You certainly did something to me through that cup of coffee. It says a lot about the power of suggestion."

"Was that all? Was it merely the power of suggestion?" Amani asks.

"Yes," Joseph replies.

"What does that mean?" Amani cries out and then, looking at Jackie, "Tell us what it was like."

"I don't know how to explain it. There was a sense of clarity. It only lasted a second, but it felt like a new door to the world had been opened. It told me nothing and I learned nothing, but somehow I knew *it* was there if I wanted it."

"What was there?" Dalia asks.

"Don't know. I don't know, how to explain it. . . . Maybe there was nothing, but since I believed Joseph, I convinced myself there was . . ."

"Can you tell us more?" Amani asks, looking at Joseph.

"No," he replies.

Zuleika leans over the table and pulls Joseph's hands into her own.

He looks at her and says, "We all must do our task, sweetheart. I don't mean any harm."

"But I want to know more. Tell me more," Amani demands.

"I can tell you a story that might put everything in context," Joseph offers.

"I love a good story," John says.

"Me too," Jackie adds. "But I am exhausted, and I feel I'll fall asleep at any moment."

"It will be quick," Joseph says. "Please, stay and listen."

"Okay," she says, resigned.

"May I have another cup of coffee?" Joseph asks and waits for Jackie to pour him a cup.

"Is it a true story or another one of your games?" Ashley asks.

Joseph ignores her and takes a long sip from his cup. "It's lovely, Dalia," he says and looks around as everyone looks at him. "It's not an exciting story, so don't get your hopes up, but it might clarify some things."

They all nod, and Joseph takes another sip, leans back, and says, "Imagine a world where gods walk amongst people."

"Oh," Amani moans, "So, it is fiction."

"It can be if you want it to be," Joseph says with a smile.

"Let the man speak," Dalia orders, and Amani sits back.

"These gods are part of the daily life of humans," Joseph continues. "They take care of people and people take care of the gods. They know each other and respect each other, but they also know their place in life's hierarchy. Some of those relationships have entered the mythology of humans, but you should know, behind each myth, there is a real world that has long been forgotten. But why? Why would you forget about your gods?"

"Because they don't exist," John offers.

"Yes, I expect you to say that because you do not know any better. But answer me this, John: would you have forsaken the gods if they were real?"

"Mr. Joseph, how could I answer a hypothetical? Were these gods good to us? Were they kind, or did they try to enslave us?"

"I can see why you might put it in those terms. To you, gods are either kind or unkind. But that's not how it happened. The answer lies in the folly of some gods, who thought men and women were ready for more. Sadly, they were not."

"So, it's our fault?" John insists.

"No. It's *the gods'* fault. You can't blame a child for failing when they are not ready for a challenge. Some of the gods decided that human beings deserved more, and if they gave them more, then men and gods would become closer. So, a few of the gods made a pact to share a morsel of their power with human beings, but only a few acted when the time came. Two of them gave the humans kernels of empathy and knowledge, hoping these two gifts would elevate them. But what the gods did not understand were the limits of the human being."

"Or perhaps the uniqueness of human beings," John offers.

"Yes, maybe so. The gods thought each person would get an equal share and they would grow it and spread it. But it didn't happen that way."

"I said the same thing earlier," Ashley says, and she looks at others for confirmation.

"You did," offers Zuleika kindly.

"These gifts spread unevenly and haphazardly," continues Joseph, undeterred by the interruption. "And worst yet, humans used them not only to better themselves as it was intended but also for immense cruelty."

"Are you saying we were nice and good before these gifts from the gods?" Dalia asks.

Joseph shakes his head as if frustrated by her lack of comprehension. "Of course not," he says. "You were always cruel, but
the gifts made you more efficient and better at it."

"Us? Not you, Mr. Joseph?" John asks playfully.

Joseph thinks about it for a moment and then says, "*Yes*, not
me."

"So, we are the bad ones?" Amani asks.

"Could we let him finish his story?" Zuleika says and then, "For
gods' sake."

Dalia laughs. "Yes, let him finish for their sake."

"Yes, gods," Joseph says. "Because in the end, these gifts also
made humans banish the gods. They didn't do it by design, but
rather the gifts made them ignore gods, and gods learned rather
too late that they can only be part of human lives if humans
believe in them. But as humans grew, so did the decline in their
beliefs."

"So human beings banished the gods?" John asks.

"Yes, and on so many levels. The two who had helped the humans the most were also banished from these lands and sent to
a place that some have come to call the Swedish Prison. Their
powers were taken and given to another god, the god of misery,
the one who had tried to protect them. And thus, the god of
misery became the custodian of not only his responsibilities but
knowledge and empathy as well."

"Who took their power away?" John asks. "God?"

"I do not know of such a being, but then perhaps. Some questions cannot be answered, but their effect is apparent."

"So, are these gods banished forever?"

"No. What I know is that after millennia, even gods get tired of
the burden. These essences should not have intermingled within
one deity. They didn't want to be imprisoned and constantly seek
their creator, and as a result, they transformed their host and became something else, neither a god nor a man. That created an
opportunity for these so-called gifts to seek out other hosts until
their true guardians returned from their banishment."

Joseph looks exhausted, but Amani is not done. "So, Ashley was right that there is a limited amount of knowledge."

"I don't know about its limit, but it is not in the shape of a mountain, nor is it given equally to each person born," Joseph replies.

"Nice little story," Dalia says, "but what about what you did to Jackie?"

"Some people can still connect with those powers," Joseph says.

"That's it?" Amani says. "The whole stupid story to say some people can connect with the gods' powers?"

"Yes."

"Then I can, too," Amani insists.

"Yes, but why?"

"Okay, boys, let's pause this. I'm honored that you think I have special connections to gods, but I'm just a regular person—one who's exhausted and needs to go to bed. It's time for me to go," Jackie offers and then gets up and says, "Goodbye, everyone. It was fun." She waves at everyone, and they all nod.

Zuleika gets up and hugs Jackie, and they both walk out of the room. But Amani doesn't want to end the conversation.

"You are wrong, Joseph. I think you're dismissing the capacity of people to learn and grow. Let's assume your story is true, and there are gods, and these gods can give their power to us. Then perhaps they picked the wrong people. If they had chosen smarter human beings, then the results would have been different."

"The right kind, you say. Like whom?"

"Like Amani, of course," Dalia and John say in unison, and they laugh heartily.

"You two think you know me so well," Amani says.

"We all do," Ashley offers.

"Fine. Make fun of me, but I can make a list of thousands of things we can do to help people if only we had the power," Amani says.

He is making a list now as he will again in a few days. Let's ignore him.

Zuleika returns and tells Joseph it's time to go. Amani is still telling Joseph why he would love to have this gift if it existed. He is getting more animated.

Ashley stands up and says, "We should leave too." But Amani is too focused and doesn't hear them.

Dalia taps him on his head and says, "John and Ashley are leaving."

Amani looks up, embarrassed. "I am sorry," he says and then, "Don't you want to stay a bit longer?"

"It was great seeing you, Amani," Ashley says and kisses him.

John hugs Amani and then kisses Dalia. He looks at Joseph and says, "You're an intriguing person, Mr. Joseph. I wish you the best." He shakes hands with Joseph and then with Zuleika.

Amani walks them to the door.

"It's my fault. I shouldn't have brought it up in such a public fashion," Joseph offers.

"Yes, it is," Zuleika says.

Amani comes back and says, "You must tell me about Spenta."

"No. Joseph has done enough for one night," Zuleika says.

"We should go, then," Joseph says.

"Yes."

"Will I see you again?" Amani asks.

"I hope you won't. I hope you two will never cross paths," Zuleika says.

"That's a strange thing to say, Zolie," Amani replies.

"I'm sorry. Yes, it was. I'm tired."

Zuleika grabs Joseph's hand and pulls him from his chair. They say their goodbyes and start to leave the room.

Let's follow them.

Dalia walks out with them and hugs Zuleika. "I'm glad you're feeling better," she says and then looks at Joseph. "It was nice to finally meet Zuleika's imaginary friend. I'm glad, in the end, you were real." She laughs and walks back into the house.

Let's stay outside with Joseph and Zuleika.

"Amani is so eager. What would happen if Amani takes it from you?" Zuleika asks.

"I don't know, Zuleika. He wants it. I can tell. I could smell the desire on his breath. He was reaching into me. He tried to convince me while you were saying goodbye to Jackie."

"Didn't you tell him that it was in jest—banter, and it didn't exist? Did you try to redirect him?"

"Of course, I did, but he didn't believe me. He senses it. And now I feel *it* wants him, too."

"Are you sure?"

"No. How could I be sure? But I've considered my choices and how I almost lost you. The gift of empathy is an immense responsibility, but it also brings joy and solace. But this other thing, the thing that you humans call knowledge, is more like a curse. I do not know what to do, but I know I must pass it to someone who will be its guardian. Is Amani that man?"

"I don't know," Zuleika replies and leans over to kiss him. "You were bad tonight, but I still love you."

"I know. I am sorry, but the energy from Jackie and Amani was too much," Joseph says.

"I know. Let's go home now," Zuleika says.

"Not yet. I need to ask someone to step forward and speak to me," Joseph says as he reaches and holds Zuleika's hand.

Step back, as Joseph will call on me.

"What do you mean?" Zuleika asks as she pans the street. "Is there another of you here?"

"Yes," Joseph says, and then lets go of her hand and steps forward. "Do you know?"

I must respond. When I step forward, you may shiver as if thousands of spiders are crawling down your spine, and you might see the moon dim. Do not be afraid.

"I should, but I cannot, in this case," I say.

"Why not?" Joseph asks.

Zuleika looks puzzled. "Who are you talking to?"

"Should I appear to her as well?"

"No," Joseph replies and then looking at Zuleika, "You cannot see him, but he is here. You do not want to see him."

"Why not? I'm not afraid."

"I've never doubted your bravery, Zuleika, but you shouldn't see him."

"Why not?" she insists.

"Because he is Death and no human being should meet Death before the Appointment Time."

"Good answer," I say. "But not the full truth. I could appear in my other self as I have done before."

"Is he here for me?" Zuleika asks.

"Of course not," Joseph replies and kisses her as an assurance.

"Then for you?"

Joseph laughs. "No, Zuleika. He is not here for anyone. He is only here as a friend. Be patient and I will tell you about him later."

"I want to see him too," Zuleika insists.

"May I?" I ask.

Joseph sighs. "I would rather Zuleika not see you in any form, but I was not at my best tonight, so I guess I do owe her."

"Yes, we certainly bore witness to your behavior. But I will do as you wish."

"Reveal yourself then."

Zuleika shivers a bit and holds Joseph's hand and then she sees me. "Oh, hello," she says.

"Good evening, Zuleika."

"I thought I would be more afraid but you look . . ."

"Normal?" I offer, hopefully.

"Pleasant," she replies.

"Well, thank you."

"So, you don't know how this will end?" Joseph asks.

Zuleika takes a step closer to me, and before I can reply, she says, "I was so angry before."

I look at her and nod. "Oh, I remember."

"I thought you were so cruel for taking my family in such a brutal way."

I say nothing as there is nothing to say to people who have lost loved ones. Joseph reaches and holds her hand. "It's not his fault, Zuleika."

"Oh, I know that now, but I had to say it. It's not often that we meet Death and survive him." She laughs at her own joke and then becomes more somber. "Death is part of our lives, and yet we don't accept it, nor do we prepare for it. I know that so well now. It brought me misery, and then it brought me joy. Now that's a paradox all in itself."

"We live in strange times, indeed," I offer.

Joseph releases Zuleika's hand and asks again, "How will this end?"

"I do not know as I do not know your full story now that you are Joseph. But we shall meet again soon, and you can tell me then."

"Do you know if Ashley was right about the degradation of knowledge amongst humans?" Joseph asks.

"Ashely was silly," Zuleika says.

"She was rather, but I do see some truth in her story," I say. "Humans are certainly less curious, less patient than before."

"We are not."

"That's not good for humanity," Joseph replies.

"Yes!"

"We are not less curious. I agree we have no attention span. But we are not less curious," Zuleika insists.

"Perhaps," Death says. "Time will tell. But I must go now."

"Before you go," Joseph says. "Why were you here tonight? Were you here for me?"

Zuleika turns to Joseph, looking concerned, "For you? I thought you couldn't—"

"I'm sorry. I didn't mean it that way. I meant, was Death here to watch over me?"

"Oh, thank god," Zuleika says.

I give a big laugh. "I found it so funny how humans can go from total panic to total calm within mere seconds. To you, everything must move fast."

"So why were you here, and with an audience?" Joseph asks.

"I was here for Amani. I had to see him myself as he interacted with you."

"Why?" Zuleika asks. "Is he going to die?"

"Be calm, Zuleika. Of course, he is going to die, as will you. That's part of your existence."

"Don't toy with her, Death. You know what she meant."

"I cannot answer that as I do not know each person's appointment until it is set. In Amani's case, something has beckoned me, and it may be you, Joseph, or could be something else. For now, I have to ponder the options, and it is time for me to go."

Let's step back. I do not want to worry you, but it can't be helped. It is time for us to leave. There is nothing to be done now.

THIS LIFE

"Go ahead and ring the bell," the woman says. She somewhat reminds me of the nurse from my multitude of visits to the Cancer Center. She is not a tall woman, her head barely reaching the counter that separates us. A small hairpin pulls her short dark hair even further back from her face. She smiles, her eyes focused, and says again, looking at the silver bell, "Go ahead."

The bell is small but looks heavy, shining under the white light of the hallway. It's secured within a polished wooden structure, dangling like a hanged man. The hammer, within it, is round, holding a thick white rope.

"Pull the rope hard but only once," she advises.

"Would it matter?" I ask.

"Matter?" She looks at me, tugging on her uniform. It looks like one of those colorful patterned garbs that medical staff like to wear now—out with the simple white and in with the statement. She tugs at her uniform again, more like a habit than the need to straighten the already fitted garb.

"Yes, would it make any difference?" I ask, hoping my insistence will result in the answer I want (I need). I'm looking at the bell and not her, but as I turn to face her, she lowers her gaze.

"I hope so," she replies. Her voice sounds thin and it fades out.

"I mean, would I be better afterward?"

"I cannot answer for you. You have to pull the rope and find out."

"But what am I doing?" I touch the rope and feel its heavy, coarse texture. I pull back immediately, afraid of disturbing it.

"You're getting ready for the next stage," she offers and then displays a quick smile behind her words.

"But what's the next stage?"

She shrugs. It feels late, and I am becoming impatient.

"Where are we?" I ask, looking around this vast unfamiliar space even though I feel it should be known to me. There is no one around, and our voices echo as if the reverberation is needed to solidify our presence.

I feel strongly that we have spent many weeks together. But perhaps it was not her but another nurse who was part of the crew that I saw every Monday through Friday and two Saturdays of the month. It doesn't matter because, at this moment, she is like my *nurse*. I feel I know her even if she doesn't know me.

Another woman appears and stands next to my nurse. She must be my doctor then. I look around to see if there will be others, but it's only the three of us now. My *doctor* is holding a large manila envelope. She is wearing a white blouse, and I notice a small tear in the seam. It's very tiny, so she must not have seen it when she dressed earlier. She was about to hand the envelope to me, but a slight shake of the head from the nurse changes her mind. She puts the envelope down on the counter, takes out a pen from her pants pocket, and prints my name on it. She has elegant handwriting. The words, large and bold, stare back at me, waiting.

"Where are we?" I ask again, hoping the doctor will tell me; perhaps the answer is hidden within the envelope. I want to reach and grab the packet, but I cannot muster the courage.

"You are where you're supposed to be," she replies and then quickly adds, "It's time." The doctor looks at the bell and then puts her right hand flat on top of the envelope to emphasize the point. Then she adds, "You did well."

"Did I?"

"Yes. You did well."

"There was the incident," I say, too embarrassed to look at her.

"True," she replies in a matter of fact tone, "but believe me, it happens."

Maybe so, but it's easier for her to say than for me to bear. It's not easy to revert to a helpless child within minutes. It is the quick transition from me to a haplessness, and back to myself again, that's jarring. What is *me* now, anyway?

I don't know. I am in a constant state of confusion. Sometimes I have dreams that I am invincible, hold powers that bring solace to others. I do recall my old self, even if it's hazy and fleeting—perhaps the real me. But those memories are as ethereal as this place. It may be the madness that has afflicted so many people now, has infected me too. Everyday realities are being debated as if truth, like other perishables, can decay. There are signs if one looks for them but fewer and fewer people do. This realization alone brings shudders to my spine.

"Was I powerful before?" I ask.

They laugh, and the sound ricochets and slaps me on my face. They stop when they see the disappointment in my eyes.

"We're sorry. We laughed because you ask this every time," the nurse says, though I am sure my real nurse would not have laughed at me no matter my question.

"Every time? I've asked this before?"

"Yes," the doctor says. "We do not have an answer for you. You must move on."

So, I ask the question that I must have asked several other times as well: "What's next?"

They have no answer. They don't know.

"You did well," the doctor offers again. "Better than we thought. You'll have to take it one step at a time. We've discussed this before." A doctor's standard answer, so perhaps she is a real doctor even if the nurse is not my real nurse.

"Yes, but never to my satisfaction."

She shakes her head. "You'll never be satisfied," she says, and then offers the same quick, mirthless smile as the nurses, as if it is part of their training.

She is right, of course. She nods and pushes the envelope to the nurse, who instinctively puts her hand on top of it as the doctor had done. The message is clear.

"I will see you *soon*," the doctor says and then nods several times before leaving.

"It's time," the nurse says.

"Will it toll for me or others?"

"It tolls for thee," she says and with no trace of irony.

"I still have a story to tell," I insist.

"Tell your story once you pull the rope," she instructs as she walks away, leaving the manila envelope and its content unguarded.

I want to reach out and look into the secrets it holds. But I don't, fearing what I might find. Not all secrets are pleasant. The hallways are getting darker, and I know what I must do next.

So I reach over and grab hold of the thick rope.

*　　　*　　　*

I stood naked in front of the bathroom mirror and stared at everything but my body. I touched the top of my head and felt the thinning hair that was once luxurious.

I had been with Dalia for over five years at this point, and per her insistence I had let my hair grow, despite the fast-expanding receding hairline. I used to have such thick hair when I was young. But that was many years ago, long before middle age, long before life, and long before the illness. Dalia wouldn't be pleased, but I was no longer me within, so why would my façade stay the same? I touched the small patch of thickness that still existed on the back of my head and then, with swift movements of the electric clippers, set to number two—though I had no context for that number—my hair changed too. Hair clippings fell on my shoulders—made me look like a hairy ape—and on the floor and inevitably in the sink, on the toilet seat, and everywhere else. The fine hair glided in the air and landed, seemingly on a whim, in every crevice of the bathroom. I should have put a sheet on the floor; I should have done a more thorough job or even done this on the balcony, but it was too late by then. I should have done so many things differently, but it was all too late.

Dalia walked into the bathroom and looked at my handiwork. She opened her mouth but closed it immediately and gave a small smile, very much like the doctors had been doing. She came closer and ran her fingers through my short hair and then, without any words, took the clipper from my hand and started to trim the back of my head.

She was fully dressed, and I felt embarrassed by my nakedness—my stomach protruding, my chest sagging, my waist, a blubber, and my genitals, undefinable.

I looked up and caught her spying on me. *The illness . . . the treatment*, she said with her eyes and then pushed my head down so she could trim the back more. It was a good excuse, but not the full truth. My haircut was nice, though.

"I'll clean," Dalia said after cutting the last unruly patch with a pair of scissors and started scooping some of the hair from the sink.

"Stop," I said, and even I recognized my tone. "I'll do it, Dalia. Just leave it, please," I added, hoping for less self-pity in my voice.

She was still holding a bunch of my hair in her hand, but she put it down on the counter. "Okay."

"Thanks. I'll let it grow, if you don't like it," I offered.

She ran her fingers through my hair again and smiled. "It feels good. You look good. You look much younger." She kissed me on my forehead and I felt her warm breath on me. She pulled back and I noticed some of the small clippings had stuck to her.

I tried to wipe her face with my fingers, and I felt her soft, warm skin beneath my own. I wasn't successful. It didn't matter anyway. Only two years earlier, the naked haircut, or even a fully dressed haircut, would have led to sex—standing, or leaning against the vanity, or on the floor on top of all the hair clippings. It didn't matter. We were always ready. I was ready. I was always ready at a moment's notice. But everything had changed.

She left the bathroom and then returned with a broom and a dustpan and put them against the door before leaving again.

If she had any expectations, she never showed them. I should have been more grateful. Most women would not be so understanding. But her forbearance left no room for me to be angry at her, so I was left to be silently mad at myself. I wanted Dalia to voice her frustration and demand more of me, so I could blame her too. I needed someone to blame because otherwise, I should have accepted it as what it was—a life's lottery—and not drowned myself in self-pity with misery as my constant companion.

I grabbed a large towel from the linen closet—and most likely shed some hair on the neatly stacked towels in the process. I hid my body under the towel. It felt good to conceal the fat and the skin and the scars under the burgundy Egyptian cotton towel. I felt safe. I swept the floor and wiped down the sink and the toilet seat. I knew Dalia would come later to do another thorough cleaning. You can never get them all, but she would do her utmost to make the bathroom pristine again.

I looked at my haircut in the mirror, and then, using a hand mirror, I inspected the back of my head. There was a small bald spot glaring back at me. It could be my handiwork or maybe even the flareup of the *alopecia areata*. The rest of my hair was too short to cover the bald spot, and Dalia's attempt to even out the surrounding areas had not worked.

It didn't matter. It was another one of life's rewards.

I threw the towel on the floor and walked under the stream of the shower, letting the warm water surround me, washing the salt and pepper hair off my body. I could see a little river of debris falling onto the bottom of the tub and then swirling around the drain before leaving the room.

The whole thing was a comedy, and if you had any sense of humor, you would laugh too. The constant struggles to order the body, to pretend there was a sense of control; the curious side effects of hormone therapy that sounded benign in the brochures, but quickly became too real; or the mass murder of the good cells, collateral damage might be the term, by the radiation—no matter the advances in the science of mathematical modeling, on which the doctor insisted—were all rich wells of comic relief.

Yet, the real funny part of it was, it didn't have to come to this. But that's another story.

*   *   *

Most of us think we're invincible when we are young, but we are wrong, of course. We live in the moment and believe the future offers endless promises, so we tend to ignore illnesses, broken bones, failures, and disappointments. However, as we get older and live in the past, observing the future as it nears us, the fantasy of indestructibility dissipates.

But that is you and not me. I *was* indestructible.

You might say, *bullshit, Stock*, and I'd expect nothing else. If my mother was alive, she would say, *Charles Stock, a good person should never lie. And you are a good person, Charles*. Well, she is dead, and I hate the name Charles.

I was a man on a mission, going to change the world. I always felt I'd be successful and make my mark and be recognized for it. I would be a Mozart and not a Salieri, though, in the end, I couldn't even take a single step toward what Salieri had achieved. I think it was the poet, William F. O'Brien, who said, "Better to try and fail than never to try at all."

What a load of shit! I look back and think I could have had a better life if only I was as contented as some of my friends were. I used to envy them, and at the same time, secretly had nothing but disdain for them. I felt they lacked the gumption to strive for more—living their little lives and missing the rewards of success. Yet, the steadfast embrace of their "simple" life is their achievement. They are the Mozarts of their own lives, while I am looking for that pinnacle, still hidden behind the clouds.

The memories of the past have become hazy in my new state, but I still attempt to look back and capture the remanence of the power that used to embody me. It feels like waking up from a sweet fantasy and staying in that state where your mind and body are still connected to the dream. And in that dream, I think I was a god with powers to bestow solace. Yet, the harder you pull, the more the thread of connection melts in your hands. So, I have tried not to pull too hard to preserve the pleasant parts, but as we all know, good things don't come alone; the wicked inevitably joins in.

This has been happening with more urgency in recent times, and no matter how hard I tried to close the lid, they came out. I remembered my mother; I remembered abandoning her because I had more important things in my life. She had my two sisters to take care of her after my father's passing. She didn't need me, and more importantly, I had my law career, and I was about to make partner, so at the time, nothing else mattered.

At least, that's what I told myself then. Nothing mattered except my singular goal. It didn't matter that I was driving a car I couldn't afford or lived a life that was a lie. It didn't matter then because I was indestructible. I was young and married to a beautiful woman—but then she left me for another man because, as she put it, I loved my career more than her. Then my father died, and I missed his funeral because I had to hide his death from the senior partners. We were at a crucial moment in a case, and you know the rest. Several months later, my mother passed away. I made it to her funeral, but by then, my sisters had stopped talking to me.

And then, at age forty, my life transformed for the better. I want to say it was because I met Dalia and most likely, that is the truth. But then I changed again and that's when I lost my indestructibility, or was it the other way around?

But what does it matter? In the end, I learned my life is as typical as anyone else's. I was never unique. I was an imprudent man who missed his life because he always lived in the future. By the time I realized my folly, it was too late, and the past had become as nebulous as everything else in my life. The sociologists have a name for it, the *hot-cold empathy gap*. I could be wrong, of course. I am a forty-something, balding man who is dying of cancer.

As are millions of other people, you might say.

True.

*   *   *

My wife's name is Dalia Smart, and she is an amazing woman. She is super smart (so her name is rather apropos) and is a powerhouse of an executive. She can build the shit out of anything and cook like a chef. She packed up and moved to New Orleans to be with me so I could have my life. Yes, she is kind and thoughtful too—it's a digression, but it needed to be said in case we get entangled in my drama and I forget to say it later. She is, in a word, fantastic.

But enough about her.

I went for a routine checkup, and people around my age group know rather well that these visits come with a battery of tests. If you haven't paid much attention—distracted by my earlier rant—you'd be surprised to know the results weren't good. By then, I had been living in New Orleans for four years, so my initial thought was to blame everything on the city.

Why not? We all become irrational when confronted by fear, and faulting the city is as good as blaming God or past sins. But later, I felt lucky to be in New Orleans, even though the end result was the same. Be patient. They will all reveal themselves; the start was a visit to the doctor.

Dalia and I arrived at the doctor's office half an hour before the eight a.m. appointment, both nervous, though neither of us admitted it. We were sitting in the waiting room with another patient, an older man. The TV was on and his gaze never left the screen. I had done the required paperwork and settled in with my book, and Dalia with her laptop to do her work.

I had opened the book when I was called in. "Mr. Stock. We're ready for you."

I looked up to see a young woman standing by the door, holding it open with her foot. She looked young, too young to be a nurse.

"Really?" I asked.

"Sure, unless you need more time," she replied, and I looked at Dalia. She was as surprised as I was. We had grown up in San Francisco, where waiting for an hour before being seen was the norm.

We both stood up and followed her in.

"You may wait in Room 2," the nurse instructed and then closed the door behind us after we entered.

Room 2 was small; it could hardly fit three people. I sat on the examination table, and Dalia took the only chair. After a few minutes, there was a knock on the door.

A man in his mid-forties walked into the room. He introduced himself and then shook hands with me and then with Dalia. We talked for ten minutes, but it was all about us and our new life in New Orleans.

He then looked at me and said, "I have the initial numbers from your GP, and it would be good to do a biopsy."

"Okay," I replied and then, "When?"

"The sooner, the better," he said and then logged on his computer and pulled up his schedule. "Day after tomorrow," he said. It wasn't a question.

"Wait a minute," Dalia said. "Aren't you rushing into this?"

"I am. It's your call, of course, but the sooner you sort these things, the better."

"Day after tomorrow is fine," I said.

"Are you sure?" Dalia asked me.

"Where would you do this? In a hospital?" I asked.

"No. We can do it right here."

"Here?" Dalia cried out, looking at the small room.

The doctor smiled and replied, "Well, not in this room but in this clinic."

"That's fine," I said.

"Good. The nurse will tell you how to prepare," he said and then stood up, shook hands with us again, and walked out.

"What do you think?" Dalia asked as we gathered our things.

"Dr. K. is good. I like a no-nonsense doctor."

"That he is, Stock. But you should get a second opinion."

"No, I'm good."

"You're not going to listen to me, are you?"

"Nope," I replied as I grabbed her hand and pulled her out of the small examination room.

Two days later, I showed up in his office at the appointed time. A nurse and a technician were the only people in the office; Dalia, to her frustration, was asked to sit in the waiting room.

I won't share all the gory details of the biopsy. It's enough to offer this: imagine a flexible thick, round nail gun going up your bum on a search mission, twisting and turning, looking for its target. And, when it finds the right spot, its needle pierces through your tissues in rapid action. Now imagine this monster not having one single target, but several, and each time it penetrates your sensitive tissues, the technician would call a number with the doctor either agreeing or disagreeing while you are lying on your side, thinking, *what the fuck.*

"You may see some blood," the doctor said when he was done torturing me.

"Where?"

"Everywhere," he replied, not looking up from his pad.

"Okay," I said. I wanted to go home. I wanted to sit in front of a TV and watch something funny and mindless.

"We will text you if it's all good; otherwise, I'll see you next week," Dr. K. said.

"Thank you," I replied. This is what we say to doctors, a common response, no matter how much they prodded, looked, and touched in and out of your body. Thank you for the sad news.

Thank you for the good news. Thank you for trying even though you are just following a prescribed algorithm, like a car mechanic. So, thank you, Dr. K., for the vague non-assurance. It didn't dawn on me until I arrived home that every day that I didn't get a text from him meant the growing possibility that all was not good. That was a strange set-up. Shouldn't they text if the results were *not* good?

And he was correct about the blood, of course, but he didn't warn the sight of crimson semen would sear deep down into your memory.

*   *   *

Options. That's what we crave in this country, and why not? Choices and more choices. We love it. This is America. We feel empowered when we can choose from a long and complicated menu of cheeseburgers, chicken wraps, tacos, and more in one shop. Even when you order a combo of something, you have more choices: small, medium, or large. Salads come with six or more dressing choices. This freedom to choose is not limited to food, of course. It expands to clothing, cars, telephones, and everything else that we must have in our daily lives.

We love it so much that we have taken this *freedom* to choose in our healthcare. You would think when your employer or social services offer you insurance, you would be done, but of course, you would be wrong. You have options. Are you ready?

I am poor but will have no choice but to pay as I need the services, formally denoted as traditional indemnity or, more euphemistically, the fee-for-service plan. There are Preferred Provider Organizations (PPOs), or Point-Of-Service (POS) plans, and of course, the HMOs, or Health Maintenance Organizations. There are options within those options. We love them, and most people would argue (fight) for these options. I pay for as much healthcare as I want, they would say. *Want* or *need*? That's the real question, and there lies the problem. But we don't see it that way.

Medicare, too? Yes. Wouldn't you expect, when you are old, that you are given medical insurance that takes care of you? Of course not. Because, even in old age, we love to plow through pages and pages of documents to find out the best *options* for us: Medicare Part A (hospital insurance), Medicare Part B (outpatient coverage), Medicare Part C (Medicare Advantage), and of course Medicare Part D (prescription drug coverage).

"Fine, then I'll get all the parts: A through D and that should cover me," you say, and that is because you are an eternal optimist. But no! There is still a gap. "Is it a wide gap?" you ask. Who knows? But don't worry, because there is something to fill that gap. It's called Medigap (Medicare supplement insurance). "So, am I covered now?" No one knows until you actually get sick. But don't worry, if you want more options, there are more.

But we love it, no matter that we hardly understand the options and the documents that go with them. We make ourselves believe we have it fine until the bills arrive, and then you learn that you are not doing fine.

There is an aphorism that a friend once offered me. Let's call it Kian's maxim: In business, you think of all the alternatives you are willing to accept or support and then package them together and offer them as options to your customers. That way, they feel good about having a menu of options, and you feel gratified no matter what they select. Kian's maxim!

But that's not the point either. What is it then? I don't know. What I know is that even doctors like to offer you options. My doctor provided me three.

*   *   *

Dr. K. didn't send a text, so it was apparent that the eventual conversation would not be fun. Dalia had not offered any opinion, had stayed away from the subject, and even worked longer hours. She knows me well.

I took a cab from our house, as Dalia planned to meet me at Dr. K's office. The taxi arrived earlier than expected, and we drove off in silence. The driver crossed Elysian Fields and made a left turn, ignoring the red light—it's more of a recommendation than a rule in New Orleans anyway—and then another left onto North Claiborne Avenue before getting on the freeway.

"I'm going to be way early for my appointment," I said without a prompt.

"That's good," the driver replied, looking at me through the rearview mirror.

"I guess, but I dread the results." I wasn't sure why I was sharing with a stranger, but it was easier with him than Dalia.

"I had cancer ten years ago," he offered, attempting to sympathize with his customer even though he had no idea why I was going to the clinic.

"And how are you doing now?"

"Fine. I was given a Gleason score of five," the driver said.

"Is that good?" I asked, having no idea what it meant.

"Yeah," he replied.

"Did you have to do chemo?" I asked, and then thought how funny, as always, this is the first question when telling people about the C-word.

"Oh, no. I was told to 'wait and see,' and we have been waiting and seeing for the past ten years," he replied.

"So, five is good then?"

"I guess. I blame the whole thing on riding bikes in this city anyway," the driver offered.

"Motorcycles?"

"No, bicycles. Riding bikes on these bad roads are the number one cause of prostate cancer," he offered, and then, to clarify, "For men."

I wasn't sure how I should respond, but perhaps he knew something I didn't. And why not bike riding? It's as good of an excuse as anything. I nodded, and his attention was given to leaving the freeway in one piece as a pink Camaro decided to exit at the same time from three lanes over. He let the car pass him and then, in his relaxed manner, left the freeway and drove toward Canal Street. A few minutes later, he dropped me off in front of the Cancer Center.

"It'll be okay," he offered as I paid him.

"Thank you," I replied and left his cab.

"It doesn't look good," Dr. K. said as he sat next to me on a small stool with his notepad. He had walked in the room followed by four other people, his interns, I assumed. It was in the same examination room as before and no chairs (no room for chairs anyway) for the visitors to sit in unless they sat on the examination bed. But that was reserved for Dalia, as Dr. K. informed them. She hadn't arrived yet; he offered to wait for her, but I didn't want to wait even though she wasn't going to be happy about it.

Before sitting down, Dr. K. shook hands with me and asked how I felt. I was not sure what he meant or whether he was earnest. I felt whatever he was going to tell me wasn't going to be good. I felt not texting for a week was cruel. I felt scared. So, I said I felt fine, and he said that it was good. He then pulled the small stool from under the sink and sat next to me.

"I hope you don't mind if we have some visitors," he said.

It wasn't a question, as they were already in the room, but I nodded my assent—that's something we all do in response to a medical authority. That settled, he shoved his notepad in front of my face and informed me that I had cancer and not the "good" kind.

"Is there a good kind?" I asked.

"No, not really," he replied and then informed me that the cancer may have spread already.

I stared at him.

He continued, still holding his notepad in front me as if to prove what he was telling me was backed by data. "It's rare for someone your age, and even more rare to have this type of aggressive cancer. But don't worry."

He said all that in one breath. I don't know how you would have reacted, but I didn't have one of those movie moments when you go through your whole life in a flash. I was more focused on his fingers on the notepad. He was pointing at charts and the data. He was telling me something about the left number and the right number. There were too many numbers on the pad, so I wasn't sure which one I should focus on. None of the numbers were more than five, and I was thinking, so why is that bad? But perhaps the cabdriver had a different type of cancer and thus the numbers didn't follow his rule. Then it occurred to me that one might either add or multiply those two numbers.

"Do you add the two numbers?"

"Yes."

"And it's out of how many?"

"Ten."

"So, nine is not good?"

"It is not."

"Is it a linear progression?"

"No."

"So, what do I have to do?" I asked, and that's when he told me I have options like a salesman might offer at a car dealer. You can get the sport package, but that limits your color options—or you can get the platinum package, which has the sport package plus keyless entry and more color options.

"You've three options," one of the interns offered. He was rather tall with a full head of blond hair. He was standing closest to Dr. K., not like the other three who had squeezed next to the sink, their youthful, eager looks focused on Dr. K. I thought perhaps he was a senior intern or maybe a full-fledged doctor. Not that it mattered. "You can do surgery, radiation, or do nothing."

I take "nothing," Alex, for $100, I thought, but I asked, "Is nothing a real option?"

"No," the blond doctor said.

"So, surgery or radiation?"

"You have options, of course, but if you do radiation first, then you can't do surgery if it doesn't work. If you do surgery first, then you can do radiation afterward if needed," Dr. K. offered with confidence.

"So, there is no option?" I asked.

"No. There are options and I can walk you through them again," he offered patiently. "You may do as you wish, but I'd recommend surgery first." The blond doctor nodded in agreement, and three young interns took some notes.

"Would that cure me?"

"I can't tell until I go in."

So, I have to buy the car before I know I like it.

"You can get a second opinion," the blond doctor offered.

"And what would that tell me?" I asked.

"Depends on whom you ask," Dr. K. replied. "If you ask a surgeon, she will tell you what I am telling you. If you asked a radiation oncologist, she might say do the radiation first because it has a higher chance of success. But both will tell you if you do the radiation, you can't, well more, precisely, it will be exceedingly difficult, almost impossible to do the surgery afterward."

"Okay," I said, but before the doctor could respond, Dalia walked in. She must have been running because she was out of breath.

"You missed all the fun," I greeted her and tapped the paper-covered examination table for her to sit down.

She doesn't like that kind of joke and had no intention of listening to me anyway. "What's the prognosis?" she asked Dr. K.

He went through the story again as patiently as he did with me. He spoke in a calm, slow manner, but he kept his words honest.

Dalia did not stop where I had. She wanted to know more. She wanted all the details of the options and why and how they are ranked. She wanted to know if there was a fourth and fifth option. Dalia liked the idea of many choices.

I stayed quiet while Dalia interrogated the doctors. I let her do her thing. Dalia is tall, taller than all the doctors standing next to the sink taking copious notes. She had refused to sit down and towered over Dr. K., but he has seen everything and stayed calm throughout. Dalia is used to being in control, and what the doctor had been telling her was she had no power here and couldn't fix me by merely ordering them around. She looked at me, and her eyes finally showed fear.

"What if I don't do anything?" I asked.

The blond doctor looked at me funny. "What do you mean?"

"I mean, how long would I live if I do nothing?"

"That is not an option," Dalia cried out.

"I want to know," I said.

"It's hard to say," Dr. K. replied.

"I won't hold you to it. Just give me an estimate."

"The way it looks now, I'd say with a high probability you shouldn't expect to live more than five years." He then pulled up a chart from the computer and showed me the mortality rate. "You're on this one," he put his finger on a black line. "And it indicates the probability curve of mortality."

"So, five percent of survival rate past five years."

"Yes, but . . ."

"We understand," I said, and stood up. "Thank you."

"I know it's a lot to digest. You need time to think about your *options*," he offered and then took out a little sheet of paper from one of the drawers. "Here's my cell number, text me if you need anything," he said as he wrote on the small form.

*   *   *

Dalia forced me to get a second opinion and then a third. We carried the biopsy results with us like one would high school transcripts when moving to a new school. The first was a surgeon, and he suggested surgery first. The second was a radiation oncologist, and she thought, given my age and the nature of the disease, radiation would "not be a bad option," as she put it. But they both somewhat agreed with Dr. K. on the limitations of surgery after radiation. The surgeon said it was possible but complicated, and I would have to go to Houston or Los Angeles.

So, there it was, a two to one vote with a possible caveat.

"Should we try for a best of five?" I asked Dalia as we came out of the doctor's office.

"It's better to have more information," she offered, not wanting to give in.

"Let's go back to Dr. K.," I said.

"If you think so."

So, surgery it was.

Major surgery, especially of this type, is a curious phenomenon. You go in as one person, and you come out a few hours later as a different person. Men are not defined by their penis—but speak to any man, and if he is honest, he would tell you that it may not define him, but it does have an outsized (no pun intended) influence on him. Dr. K. had assured me that he would do his best to preserve my *normal* quality of life. But what is normal?

"I'll do my best," he promised as I left his office, two days before the surgery. Then he added, "I will know more when I *go in*." That was the fine print.

It was all an abstraction at that point, and my first thought after he talked about the small cameras and robotic arms was not about the potential loss of all manner of bodily functions, but if there would be a video of the surgery and if he would be willing to share it with me. And you would think everything about your *everyday* life a few days before the surgery would be memorable; they were not. Everything was an abstraction jumbled together. You try not to think about the consequences of your decision as you get ready to go to the hospital voluntarily. I drove, even if it made Dalia upset, because I wanted to show the world I was calm and in control. I walked to the surgery and obediently followed the instructions of the attending nurse: take off your clothes, put on a gown that does nothing to cover you, drink this horrid liquid (all of it), give me your arm, stand up, sit down, and then finally lie down.

"It'll be all right," Dalia assured me.

"He'll be fine," the nurse assured Dalia.

I was no longer a thinking, independent adult. I was an object on a narrow bed, pushed by an orderly through the corridors of an old hospital. And before I could blink, I woke up in a different room with Dalia next to me.

She smiled and said, "Do you need anything?"

I shook my head. "Where am I?" I asked.

But before she could answer, Dr. K. walked in the room and sat next to me, and immediately three of his minions followed him in.

"I think it went well," he said.

"Okay."

He looked at me for a second and perhaps thought I didn't understand the gravity of his comment. He added in his calm, authoritative tone, "We had to remove more tissue than expected."

"Why?" Dalia asked.

He looked at her and said, now in a lecture mode, "At each step, we take a thin slice, freeze it and send it to the lab for an immediate assessment. If there are traces of anomalies, we take another thin slice. We had to keep cutting as there was more evidence. I was forced to stop as cutting further could have damaged his other organs."

I had zoned out a bit but heard Dalia ask, "But, will he be okay?"

"He is fine now," Dr. K. said. "But we'll have to see."

"What does that mean?" Dalia stood up and put her hand on my shoulder. I was an object again, while the two discussed me. But all I wanted to do was go back to sleep.

Dr. K. tapped my shoulder and said, "Drink some water."

"Okay."

Dalia handed me some, and I took a sip, though I wasn't thirsty.

"Your skin may feel like bubble wrap for a day or two. That's normal. It's the gas we used."

I touched my chest, and it did feel exactly like those wraps with small little bubbles. I wondered if I pressed hard, would they pop? They didn't. They moved around as if thousands of tiny bubbles were floating on a shallow liquid.

"You didn't answer my questions," Dalia said.

"There is no more to say now. We have to wait and see," Dr. K. replied.

They let me go home a few hours later. There was no reason to keep me, and the less time you spend in a hospital, the better; hospitals are the most significant source of infection.

The surgery was scheduled for two hours, but it ended up lasting for over five. I felt bad for the doctors in that surgery room, meticulously slicing little pieces of me using the robotic arms that went in and out of the small holes that had been drilled on my lower torso, four round holes plus one straight thin cut across my abdomen. I wondered what they did while they were waiting for the results from the lab next door. Did they fiddle around with the robotic arms to check out other parts of my body? Or did they sit back and wait the few minutes needed for the lab to report, chatting about the Saints? They were probably drained on the fifth hour, and I wondered if it crossed their minds that perhaps they should take thicker slices and be done with it. I hoped not, and I was glad he had stopped where he did, because any further cuts would have meant a colostomy bag for the rest of my life. That was my red line with him. I had warned him that I would not do the surgery, would rather die than have that kind of life. Dalia had strenuously objected when I tried to make that deal with Dr. K., but in the end, she had no choice. Though I am not sure if Dr. K. officially agreed to my deal, it's moot now.

The recovery was easier than I had expected. The postop nurse had warned me about the possibility of a UTI (which I got, but a quick dose of antibiotics solved that), hernia, and tears in the urethra (which I escaped). I did cry like a child because I couldn't find the strength to get on the bed by myself. I felt utterly ashamed afterward and wondered if Dalia thought less of me. The little bubbles popped on their own, making me feel like a man possessed with tiny insects. But perhaps the funniest part of the recovery was when Dr. K. decided it was time to remove the catheter that had been my friend for two weeks.

The hospital had given me pages of instructions, and one of them indicated that you must bring a disposable pad for the drive back home on your first visit. Dalia dropped me off in front of the doctor's office and went to look for parking. We were early again, and I told her I'd wait for her in the front office. But clearly, we hadn't learned our lesson because the doctor was ready as soon as I walked in.

"Let's take this catheter out," he said as soon as he walked in the examination room, followed by a nurse that I had not met before.

"Should I lie down?" I asked as I took a step toward the examination bed.

"No, I'll do it right here."

I need to explain something because what happened next is not my fault. The little instructions on the guides that held the tubes and the bag in place clearly stated: "remove with rubbing alcohol." But what did Dr. K. do? He grabbed hold of these rather large plastic holders and pulled them hard like one does with a band-aid, no alcohol applied to loosen the adhesive. Then he grabbed the catheter and pulled it out of my body. I didn't have time to scream or yell at him for being an asshole because as a reward for his action, my bladder emptied itself in a gush on him and everything else.

The nurse grabbed for a garbage can from under the sink and put it under this seemingly unending stream of urine, but by then, Dr. K.'s pants had urine stains, as did the nurse's uniform, and a yellow puddle had formed on the floor. I kept uttering my apologies, but I had zero control, and there was no end to it—I was like a bull in a field.

"I deserved it," Dr. K. said calmly after I was done, and the bucket was glowing with my pee. The nurse left the room, I assume to change his whole outfit. Dr. K. washed his hands and threw tons of paper towels on the floor

"I am so sorry," I said. "I don't know what happened. I couldn't control it."

"It's not your fault. I should have anticipated it, but I thought you may have more control."

I wanted to ask why he thought so, but before I could speak, Dalia walked in and looked at me still naked, and then the bucket and then the stain on Dr. K.'s pants. "I have your pad," she said.

"Too late now. You missed all the fun," I said, trying to be brave.

In retrospect, it was a funny scene. Dr. K. had seen it all, so he was not angry about it. And whatever embarrassment I felt at the time was quickly replaced with the sad realization that I would never be the same. I was no longer me.

The advertisements for adult diapers were no longer amusing, as they had become my reality. I went to buy a Costco-size box because I wasn't sure when or if I would stop needing them. As I put a box in my basket, I felt everyone was looking at me. I wondered if they thought I was buying it for my aging parents. That was a brilliant idea, I thought: I should pretend I was buying it for someone else. And I should buy a year's worth, so I wouldn't have to do this again. So, I piled boxes and boxes of them in my basket. Now, I looked like one of those merchants who shop at Costco because it's cheaper than wholesale prices. Then I thought, I can't go to the cashier with a cart full of adult diapers and nothing else. I should buy other things as a distraction, like when teenage boys buy their first Penthouse magazine. You never buy the magazine by itself; it looks perverted. So, you purchase a can of Coke, a packet of gum, a couple of chocolate bars, and a bag of chips too—and you think you are smart. But now it's clear it looked exactly like what it was: you were having a party by yourself.

A month passed, and I thought this new life would be my reality forever. I wished I had taken the wait-and-see option. I thought I always smelled like pee, and perhaps I did. I asked Dalia, but she told me I was silly, but she wasn't convincing. I texted Dr. K., and he assured me it was going to get better. I didn't believe him, and empty boxes of adult diapers spoke of a forty-six-year-old man who was worse than an infant.

Dr. K. had warned me not to search the Internet on this issue. That only made me want to learn more, but now I understand his motive. The chatrooms were filled with sad stories of men who had zero control over their bladder even after more than a year. One said, "It's been more than two years, and it's still the same. I drink, which makes me lose the little control I have, so I drink more to forget, but how can I forget the soaked bed?" There were women participating in these conversations, too, frustrated with their husbands or boyfriends who would ejaculate urine from their flaccid penises.

"I can't stand it anymore," I said as I changed for the fifth time in the day. I had given up hiding it from her as I had done in the first week. There was no point.

"It'll be fine. I'd rather you live a long time."

"Not like this," I said, "Not like this."

"Don't say that, Stock. Be patient," she said.

I wasn't being honest with her. It wasn't just the temporary incontinence; it was the loss of self. I had become a new person with different thoughts and feelings. I had gone further within and couldn't find a way to get out.

"I am no longer me, Dalia."

She stared at me for a moment. She had become more cautious in her responses, wary of my short temper since the operation. She wanted to accommodate me, but my cryptic conversation confused her more. I knew she was frustrated, but I didn't know how to explain the gravity of what I felt.

I had always told Dalia, if you find me dead, it's murder, because I could not think of any reason to kill myself, ever. I had told her this with a sense of invincibility that I should have never possessed. I would kill others before I'd kill myself, I told her. A month of heavily soaked adult diapers doesn't necessarily make you suicidal but add that to all the other changes to your body and mind, and it does make you start to think of it as an option.

In the end, Dr. K. was right. After a few weeks, there were improvements, a near full control, even though I was stuck with a year's worth of adult diapers. But they won't go to waste, I thought, as old age was around the corner.

"I was worried a bit," Dr. K. said when I went to see him for a checkup and reported that I had finally reached a certain level of control.

"But you told me not to worry, and it's normal."

"I was trying to be a good doctor."

"So, you lied?"

"It wasn't a lie. It's just that at your age and health, I was expecting a quicker recovery," Dr. K. replied.

"So, what's that mean?"

"It means nothing. It means it took you longer to recover. That can happen too."

"It'd be nice to get the honest answer even if it's not positive."

He nodded and then added, "Since you asked. Your blood work came in today, and it doesn't look good."

"Fuck," I said.

*   *   *

In New Orleans, when there is a hurricane coming your way, you never wish for it to go somewhere else. It's bad juju to wish it upon others. And in a traditional city that has immersed itself in Voodoo, you tend to obey such unwritten rules. You want the hurricane to not come to you, or will it to dissipate, but never desire harm on your neighbor because it will come back to you some other way. So, I don't wish my disease on anyone. I haven't asked the why-me question, not even in private thoughts. I have a friend who continually asks that question every time I see him. His wife says the same thing.

"Why him?" she asked me. "He doesn't deserve it," she added as if others did. I wondered if she thought I deserved mine. I tried to be understanding though. He was dealing with a cancer even more serious than mine. My other friend's illness started as *common* bladder cancer, but then it went to her lungs—but she never complained, nor did she ask why me. It's funny how these things come in threes.

Some time ago, my lung cancer friend and her husband visited us in New Orleans. Let's call her Gladys. It's an old person's name, but she won't mind. She was young, a few years younger than me. Gladys and I were friends long before she was married, but we drifted apart, and by the time she was diagnosed, we hadn't seen each other for years. She had sent a mass email informing her friends of what she called "my status." The email led me to call her, and we reestablished our friendship. Gladys told me she always wanted to come to New Orleans, so this was an excellent opportunity to visit me and meet Dalia.

Dalia and I went to the airport to pick them up. They had offered to Uber to our house, but we hadn't seen our new airport, and we thought it was an excellent excuse to explore it. The old NOLA airport was nice but definitely hoary and small. This one is large and beautifully designed with its massive windows and terraced levels.

Dalia and I were leaning over the railing on the third floor, where you can see all the departures and arrivals, and we spotted Gladys and her husband, Carlos. We shouted, but they didn't hear us. We ran downstairs to meet them. They came out of the exit, trying to spot us in a mass of people.

"Gladys," I shouted, and she spotted us and smiled. I remembered her welcoming smile.

She moved ahead and hugged me tightly and then hugged Dalia, who had stretched out her hand for a handshake.

"It's so lovely to finally meet you, Dalia," Gladys said. She then grabbed her husband and introduced him to Dalia.

"It's a beautiful airport, Stock," he said as he gave me a hug. Carlos is a small man who looks so fragile that I always worried that I might break him.

"It's nice. It took a long time to build, but it's finally done."

"What do you guys want to do while you're here?" Dalia asked.

"We don't care. It's just nice to get away," Gladys replied, and with that, she grabbed my arm and said, "Let's go see your city."

Gladys and I walked ahead, and Dalia and Carlos followed us to the parking lot. "You look good, Gladys," I said.

"Thank you, C., you do too," she said. Gladys knew I hated my first name, but she also didn't like the idea of using my last, so her solution was to call me by my first initial.

I wanted to ask her about her cancer and how she was doing, but I didn't think it was an appropriate first question. She looked good. She looked healthy, even though she had lost some weight. Her hair was short but looked full enough.

We spent the first day biking. New Orleans has lovely bike paths that take you all around the city. We biked from our house on Dauphine Street toward the French Quarter, and from there, through the Warehouse District, and then down the Garden District and the Irish Channel. Gladys rode slowly, and we tried to stay at her pace. She didn't look tired, but we didn't ask either. We had breakfast at The Camellia Grill, not the best place in New Orleans, but Gladys likes old fashioned diners, and this one was that. Camellia's is counter service only with bow-tied servers and cloth napkins. It's been the same design since the late forties, and it continues to serve the same greasy food.

After breakfast, we went straight home and Gladys went to her room. When I checked on her a few minutes later, she was fast asleep. She didn't get up until it was dark outside but came out of her room dressed up and looking refreshed. "Am I late?" she asked. We had a reservation for Commander's Palace and only fifteen minutes to get there.

"Of course not. This is New Orleans, and everything is only ten minutes away," Dalia replied.

This is a city that you can do so many things in one day. In San Francisco or Los Angeles, one task a day is the rule. In San Francisco, looking for a parking space is an event in and of itself, and an easy, five-mile drive from Santa Monica to West LA could take more than an hour.

We arrived at Commander's right on time and were greeted immediately and formally. When I lived in San Francisco, I used to tell any visitors who insisted on going to some trendy restaurant that we couldn't go because it was *too touristy*. No one in his right mind would go to a place where tourists from Idaho might go or, worse, people from the Peninsula. Those people only came to the city because they had read an article on a new, all-that restaurant, and they had to try it.

In California, it was a worthy rule to follow, but it definitely did not apply in New Orleans. These restaurants are reputable because they have been excellent for decades. Commander's is one of them; every tourist wants to go there, but locals have their own tables too.

We were led through the first dining room, then through the kitchen, the backyard, the next building, and up the stairs to the second-floor dining room. Dalia knew the owner, Ti Martin, and as soon as we sat down, she showed up and asked if we wanted a tour. Carlos was keen, but Gladys didn't want to move again.

I stayed with her while Dalia and Carlos got up to leave with Ti. "I'll send you a couple of martinis," she said before leaving.

"This is a lovely place," Gladys said.

"It is. It's a city of awesome food."

"And you know how much I love eating."

"We can try the Joint tomorrow if you want perfect BBQ," I said.

Our drinks arrived, and we sipped in silence. It had been months since I'd had anything alcoholic.

"This is good," Gladys said, "It's my first drink in a year."

I laughed. "I try not to drink either. It takes away my muscle control if you know what I mean."

She laughed too. "Now you know how women feel after pregnancy. After my second, I could hardly laugh without losing control."

"Can I ask you something?"

She looked at me funny and took a subtle defensive stance. "Sure," she said.

"What do you tell people when they ask you about your health?" I asked.

"Oh, that," she laughed.

I had done what Gladys had done a few years earlier: I announced my disease to the world. I wanted to own it and not hide it like my other friend had, the one who continued to moan *why me*. I am not judging him. In cancer, like most things in life, there is a hierarchy, even though each of us is on a different journey. The problem with announcing such things is that people react. Some can't deal with it, so they pretend it's all good and never mention it. *It* becomes a taboo. And there are some who continuously want a status update. At first, I told them everything about the difficulties of the disease. But then I realized their inquiry was more about them than me. They are genuinely worried about you, but they don't want to hear the truth, not really. They are looking for assurance. It bothered me at first, but then I comprehended the reality of it. They are concerned, but they can't do anything to help you, so telling them the truth only adds to their anxiety without alleviating your own. It's somewhat of a lonely journey.

Gladys took a sip of her martini and held the liquid in her mouth for a second before swallowing. "You know what the best day has been since the cancer has moved to my lungs?"

I shook my head.

Gladys gave a tiny smile and said, "I had a friend who had stage four breast cancer. Isn't it funny that as soon as you get cancer, others with it come out of the woodwork?"

"I always thought they come in threes," I replied.

"Maybe. Anyway, a few months before my friend died, while she could still stand up and walk around, she and I spent a day together. At first, I dreaded seeing her. I knew she was going to die soon, and I wasn't sure how to react to her."

"I know," I whispered, thinking that Gladys may only have a few months left herself.

"But it was the best day. I met up with her at a café, and as soon as we kissed hello, all my fears disappeared. I realized with her, I could be me, Gladys, the person and not Gladys, who has cancer and may die. We spent a day together without ever mentioning health or drugs or radiation or chemo or any of the shit that goes with every fucking treatment that we go through. And you know how it is with cancer. You look fine from the outside, so to those who don't know about you, you are fine and healthy. On that day, it was just us, two girls having the time of our lives in Manhattan. Do you understand?"

"I think so."

"So, to answer your question: I always tell people I am fine. This is a lonely journey, C., no matter how much people love you and want to accompany you."

I wanted to ask her more, but Carlos and Dalia came back, and we didn't want to talk about cancer anymore.

We ordered our food and for dessert, I insisted Gladys order the bread pudding soufflé. She did and loved it. It was a lovely night, each of us trying to be ourselves.

They stayed for two more days, and then we had to take them to the airport.

"This was great," Gladys said as she kissed Dalia goodbye.

"I hope you will come back soon."

"We will," Gladys replied. She then stepped toward me and hugged me. "I'll see you on the other side," she whispered, and without waiting for me to respond, grabbed Carlos's hand and joined the queue for security.

We ran to the third floor and watched them go through the process. Gladys looked up and waved at us, and we waved back. She was smiling. She'd had a lovely visit, and I was glad she and I had had a moment together. They cleared security and walked hand in hand toward their gate. Gladys looked up again before turning the corner. She was still smiling.

As she knew it would be, that was the last time I saw her.

*   *   *

It started, as it did every day, with a soft groan as if it was resist-
ing waking up from a long, deep sleep. And then after a while,
the whine was replaced with a crunching sound that sand might
make if crushed under the heavy weight of a grinding stone.
Then an eerie silence, followed by a mechanical whirl of engines
extending two gray arms, each holding a rectangular plate, one
clean and smooth that you might find in an Ikea store, and the
other dotted with little knobs and lights, along with wires that
were unnecessarily exposed, looking like old electronics bought
from a secondhand store. On top sat a large square gray box with
green laser light dividing it into two parts. One could call it an
Overseer, as it sat high up looking down at the room and the arms,
as they stretched forward from the main body.

The arms extended noisily as far they could and faced each
other as if wanting to cradle their cargo, a large, bed-like gang-
way protruding from the belly of the machine. And then once
again, there was total silence in the room.

It didn't last long, and new activities started with what sounded like a heavy door shutting with a bang in the distance, followed by an electro-mechanical spinning of a large coil within
the Overseer, as it built up its linear accelerators to its full capacity. The Overseer moved slightly to adjust its position, and
the arms started whirling counter-clockwise. As one arm passed
overhead, a large round head hidden below the bed rose from
the right following the arm. When it reached its zenith, it had the
appearance of a giant seal embosser used (perhaps long ago) in a
notary office. The rotation lasted about sixty seconds, and then it
all stopped with a thud, and once again, the Overseer sat on top,
looking across the room.

The two arms pulled back loudly and grudgingly, but in the
end, they both relented, and they sat back against the body of
the machine. Another sixty seconds of pause with soft rock music
piping from somewhere in the room. If everything was fine, and

sometimes it would not be, then a new buzzing sound began, like thousands of bees swarming in the room, indicating a change of the application. The seal embosser rotated again, now clockwise, without the two arms chasing it, for another sixty seconds, sending mathematically modeled, concentrated deadly radiation. Then twenty seconds of silence, the accelerators charging, followed by the repeat of the cycle, in the opposite direction. Then, one more to complete three processes of dispersion of the beams, each time in a different order but with the same rotational speed, sixty seconds per revolution.

Then I was done, at least for the day.

And through it all, I lay flat on the bed, forbidden from moving, while holding a blue rubber donut with both hands as it sat unnervingly on my chest. The donut had frayed in places from its users' nervous pressure, and I was afraid it might break in my hands at any moment.

It always started fine as I looked at the ceiling, lined with green, crossed laser beams that were supposed to help position my body as technicians tugged and pushed at the sheet beneath me to adjust me *just right*, though I always doubted the accuracy of their result. Then the light dimmed, and the technicians left the room and closed the heavy metal door, a door as thick as a tree trunk. Then another moment of quiet. The red light on the sidewall was turned on, and it beamed across the darkened room. And this was when the machine was awakened.

There was no physical pain with the first rotation; it was a simple test of the bladder's fullness. There was overwhelming mental stress, though, as I waited for the results. I started counting the seconds as soon as the two arms retracted: One, two, three, four . . . fifty-nine, sixty. I would start to panic if I reached the minute mark, because if the wait was much longer, then it meant my bladder was not full enough, at least not for them, despite the tremendous pressure on my lower abdomen. And if this were the case—and it often happened early on in the treatment, before I was able to find an optimal balance of liquid intake and output by each procedure—it meant giving up my turn to someone else, and waiting outside for another fifteen minutes or more, in which time my bladder was so full that no amount of Kegel exercises would stop the inevitable. But if I had timed everything correctly, then the bed would adjust slightly at around sixty seconds, signaling the machine's readiness to emboss me with radiation. That was when I could concentrate on the pain that was growing to an excruciating level as my full bladder with its missing sphincter assigned the task of urinary control to other parts of my body.

At the time, it felt like an eternity even though the entire process was less than ten minutes. And in those *short* minutes, your brain could pack so much in. I had read the human mind merges separate distresses into a bundle. People who have been tortured have reported that the number of days, no matter two or ten, meld into one significant trauma in their memory. They had forgotten if they were in pain for an hour or for a thousand hours. Their mind remembered the images and sounds and stress but not the duration of it. It's definitely not the same, but I believe your brain deals with a certain level of poverty the same way. That is assuming you have come out of it. You remember being poor, and you remember the stresses that poverty brings, but you cannot remember the actual feeling, that utter hopelessness that you have at the moment when you realize you are only one paycheck away from homelessness or that if your twenty-year-old car breaks down, you will sink even more into debt.

I have forgotten all those feelings, and as I am writing this, I cannot bring them back. It has become an abstraction again but then—and only for a moment, when the side effects of radiation had weakened my defenses—in that ten minutes of waiting, I had an eternity to let my mind wander, and the feelings came rushing back. I didn't will them nor did I welcome them, but they were there, and as if a black hole had opened up, I was sucked into deep despair, the feeling that no matter what you do and no matter how hard you work, you will stay in the state of destitution. I had tried hard to conjure the feelings months after the last session of radiation, but they were gone. I wondered if it felt like getting lost in a supermarket when you are three, old enough to know but too young to manage. The panic is at its zenith in those few moments of recognizing that you are alone. Those seconds or minutes must feel like most poor people feel most of the time, the panic of knowing there is no safety net if you fall.

I tried to hold onto that feeling, or at least the ghost of it, every time I received test results that brought tears to Dalia's eyes.

*   *   *

Well, I think I am at the end of my story, as Death has appeared. He looks as surprised as I am. I never thought such a being existed, but here he is, standing next to me. He doesn't look scary, like stories have you believe, nor does he look like the character in Bergman's *The Seventh Seal*. Though I wouldn't be surprised if he was a good chess player. He looks genteel and is now watching over me.

I look up, and he says, "I *am* a good chess player. But finish your thoughts, Stock."

"You looked surprised to see me," I say.

"I was."

"Is that normal?"

He shakes his head but doesn't reply. He walks over, stands on the other side of the counter and stares at the manila envelope.

"Are you real?" I ask. "Or perhaps I am dreaming you."

He waits for a moment as if wanting to make sure I am finished, "I can be as real as you wish me to be."

"Would it matter?" I ask.

"Not really."

"Where am I?" I ask the unanswered question once more.

"You are where you should be, Stock."

"No, I mean, what is this place?"

"This is a place with many names, but you may have heard it called the Swedish Prison by some of your friends."

"Oh, yes. . . . Joseph and Zuleika. How strange of a tale is our story."

"Yes, you all have a peculiar connection. Do you remember everything about them now?"

"Yes. Dalia introduced me to Zolie, not knowing that she and I had met once before. Though at the time, neither Zolie nor I remembered our first encounter. We both felt that we must have crossed paths, but it must not have been pleasant, as we had both tried desperately to eliminate it from our memories. We limited our interaction for the longest time as if we repelled each other. But eventually, we became friends. We could never fully remember or understand everything. But we learned of our small roles in the worlds of gods and their hubris."

Death nods, appreciating my understanding of his world, spoken and unspoken. "Yes. We have so much to remedy. But for you, the story must end soon."

"You know, in the end, I blame myself. I am a victim of my own vanity, my own hubris. Do you know what I mean?"

Death shakes his head. "At least you have all your faculties back."

I laugh. "A bit too late. And not my mind really. It's still a jumble of half thoughts. Now, do I have time to tell you why it's my fault?"

"You do what you need to do," he offers.

"If I had not been so concerned about my looks, I would not have taken medication to regrow my hair. Or I at least could have paid more attention to the fine print, where it listed its side effects. I took the pills, even though it did nothing to slow down the baldness. But it did mask the antigen, and by the time it was discovered, cancer had gone too far."

"You cannot be sure," Death says.

"True, but one's vanity is as good as anything if you are looking for something to blame."

He sighs but doesn't respond.

"How long?" I ask.

He still doesn't answer at first, but then looks at me and says, "I am sorry, but we asked for a reprieve, and I was certain that you were given one."

"I didn't know such things were even possible," I say.

"It would have been here, in your story," he replies. "Though at this point I can see that we merely assumed there was going to be a different ending for you. But that was never explicitly promised. I am sorry."

I don't know what to say, so I say nothing. You must think I am delirious and dreaming all of this. You may be right, but Death is still here, trying not to look at me.

"Do you know how much more time I've left?"

"Not much, now," Death replies.

"But what about my story?" I ask and then quickly add, "I know after everything and how the world has turned, I should be less selfish, but clearly, I am shameless."

Death shakes his head and puts his hand on the envelope. "Your story is here and will be told. You have done nothing to be ashamed of, Stock. You have done well."

"I am glad I was able to say goodbye to Dalia. I am glad she forgave me for all my follies."

"She will be fine, Stock," Death offers solemnly. "She is a strong link in the bond that holds your friends together. Her story will continue."

"And the woman in the BART? Jackie."

"I am glad you remembered her. She is the most important player in this adventure. She will decide the future for you and me."

"Oh. I would have liked to know her."

"Me too, and perhaps it will happen."

"I wonder if I should pull the rope," I say. I look down, and I am still holding it in my hand.

"You have no choice."

"I don't understand."

Death gives a warm smile and says, "You will. The bell tolls for you as you enter the next stage. It's your reward as the faithful custodian of empathy for those many years."

You are now wondering how it's even possible to tell this story if I am dead. But I am not finished yet. I am still holding the rope.

Death nods, and I pull the rope hard.

THE SWEDISH PRISON

"In the beginning, you will sympathize with me, and try to feel my pain, and you might even cry for me. But as I tell you more, you will realize the cruel joke and you'll be angry and you'll curse me; yet you will still want to hear more because you know it's true, even though you don't want it to be.

"My name is Jackie Goodwin. Do you know me? Do you remember me? Don't worry if you don't, because no one else does. To be honest, I'm surprised I still know *me*. I've been given five to seven years. I don't remember the judge or the jury, but I vividly recall the judgment.

"*Five to seven years.* I was in my little apartment in the periphery of San Francisco one day, and then as if by magic I was here, living in putrid yellow cinderblock housing. *Five to seven years.* Did I say that already? I'm sorry, but it echoes in my head every minute, and I sometimes feel compelled to say it out loud as if it's a release valve and without it I would explode.

"I walked in . . . or rather appeared in my new abode with somewhat of a fanfare. The smell of dust and dank hit my nostrils first, and then, the wind picked up, which brought the added acrid air of the massive construction across the river. I laid on my new bed, small and narrow, but surprisingly soft. The ceiling was low, and I thought if I reached up, I could touch it. Someone had drawn a cloudy sky on the ceiling, making it appear even lower than it was. The clouds were gray and heavy, and it seemed at any moment they might release their burden on me. I have a small kitchenette on the side, and the lone cupboard holds one cup, one plate, one fork, and one knife. Food appears and then disappears with the same rhythm as the rest of the world around me.

"I'm not the only occupant, though. You are here, of course, and there are other men and women (where are the children?), each relegated to their penance. They see me and I see them, but we don't connect. They fear me. I don't know why, but once when I was behind a building, I heard them talking and they said a whisper from me would end the little solace this place has offered them.

"*Whisper?* Is this possible?" You nodded. It was done slightly and reflexively but I saw it. So, I should believe it too? Do you think mere words have such power? It sounds like an old cliché; *words are mightier than the sword* bullshit. Well, this isn't like that. I'm not like Medusa with words. I'm like a regular person (most times) and I can speak normally to others, though not for too long because I don't have the patience. You know, how they say we're only using ten percent of our brain, and if we could use 100% of it, we would be gods? This is ridiculous because we *are* using our brain, all of it, fine, and gods are no better than us anyway. I see you agree. But how do I know that?

"I miss my old apartment though. I miss the city. I miss the steep streets sleek from the fog and the rain. I miss the morning seabreeze, sitting in the Cliff House, looking at the ocean. I miss my old life when I was free, and I only knew as much as one should know. *Knowledge* is only power if there is only a bit of it; too much knowledge is a curse. No, it's like a poison without an antidote. And I feel I've been poisoned. You're not convinced, are you? Doesn't matter.

"Every morning I walk to my car and open the left front door and sit on the driver side. The car is my only link to the past and when I sit in it, I feel I'm back. I am normal again. The old leather seats and the now antiquated dashboard and the rusting body are all that's left of my car, which is the only tangible item in my prison.

"*Five to seven years*. But how does one count time in this prison? Certainly not by the erosion of the remaining metal in the chassis of my car, and not by the images in the mirror."

I've been listening to Jackie's tirade as we stand side by side in the yard, staring at the metal fence that surrounds the field. We can see the construction across the river, as large machines pierce the earth making room for something giant. She looks at me with her *piercing* eyes for a moment and tries to read me. She frowns a bit and pulls her long hair away from her face. She wants to concentrate on me. Her hair used to be dark, but hours of standing under the intense morning sun in the yard have produced light reddish strands that glisten as she turns. She purses her lips in concentration, but nothing happens, and she gives up, as she has done many times before.

"Five to seven years," I say it for her, knowing that she would again.

She looks across the yard and then spits on the ground as if she had tasted something foul. Her saliva hits the blades of green grass and spreads like a spiderweb, then slowly moves over the surface of the grass, forming a white, translucent sphere before disappearing into the earth.

Jackie only speaks to me as if she feels she has known me or has some connection with me.

She turns around and faces me. "Did you arrive before me or after me? I can't recall. Is that strange?"

I shake my head and smile. "It's the nature of this place."

"How long have I been here?"

"Not long enough, if you still have to ask."

"Still?"

I nod but don't know how to respond. There isn't anything I could say that might help her. The large machines continue to pound the ground and at times the earth trembles beneath our feet.

"It feels like an eternity," Jackie says.

"You don't know what eternity is until you're condemned like I was." My response was harsher than I meant it to be, but I had spent a lifetime waiting and then another one looking for her.

She turns again and stares at the hills beyond the parameter fence and asks, "How long?"

"Do you know why you're here?"

"Because I've done something bad. . . ."

"No. You're a victim."

"Am I, now? I don't think the judge and the jury felt the same."

I nod with a certain understanding, remembering my own judgment. "Do you know me?" I ask.

"Are you Joseph?"

Her question brought a smile, but I shake my head again. "No, I'm not Joseph, though I can see why you would think I am."

"Then who are you?"

"I've answered that question many times already."

"Tell me again then."

"No. You must first tell me how you got here."

"*How I got here*? How would I know that? Why should I know such things when I know nothing else?" She takes a deep breath and thinks for a moment. "I remember my little planter box on the balcony of my apartment. I used to grow tomatoes and basil. I had to cover them with plastic wrapping to protect them from the wind and the cold of the city. I can still smell the turned earth, the sweet, green aroma of the plump tomatoes, and the subtle licorice fragrance of the basil leaves as I rubbed them between my fingers. That was heaven."

I had closed my eyes and joined her reverie but then she stopped. "Please try and remember how you got here," I press the point as I have done so many other times.

"Weren't you the one who brought me here?"

"You must be certain, Jackie."

"Why must I? I'm certain of nothing but my old car. That junk of a car is the only certainty here. It exists, and as long it does, so will I."

"And what you hold?" I ask even though I know it would not resolve this.

"What I hold?" She asks, now uncertain, and then she pauses and taps the side of her head with her fingers and for a moment she remembers. "Oh, yes. My little secret."

"Yes, the Gift."

"It's no *gift*. Who told you it was a gift? What kind of person would consider what I was given a *gift*?"

What do you do when you know you have the answer? *The* answer. The answer to the secret. Do you have to know the secret first to know the answer or the answer leads you to the secret? Or the secret is the answer? It doesn't matter, at least not to Jackie, because it's all poison to her, tearing her apart, corroding her body. She is strong so she is protecting herself from it by forgetting it. But it's still within her and the end is inevitable.

She hasn't eaten properly for a long while, even though she claims she has. She used to have full lips with a heart-shaped face, but now she looks drawn and tired. Her skin has lost its luster and her hands tremor as she speaks. She is now in the habit of lacing her fingers together to stop the shaking, but it doesn't always work. Her strength lies in her eyes. They still hold her power.

"Do you still have it?" I ask. I can no longer feel it as she has put solid protection around herself. She is powerful but she doesn't want to recognize her power. It took me a long time to find her and this place, and then even longer to gain entry.

"I don't know. This place is so bland, and no one speaks to me, so I don't know if I have it or not. How would I know?"

"You know when it's gone," I tell her, hoping she will lower her guard.

"Who are you?"

She wants to know. She has been asking the same questions from the moment we met. How does a god tell a mortal that he is a god? You might think it would be an easy task, and there was a time when that was true. We told them we were gods and they believed us, and they worshiped us, and we roamed with them.

But no more. We are relegated to the past and the depth of human minds, replaced by imagination and doubt.

I gave them the tiniest piece of me. I gave them the seed of knowledge to help them and they took it and spread it amongst themselves, but like most things in nature, it didn't grow evenly. Knowledge became both a blessing and a curse. They used it to help each other and to hurt each other, and then they used it to dismiss us and then forget us.

They were not ready when I gave them this gift, and as a punishment, I was banished from them for almost two millennia and my essence was given to another, and he became Joseph. And this custodian of my power performed his task well and guarded my soul as long as it was possible. But in the end, Joseph too succumbed to the lure of humanity and abandoned his duties. He bestowed my precious gift to a man who wasn't ready and would never be ready to take on the immense power of knowledge and what was meant to be a gift became a poison to him. The man—Amani was his name, was weak and not worthy of the gift. So, he ejected it and, in the process, poisoned Jackie. Now she is being tested as I wait for its return. *Five to seven years* is not her sentence but ours.

Jackie is still looking away from me, perhaps having forgotten the question, as she has done many times before. But I was wrong. She shifts her weight and leans closer to me. I can feel the warmth of her body and the energy of her power. "Who are you?" she asks again.

"I was the custodian of what you hold. Knowledge is my essence."

She laughs and shifts her weight again and looks across the metal fence. "I thought Joseph was the custodian?"

"He was for a time while I was banished. But I'm the creator of it."

"Banished? How? Where?"

"You might think I would know the how, given that I am knowledge, but I don't. And the where is not so clear either. I could have been here in this place, but I am not certain."

She takes a deep breath and considers what I've said for a moment. She closes her eyes and taps her head with her fingers a few times as if settling her memories. She opens her eyes and looks at me intently. "I know what you mean. Ask me to solve Maxwell's Equations, and I wouldn't even know how to start. Ask me the distance from the earth to the moon and I wouldn't know if it was two hundred thousand miles or two hundred million miles. And yet, at times, I feel I hold the answer. At moments like this, I remember that I have the answer. How is that possible?"

"Because you're not ready."

"What does it mean?"

"It means your kind was not ready for this gift, and as you often like to point out, it became a poison to you," I tell her, and I am ashamed of my own hubris.

"Then why give it to me? Then why infect me so cruelly?"

"That was not our intention, and you can give it back to me if you wish, Jackie."

"Give it to you? Why would you want this poison?"

"It's not detrimental to me. It's my essence," I plead and for a moment I think I have reached her.

She shuffles a bit and then turns around and looks at me as if debating her next move. She opens her mouth and then closes it sharply, and before she can say anything, it's time to eat, and her memory is suppressed again.

I nod and allow her to walk back to her little house. She will go in and take out her single dish from the cabinet. She will take out her single fork and put some of the food into her mouth. She will think it is Chinese food because that's all she remembers, though she is never sure. She can never be sure about the food she is eating, not that she eats much. She believes it is Chinese, and therefore it must be. She will come out again shortly and will wonder out loud what others eat though no one ever eats with another. We will stand side by side, and we will begin our conversation anew.

*　　*　　*

Jackie comes out and stands next to me as she has done before. She takes a deep breath, no longer bothered by the acrid smell of the construction from across the river.

She stares ahead, observes the giant machine as they molest the earth and says, "As a child, like most children, I thought I was special. I thought God had special plans for me and I'd be called to fulfill my destiny. But I was ordinary, like most people, and I only imagined a life that was never to be. Memories of my old life have become hazy, though I still remember some things . . . I think. I was a regular person, living a simple life. But it was my life. I owned it. And then, within minutes, it was taken from me and I was put here.

"You know who did it to me? I remember it now. It was no other than my love. And to top it, I asked for it. I walked into it, blinded by my feelings for him. I wanted to save him, so I begged for it. I loved him but more than that, I admired and trusted him. He was the man I knew I could rely on to save me if I ever needed saving. But in the end, I was wrong because he proved to be a coward and fiend. He molested me and then he kissed me to seal it.

"Wouldn't you step in front of a bullet for your child, for your spouse, for the person you loved the most? Wouldn't you consider your own life trivial if it would save your love? I did. But what if your action, the armor you provide to stop the bullet doesn't protect them? Do you still make the conscious decision and step in front of them, knowing that nothing could save them? I had asked myself these questions days after my lover infected me, having realized that what I had done had not protected him after all.

"He put his lips so close to my face that I could feel the prickles on my skin, and he whispered as if making love to me, but what he delivered was brutish and pungent. He ejaculated words, simple, meaningless individually, but infectious and malignant together. It didn't take long for him to deliver his venom and when he was done, I felt bewildered and he felt free.

"He had only savored his freedom for mere hours. In his desperate attempt to save himself, he chose me, and like a willing
savior I took on the task. He impregnated me and then walked
away from it with a soft kiss, like a vagrant. And then he killed
himself, because without this poison he had become an empty
shell. Then why give it to me? Why would he burden me with it
if he was going to kill himself over its loss? He left me with the
power of knowledge that is bigger than me, bigger than the rest
of humanity. All on me. Why me? I have no answer for that."

Jackie stops and we continue to look past the fence at the construction across the river. Jackie is standing close to me, and I can
feel her right arm against my body. Occasionally, her hand will
tremble, and her fingers will brush my hand, and I can feel her
skin—warm, as if she has a fever. (Even gods crave a touch.)

The irony is that she will not die while she keeps this so-called
poison, the seed of knowledge, in her body. It protects her all
while it tries to destroy her. Part of her knows this well and can
see the future, but the other part is oblivious to everything but the
present. It makes no sense, but nothing does anymore.

"Five to seven years. That's not long, is it?" Jackie asks, bringing
us back to the origin of our conversation.

"What do you want?" I ask.

"I want my old life back."

"That is not possible."

She turns to face me, and I do the same. I'm delaying the inevitable, but I am torn between getting what belongs to me and
spending more time with this woman. She would have been a
god in a different epoch.

"Are you sure?" she asks and then, as if wanting to confirm my
presence, she reaches and touches my face with her fingertips.
It is the first time she has voluntarily touched me. I feel the raw
power of my gift through her fingers and its urge to leave her, and
yet my gift is weak against her resolve.

"That world is no longer available," I inform her, again.

"What does that mean? Was the world destroyed?"

"It's difficult to explain but suffice it to say humanity is losing its place without the nurturing power of knowledge." I expect her to insist to know more, as she had done before, but she poses a new question.

"What choice do I have?"

She is looking at me carefully as if reading me—as if she were deciding my future rather than I hers. I want to cry out for her in pain. I want to give her life back to her. I want her to be a regular human, and part of me wishes the same for myself.

She turns her head and looks beyond the yard, and I know she will start on her rant again. She takes a deep breath.

"If you give me a calculus problem, I couldn't solve it. If you ask me how many countries are in the United Nations, I wouldn't know. And yet, I know I have the answer. I have the answer to the secret all of us are trying to decipher. Scientists, philosophers, intellectuals, and prophets all have been searching for the answer without success, and yet I have it. But what do you do with it? Do you cure all the social ills? Do you solve poverty, war, and hunger? Now, that simple answer eludes me. It is the cruelest of jokes to have the answer but not be able to use it. If God meant to be cruel, then she has succeeded with me."

"Then give it to me."

"Give what to you? This poison?"

"Yes."

"You want me to give this curse to you, and to be callous like my lover was. But I cannot. I cannot infect you like he infected me. I cannot be so heartless."

"We're not cruel. We have a job to do and we do what we must," I reply like a schoolchild repeating the oft-used mantra. "We made a mistake. We cared too much, we gave you gifts that you were not ready for, and our acts of kindness corrupted you."

"Me?"

"No, humanity."

"Then why are you punishing me by keeping me in this prison?"

"Tell me about your life," I say.

"My life? I've said all I have in me, haven't I?"

"Yes. But tell me more."

She turns around again and looks at me and holds me in her eyes. She may be an inmate in the Swedish Prison, but she has managed to imprison me too. Five to seven years is an eternity when time is not measured by the orbit of the Earth around the Sun.

"*Tell me more*," she echoes, her voice raspy. "Once I said those words to my love, and that was the end of my life. And then once again, another said those words to me. It would have been so easy to lean over and whisper to her and free myself of this poison."

"Why didn't you?" I ask, though I would've been devastated if she had.

She shifts her weight and stares into the distance for a moment. She moistens her lips with her tongue and they glisten under the sun. "I almost did. I don't remember her, but I still feel her kindness."

"She was your boss. She was worried about you when you didn't show up for work for days and wanted to make sure you were all right."

"Oh, yes," Jackie replies, recovering another piece of her memory. "My darling boss. She was so understanding. I told her my story, but she didn't believe me. She wanted to know more. She wanted me to tell her more. She insisted and I leaned over and brought my mouth close to her ear, the same way my love had done to me. I could smell her perfumed hair. It was so inviting. It would have been so easy."

Jackie turns around again and tilts her head forward toward me, but I'm much taller so I lean down so she could reach me. She comes even closer and I can feel her warm breath on my earlobe, feel the power of the gift on her lips. Her hands are on my back and they tremble either because of her frailty or because of what she might decide to do.

"I was about to give her this so-called gift," she whispers in my ear. "All my being was crying out for what would be an immense release."

I wait but she does nothing. I don't want to move as it might break our connection. "Why didn't you?" I ask in a faint voice as the moment demands a certain solemnity.

Her lips move without a sound. As they tickle my ear, I feel it throughout my body. She suddenly pulls away, as if realizing the danger of her proximity, and I feel a chill down my spine. I look around expecting to see Death, but there are only the two of us, and the morning sun is shining across the green lawn.

"Why?" I ask, though I should know the answer.

"Because I felt the goodness in her, and I could see the devastation I would cause. Perhaps this is my hell for all my sins. I must have been a bad person, but if there is a bit of goodness in me then I would preserve it by keeping this poison. Do you understand?"

"Yes, but I'm different. You can give it to me, and you will not infect me. Do you understand?"

She smiles and pats me on my head as one does to a small child. She doesn't want to believe me.

"It's time for bed," she says and walks away.

I follow her with my eyes as she ambles toward her room, her hands pressed together to keep her steady. Her blue and white dress showing its age as it brushes against the cinderblock walls. She turns and looks at me before walking into her home. There is no recognition in her eyes, and then she is gone.

*   *   *

"I've been thinking. If we're prisoners here, where are all the guards? I don't recall seeing a single one. And the fence is not high or menacing. I bet I could climb it and leave this place. Then I thought perhaps I'm here of my own volition, and this is not a prison at all but an insane asylum. But then where are the doctors and nurses and the orderlies? Or perhaps I'm inside my mind. I have gone crazy and I must be in a padded room, talking to myself. Or I'm talking to you and you're my doctor, but you've created this elaborate prison in my mind to cure me. But then that doesn't make too much sense either. Therefore, the logical conclusion is that I'm indeed crazy and I'm either in a hospital or somewhere else, but I am certainly imagining you. But why you? Who are you? I think I know you, but I don't recall ever meeting you until I saw you here.

"I dreamt about you last night. Is that odd? I had a long, vivid dream about you. You and I were on Spenta Island, just the two of us. Why there? And why five to seven years? Why make it sound like a prison sentence and even call this place the Swedish Prison?

"If I haven't told you, my name is Jackie Goodwin. But I'm sure I've told you this already, since I've created you in my mind in the first place.

"My love betrayed me viciously in the end, but I was cruel to him as well. I met him when I was young, seventeen or eighteen, our first year in college. He was my first, and at the beginning, like most love affairs, it was blissful and fulfilling. But after a few years, I wanted more. I wanted to be loved differently. I didn't want to give up his attention, but I wanted others too."

"So, I slept with the first person who paid extra attention to me. I was naïve and took it to be real but of course, it wasn't. He was older and single, and he wanted to try me. And I failed in every account. The sex was hurried and sinful, and then I made a mistake of confessing to my love because the burden of keeping it was too much. I was a coward too. I couldn't handle the pain of the lie, so I confessed my sin and put the burden on him. I told him and saw how the weight of my wickedness lifting from my shoulders and landing on his, crushed him. I saw his eyes change and I knew we would never be the same.

"I wonder if that was how he felt when he poisoned me twenty years later. Was it his revenge for what I had done to him?

"We reconciled of course, and we went on with our lives, as lovers and friends. So, yes, perhaps I'm as guilty as my lover, but I thought I had been punished enough already. My love and I wanted children. But, after several miscarriages, I had to have a hysterectomy. No chance of children. I left him to offer him a chance at happiness with someone else. And when he married a better person than me, I thought I deserved it for all my sins. I thought I had paid in full and more. But maybe not, as my love decided to poison me and not his wife. She was too clever for that anyway."

Jackie stops talking. We start each meeting with her rant. She comes out of her room, looks at the yard, strides toward me looking straight ahead, stands next to me, stares at the construction across the river, and then starts speaking without a prompt. It's her way of adjusting her mind to the situation, and I let her talk as long as she wants without looking at her. Sometimes, she stands close to me—and I relish that momentary closeness—but other times she stands afar. In such episodes, she introduces herself as if we had never met and tells me about the terms of her imprisonment.

But today is different. She is standing right in front of me and awfully close, and I have to lean down a bit so I can see her face, and as she speaks, I can feel her warm breath on my face. It is the first time she has questioned the sanity of the situation, and I am wondering if we are a step closer to a resolution.

She is staring at me and I'm thinking about the change in the rhythm when she leans close and kisses me. Her lips are soft, and billowy and warm. She lingers, holding me to her and for a moment I am not a god, but a man entrapped by his emotions.

She releases me and I step back, wobbling, my knees too weak for full control of my body. I reach and steady myself against the wall behind me.

"I had a dream about you," she says with mirth that had been absent since our first encounter.

"What?"

"I wanted to make sure you were real."

"I'm as real as you want me to be."

"Did you feel it?"

I thought she meant the kiss and was trying to find a way to respond, but she is looking past me as if searching for something.

"Did you feel it?" she asks again with more urgency, still looking to her left, and then adds, "I felt the presence of another being. I haven't felt that sensation since my father died."

I'm about to say something about the kiss and how it couldn't have been that horrible, but then I realize the change in the sun, as if it had dimmed for a moment. I turn and see Death standing tall with his regal cloak.

"Why are you here?" I ask.

Death nods and smiles shyly. "Any progress?" He pushes the large hood off his head and takes a deep breath.

"Doesn't your presence here indicate such?"

"I'm here on my own accord and without any intentions, but you know that already."

"Yes. And yes, we're making progress. I don't want to push her too hard. I don't want to harm her," I say.

"We both know we're past all that. We're at the point of no return, and yet you waste time by bringing her here."

"Bringing her here? Can't you see she is the one who brought us here and not the other way around?"

"I only see the end and nothing else," Death tells me, as he has done often. "And what I see now is the end of humanity, because she holds the seed of knowledge."

"If I force it out of her, she will surely perish."

"Her end is inevitable. But time is moving slower here than in the world, and the decay is set. It started slowly and imperceptibly at first, but now after so many decades, its foul effect has erased years of progress," Death warns.

"I gave part of my essence to them, believing that they would do good, but I was wrong. This so-called progress has only upended what little good was in them," I say ruefully.

Death gives his fatherly smile and does not remind me of his warning eons ago. He knows I do not require a reminder.

"They have done many good things with your gift," he offers generously. "And there are people like Jackie, kind and honorable."

"Yes, there is Jackie."

I was so absorbed with my conversation with Death that I forgot about Jackie, who was staring at me patiently. But now she steps forward and reaches in the void where Death stands.

"Who is here? I sense its power but cannot see it."

"'It?' Have I become a thing now?" Death asks. "Should I reveal myself?"

"No, not yet. Go away for now and let me work on her."

"You must move quickly. It's not only humanity's concern but ours too," he warns.

"Don't you think I know that? Don't you understand?"

"I understand well. I know you have grown fond of Jackie, even love her. She is a powerful being. In a different world, she could have been one of us. I love her too, as did Joseph when he met her so many years ago. But it's time for you to do your job. You know you have the power to extract your essence from her."

"I cannot," I tell him. "Not without her consent."

"You must, my young friend."

"No. I will find the way to have them both."

"There are no options here and you know that. Perhaps you will meet her again in a different domain."

I shake my head, but I know he is right. I have wronged humanity once, and I cannot do it again because of Jackie. She would expect no less of me.

"She has done nothing wrong," I tell Death. He has no response as none is needed.

"Something powerful is here," Jackie insists.

I step forward and gently pull her face toward me. It's the first time that I've touched her, and I feel like a teenage boy, giddy and awkward. She looks at me with her powerful eyes. "What's happening?"

"We are near the end, sweetheart." I didn't mean to use such terms of endearment, but my words are no longer mine.

"What do you mean?" she asks, still peering over my shoulder.

"You need to remember," I say, hoping the urgency of my tone penetrates her defenses.

"Remember? Remember what?"

"You need to let go of the gift you hold, and to do that you will need to remember what I have done to destroy humanity," I say and I want to cry like a human might.

"You? Am I not the guilty one here?"

"No. I am the guilty one. You just need to remember who you were and what you were holding. I will help you remember, but the decision is yours." I put my hand on her shoulder to provide her courage and guidance, but in reality, it is Jackie who has given me the resolution.

She closes her eyes and taps her head several times like she had done before. We wait patiently. A small wind picks up, which brings the putrid smell from across the river. The giant machines pound the earth relentlessly, the water glistening under the bright morning sun. And we wait.

She opens her eyes and faces the river for a moment, then she turns toward me and puts her hand on top of mine. "I remember why I chose the Swedish Prison as my home: it's a place where I don't have to know, and no one can be harmed."

I take hold of her hand and lace my fingers through hers; for a moment we are one. We stand there and stare at the river beyond the fence. The giant machines, oblivious to us, continue their pounding. We wait.

Death steps forward and faces her; the sun dims and the whispers die across the field for a moment, and then he is with us.

"Oh, you are Death," Jackie offers with a waning smile and pulls away from me.

Death nods and bows slightly. "I'm here to help you make your decision, Jackie."

Jackie thinks for a moment and then asks, "Will my life save others?"

"Yes."

I reach out and hold her hand again and force her to face me. "There is another way." And then to Death. "You shouldn't have come."

Death closes his eyes. "There is no other way, my friend."

"Yes, there is," I say, hoping my harsh tone will make it so.

Jackie hasn't moved, still holding my hand. She has the patient understanding of an ancient sage.

"I can go back with Jackie," I say.

"And then what? What do you think will happen to her?"

"Jackie can keep my essence, and I will guide her, and I will protect her. I will stay with her."

Death gives a sad smile at my childish grasping to hold onto something I know I cannot.

Jackie lets go of my hands and smiles. "It's sweet to think we could have that." She shakes her head. "And though my mind is still hazy, I know I can't go back like this. I will not last long. I will go mad. I had to use my imagination and knowledge to find the key to this place, so I can protect them and keep my sanity."

"I'll be your safeguard, Jackie."

Jackie faces Death. "Is this possible?"

"No."

"Don't listen to him," I cry out. "He doesn't have all the answers."

"That is true," Death offers. "But I know as much as we want to make this solution real, we all know the imprudence of this action.

"Will I get to see my friends?" she asks.

Death stares at her for a moment and then looks down shaking his head. "No, Jackie. Their time has come and gone."

She falters. "All of them?"

"Yes."

"How long have I been here?"

I hold her hand again. "A long time, sweetheart."

Death walks around and stands behind us. "Turn and face the other side, Jackie. Face the now and the future and not the past as you have done."

Jackie looks at me, and I can see the slow return of knowledge. Nevertheless, she asks as if she doesn't trust her memories. "Have we been facing the wrong side all this time?"

I refuse to face her. We are still staring across the field and at the river, and the machines, as they build the past. The river shines under the bright morning sun and moves leisurely through the fields. The blades of grass undulate happily as the breeze maneuvers through them.

"Where are the children?" Death asks.

Jackie turns around and faces him. "What does it mean?"

"Step forward and look at the other side," Death tells her.

Jackie looks at me and I shake my head. "Don't."

She takes a step forward and like a man pulled by a leash I follow her. She takes another step and I do the same, and I see in Death's eyes that he finds no solace in his act.

We walk past the building and stand next to each other as we had done many times before, but this time, we are facing a different side of the Swedish Prison. I close my eyes for a second, refusing to acknowledge what I had known already. Jackie looks at me and then at the brownfield ahead of us and shivers slightly in the dimming evening sun. The wind picks up rolling the tumbleweeds through the dust devils.

She points to the field and asks, "Is that now or the future?"

"It's now to you and the future to others," I tell her.

She closes her eyes and taps her head with her fingers as she has done so many times before, concentrating hard. Then she lets go and floats freely as her memories flood back. I trace her face with my fingers, and she leans her head against my hand and presses against it, and I feel her, and she feels me back.

Suddenly she opens her eyes, and I know she has succeeded in reaching the depths of her memory, that she knows as a god would know. She knows everything.

"It's all because of me," she moans.

"You kept the seed of knowledge and therefore nothing grew, and the decay followed," Death offers in a monotone voice.

She looks at me horrified with a dawning understanding. "I meant to protect them."

"I know," I say.

"It tricked me. Your gift tricked me."

"It was no trick."

"It poisoned me with all the knowledge, and I walked the city like a mad person knowing but not being able to tell. How could I have told when I knew the knowledge would have destroyed them? And yet, I destroyed them by holding back."

"It is not your fault, Jackie. The fault has and will be with the gods, with me. We wanted more. We wanted you and your kind to have more empathy, to have more knowledge, to have more. But we made a mistake as we have done so many times before. . . ."

I pause, not knowing what else I could tell her. Admitting to our guilt would not take away her pain nor mine. Death looks at me and then at Jackie and says, "In all of our lives we had never encountered a being like you. You are powerful beyond any human and now you must save your kind by doing what must be done."

"No," I cry out. "There may be other ways, Jackie. Turn around and face the river and the green grass of the past. I know with more time, I can find a way to take the gift from you and keep you whole."

Jackie looks at Death and asks, "Is this a possibility?"

"No."

"I have told you, he doesn't have all the answers, Jackie," I shout. "He is a servant like me, and he doesn't have the answers.

"It's true that we are both servants, and it's true that I do not have his knowledge, but I see humanity and I see its end."

Jackie takes a deep breath, looks at the yard and the fence and the houses in the Swedish Prison. I can see she knows that they do not need to be there, and she can be free.

"I know," she says with the bitter weight of what has happened to humanity. She looks beyond, sees the world as it is, and tears roll down her face.

"It's not your fault," I offer again.

"I know."

"It had to end sometime, but we can prolong it and perhaps even save it," I promise, though I have no justification for my claim.

"That may be true, but I can no longer be part of its end. No one awaits me there. My time has come and gone too."

"I will be there for you."

"I wish that was enough. I wish I could stay here with you, but I cannot be so selfish and cruel. And I cannot go back knowing what I know now. There is only one solution for ending this misery."

"The world will not be the same without you," Death offers.

"I am hoping it will be better. Am I free then?"

"Yes," I reply with an utter sense of loss.

Jackie reaches out and holds my hand and I feel her soft skin and the warmth of her body. "I know," she says again. "I know and for the first time I can tell you."

Death nods. "We've waited so long for you, Jackie."

"I'm here now and I am here for you," she says.

"Don't, Jackie," I plead. "Stay in this place and we will find a way. There is always a way."

She ignores me and continues to focus on Death. "Will everything be as it should be when I'm gone?"

"It will."

"As it is meant to be?" She wants to be sure.

"Nothing is ever planned."

"I didn't mean to keep this poison for this long, but I didn't know what to do, and this place gave me such solace. If I had known, I would have summoned you myself."

"It was not your fault," Death says.

"I know everything."

"Not *everything*, as your predicament here proves."

"Will humanity survive?" Jackie asks.

"At least for a while longer."

Jackie looks at me and offers her other hand and I pull her close and she kisses me. "Are you ready?"

"I don't want to be."

"I can feel it. It wants you. I knew this from the beginning, but I was so afraid that it might poison you as it had me."

"It cannot harm me. It is a gift to me."

"Then I will whisper it to you," Jackie says.

Jackie leans close, and I know I have no power to deny her. She puts her lips on my ear and I can smell the morning dew on her hair. I don't want this intimacy to end, but she whispers what she knows is poison, and then she is done.

She withdraws slowly. I feel my strength coming back and I can see, for the first time in ages, and she feels free and light. She looks at me with her normal eyes, and I can see the beauty and a different kind of strength that only she could hold. She leans closer and kisses me on my mouth and all at once I taste her joy and love, and disappointment and loss. She pulls away and holds me with her eyes.

Death takes a small step and touches her shoulder.

"Please give me a moment," she says.

"Of course."

And then when the moment is at the end, she is too.

WHAT HAPPENED TO THE SPENTA STORY

Marshall walked in heavily and sat on a stool at the end of the zinc bar, and without words the bartender put a large Bruges glass of beer in front of him. Marshall eyed the amber liquid with slight trepidation, but then took hold of the glass with both hands and downed half of the content. To make sure that no foam was stuck to his large mustache, he wiped his face with a white linen napkin the bartender had provided with the beer.

Marshall was a small man who always wore a crisp white shirt with a pressed dark suit and wide, patterned tie. He was sporting the same today. Marshall was wealthy and had busied himself with directing a small theater in Williamsport, Pennsylvania, where he had lived all his life. Marshall believed in his profession and had conducted himself with the zeal of a real artist for almost thirty years.

The heavy wooden door opened, and someone sauntered in and went to the side of the room and sat at the table next to a large window. A small lamp was installed on the wall below the windowsill, which the man turned off. He didn't look up and no one paid any attention to him at first.

The warm sunshine penetrated the dimly lit bar as the Universal Hardware door-closer pulled the door in a smooth movement. The trees outside had begun to blossom, pink and red buds painting the barren trees. From the large windows on the side, one could see the green hills across the meadow and the grass undulating with the breeze. The exit sign on top of the door was off, and when the door finally closed, it turned red.

Marshall looked over and was about to say something, but thirst had overtaken him, so he grabbed the glass again and drained its content. The bartender smiled and put another one in front of him. Marshall nodded but didn't say anything, but one could tell from his eyes he was bursting to speak.

It didn't take long.

He leaned to his right, looked at the man, and said from across the room, "I don't understand you. Why can't you tell the story of Spenta, Z.? I mean, it shows up in every other story for God's sake. If you weren't going to tell its story, then why even mention it?" Marshall paused and took a gentle sip of the beer, then looked at the bartender and asked, "Don't you agree, Gustavo? Don't you think he should at least tell a short story of Spenta?"

The bartender nodded but didn't say anything. He was a handsome man with an easy smile and rarely involved himself in such disputes. Gustavo was a bartender by design, and his expertise was in pouring the *right* drink for his customers.

But Marshall insisted. "Come on, Gustavo. You must have some opinions. You're the one who insisted that you know people. I remember your conversation at the pool bar in Los Angeles with that great lady. Wasn't she called Vera or something?"

"Yes, Vera Pacient," Gustavo replied with a hint of melancholy.

"So, tell me, don't you think people want to know about Spenta?" Marshall insisted.

Gustavo looked across the room, and for the first time Z. looked up and nodded as if giving Gustavo permission to speak. He then turned his head and stared through the window deep in his thoughts.

Gustavo wiped the counter with a towel for a second and then mumbled, "I don't know. . . . I think Z. tried to tell that story but couldn't get it going. I guess he felt there was no point to it. But who am I to say?"

"No point to it," a tall, young woman from the other side of the zinc bar interjected. She had long, black hair with an oval-shaped face and leaned against the bar, looking at the bartender.

"No point to it," the woman said again. She had small eyes, which took a bit away from her otherwise beautiful face. "Z. forced me to learn a whole book on soccer and then didn't even give me a chance to talk about it. I had to pretend I didn't know anything about the game while my boyfriend and others were having this great banter on the subject. And now, he can't even tell a fucking story about Spenta even though it's injected in every boring story. It's bullshit. Come on, Z., don't just sit there and be coy. Say something."

They all looked at Z., and you could tell they were worried they may have pushed too hard. The man continued staring out the window, clearly ignoring them.

"I agree, Alice," Marshall added softly and then louder, "And since we're on this subject: it is bullshit that I'm being served beer when everyone knows I like a glass of Chardonnay. And . . ."

He stopped as he had felt a chill in the air, and the place became silent and still for a moment as the sky dimmed. Then, as if nothing had happened, time moved forward.

"Oh, it's you," Marshall cried out, shaking his head.

Death sat on the stool in the middle of the bar and smiled back at Marshall, waiting. He wore a black cloak that draped around him. He was massive, and the cape made him look even more prominent. He had a large, strong face with dark and powerful eyes.

"Why can't you walk in the room like everyone else? Why such drama every single time?" Marshall admonished.

Death smiled again and shook his head. "I am sorry. I don't mean to. I try to appear as quickly as possible, but the air molecules react differently to me. I didn't mean to disturb you, Marshall. You were saying?"

"Oh, nothing. I was complaining about not getting a glass of Chardonnay in my tavern."

Death looked at him with a sense of appreciation but didn't respond. He wasn't going to remind Marshall that this place was not *his* tavern.

"Is Z. here?" he asked.

They pointed behind him, and Death turned around. "Oh, hello. I was hoping to get in earlier, so we could strategize without you, but no matter. You probably already know everything we are going to say anyway."

Z. faced Death and gave a small smile, happy to see his old friend. "No one knows everything, Death," he said. He spoke with a slow, calming voice, and they all felt the certain assurance that only Z. could give them. "No story is fully written until its final moment. You know that better than anyone." Z. panned the room and added, "Our stories, and yes even mine, are like rivers, sometimes calm and other times raging, twisting and turning— but always moving until they reach their end."

Death smiled. "Though you do guide these rivers, to put it mildly."

"True, but I try extremely hard to let them follow their natural course. Many have surprised me in the past and I am sure many more will continue to venture onto an unintended path," Z. said and then added as a warning, "Though this may not be the wisest choice for everyone. Now, you go on with your conversation and your strategies and ignore my presence if you can."

Death nodded and looked up at Gustavo, and the bartender, ever ready, put a small cup of espresso in front of him.

"Oh, thank you," Death said and picked up the little tulip cup and put it under his nose. He took a deep breath. "How wonderful," he said.

Marshall shook his head and said, "I never get you and your ilk's obsession with coffee. Why coffee?"

"Don't you know?" asked Alice, as she walked over and sat next to Death. "It's the Devil's brew."

Death laughed. "That's great," he cried out and patted Alice on the back. He then extended his hand with its long, manicured fingers, and Alice took it into her own. They shook hands and Death said while staring into her eyes, "We've never met. I am Death."

"And I'm glad of it, for certain. My name is Alice, but you knew that already."

"I'm not *all-knowing*. I know of people when the time is right and not before."

"Don't listen to him, Alice. Weren't we talking about bullshit? Well, he loves to deliver it almost as badly as Z. does," Marshall offered as he accepted his third mug of beer from Gustavo. He took a small sip. "Go on, tell Alice about my appointment with you."

Death was still focused on Alice and took his time to extricate himself from her. He then looked at Marshall with incredulous eyes and said, "I thought our meeting went rather well."

"That's funny, because I remember you showing up on the passenger seat of my car while I was paralyzed with fear as my car tumbled down the cliff and into that horridly *deep . . . dark . . . cold . . . gorge.*"

"Yes?"

"Horrible, deep, dark, cold, gorge," Marshall repeated, enunciating each word. "And you sat there laughing, and I could see you, and I knew I was going to die of this painful death." He exhaled sharply as if he had tasted each word. And then as if to reemphasize its import. "And you sat there, laughing."

"So, it seems you are still bitter about your plunge down the gorge," Death said.

"Are you deaf? Didn't you listen to what I said? You were laughing as I was petrified."

"I was not laughing. I was amused because Z. led us to believe it was not you inside the car but someone else. So, when I saw you, I was surprised. I apologize if I looked scary."

"Scary? It was a horrible . . . painful . . . experience," Marshall moaned.

"You are exaggerating, Marshall. It was a quick and painless death."

"How would you know? It certainly was not, and even if had been, why did you need to show up so early? Why couldn't you have come at the instant it happened? Why did you sit there smiling at me, while I was engulfed in agony? You're shameless, Death."

"So, was I smiling or laughing? Make up your mind, man."

Alice leaned over and inspected Death's eyes. "Is it true?"

"Yes and no. I show up when I am called. Marshall feared death was coming, so I did."

"Is that true for everyone?" Gustavo asked.

"No," replied Death.

Marshall was not satisfied but also unsure of the next step, so he asked, "Why do you have to always wear that black cloak anyway?"

Death looked down at his attire. "I think it looks good. I've added these new stripes," he said, pointing at the royal blue velvet adorning his long sleeves.

Marshall shook his head but didn't reply.

Alice touched the stripes and said, "I like them. It's a nice touch."

"You see," Death said, looking at Marshall.

"Could I ask you something?" Alice's tone was hushed, and the joy on her face was gone.

"Only in this place, Alice," Death replied.

"I'm not sure how to ask it, and maybe even whether I should, but I feel I must."

"About your mother?"

Alice averted her eyes, and it was clear that she was trying to hold back tears. "Do you remember her?"

"I remember everyone I meet."

"Did you . . . Did she . . ." She trailed off.

Gustavo stepped forward and put a dry Martini with two olives in front of Alice, and she looked at him and then the glass and took a grateful sip.

"This is good, Gustavo," she said, relieved for a moment by the distraction and the liquid courage. Gustavo nodded and then stepped back, busying himself cleaning the counter that was already spotless.

Death finished his espresso. "May I have a cortado now?"

Gustavo nodded. He made a double espresso in a purple tulip cup, added two dollops of silky, hot milk, and then put the constructed Cortado in front of Death while everyone watched him.

Death took a small sip with his eyes closed, and when he opened them, Alice could see the power behind them. "I was there a few seconds before she died," Death offered. "She was ready."

Alice frowned and replied, "I don't understand why I had to have this experience as part of my makeup. It wasn't necessary, and it was always kept in the background. So why add this miserable memory to my history?"

"Z. is cruel," Marshall shouted.

"I think so. At first, I was glad to have been sent to Los Angeles. It would give me some perspective about life beyond my little world. But then my mother died while I was away, which was somewhat expected, given her health. I would have accepted it, but the cruelty was not in her passing, but in the way I was informed.

"I received a text from my brother-in-law conveying his condolences. He didn't know I was out of the country, so he had assumed I knew. It was a plain text: 'My deepest condolences.' That's how I learned of my mother's death: through a text in the middle of Target. I was hoping I could be there for her. Her last moments were with you, Death, and not with me."

Death pursed his lips and took another sip of his coffee before replying. "It's true, but that is always the truth."

"Did she say anything? Could you tell me that?" She tried to wipe away her tears, but they kept coming.

"She did not speak. She was old, and her mind was gone. Your mother gave me a look that I have not seen often."

Alice laughed. "Oh, I know that look."

Death leaned over and wiped her face with a soft linen handkerchief produced from under his black cloak.

She took a deep breath and then exhaled, trying to stay calm. "I stood in the middle of the store as people pushed their carts

around me, smelling the store's oily, stale popcorn. You can't remember smells, but you can certainly recall the nauseating feeling
it invokes. I wanted to cry, but I held it back. I told myself that I had
been expecting it. We all had been expecting it. She had dementia
and could barely remember any of us. But she was still there; at
least her essence was present. She still talked about a childhood
that could have been real or imaginary—not that it mattered. So,
what if she could no longer recognize her children? So what? She
was the center. She was the fulcrum that kept each side balanced,
and now she was gone. And I will never see her again."

Death nodded but didn't say anything, knowing Alice wasn't
finished with her soliloquy.

Alice continued, "The text didn't say it was my mother who
had died, but I assumed it. Isn't that horrible? I didn't call my
brother to ask; I assumed it was my mother and accepted it. I
hate myself for it."

"We all grieve differently, Alice," offered Gustavo as he put a
fresh new drink in front of her.

"What is it?" asked Marshall.

"I call it Pacientè. It's named after my friend, Vera. It's gin, a
bit of Dom Perignon champagne, freshly squeezed orange juice,
and Grand Marnier. It's what Alice needs."

"Then make me one too, please," ordered Marshall.

Gustavo nodded but put a pint of stout in front of him. Marshall looked at the glass and then at the bartender. He scowled
but took a sip of the deep, brown liquid anyway.

"I miss that look," Alice continued as she drank her Pacientè.

"Yes, very intense," Death offered.

"I don't get it," said Marshall.

Alice said, "It's like when I was twenty, and I was complaining
profusely to my mother about something, like how life was unfair
and the world should do this or that. I was sort of lecturing her
and she took it all, nodding and smiling and asking encouraging
questions. She had that look, and I initially thought it was the
look of being impressed. That I, at twenty, was impressing this

experienced woman with my deep, well thought out argument. But years later, when I remembered that look, it dawned on me that it was also a look of a person who had seen and known so much that she didn't need to show her knowledge. She wasn't condescending but rather patiently tolerant of my ignorance. Does that make sense?"

"It does to me," Death replied. "She gave the same look when it was time for our appointment. Your mother looked at me like she was looking at a child, even though I had thousands of years over her. She welcomed me to her bosom, rather than allowing me to lead her into the other world. She understood my job and gave the same patient, tolerant look as her life ended."

Alice nodded with understanding. "She was a good mother. Patient and kind."

"Yes."

Alice leaned over and kissed Death on the cheek. "Thank you."

Death touched his face as if holding Alice's kiss in place and then gave a faint smile. Alice stood up and looked at Gustavo, who had been staring at her all this time.

"Don't go yet," Death said.

"I need to sit at the other end for a moment," she replied and then walked to her side of the zinc bar.

"I'm glad you didn't ask about . . . him," Gustavo said as Alice sat on the stool.

"Him? Is he still 'him' to you?"

"Okay. Your boyfriend. Your Daniel."

Alice glared. "Don't get mad."

"I am not, Alice. As I said, I'm glad you didn't ask about Daniel. I couldn't see you reliving it again. I don't want you to get hurt again."

Alice reached over and held Gustavo's hands in her own. "You are sweet. There was nothing to ask anyway. What could Death tell me about Daniel that I don't know already? He lived his life the way he wanted to and died as he had lived. We should all be more like Daniel, though his impatience brought his end."

"I know you miss him. . . ."

"Of course, I do. And the way it ended so abruptly and so brutally. It has marked me forever, Gustavo. He made me a better person when he was alive, and his death crushed me. I could have saved him if I was allowed. If I was given more space to speak to him, I think I could have made him less impatient. But Z. didn't allow it. I was given such a limited role and was there for a brief time, and then nothing. I wasn't even allowed to grieve him."

"We are who we are, Alice. We cannot change our destiny. As much as it hurts me, I know we cannot change who we're supposed to be."

"We had our time together in Los Angeles, didn't we? You were there for me when I needed you. You were the only one I could speak to about Daniel. You understood me."

"Yes, but it was a fantasy. It was a background story that was never given a second thought. We were not allowed to mature and make something of it. I wanted so much to step over the barrier and touch you, to hold and to make love to you."

"Why didn't you? I wanted it too. I needed it more than anything."

"But our tale never made it, did it? We were not allowed to tell it. It was kept between us. Z. kept us invisible."

"So what? Who cares? You and I know about it, and that's what matters, Gustavo. I was there and so were you. Shouldn't that be enough? Why do we have to live for others?"

Gustavo looked across the room, but Z. was not paying attention to their conversation.

Alice pulled Gustavo back to her and said firmly, "We don't need an audience, and we don't need Z.'s approval."

"You can never get over your first love," offered Gustavo with no preamble. "You should know that."

"I do know that and that's the point."

"I wish it was as you paint it, Alice. I wish it was as simple as that. I wish we could fall in love as we have and become untethered as we hoped."

"We are not two-dimensional beings. We can cross the threshold, and nothing will happen to us."

"Are you sure? You heard Z.'s warning."

"There is only one way to find out. Make me a drink, Gustavo."

Gustavo brightened up visibly as if her order for a new drink was all he had needed. "Of course, and I know what you need," he replied with a mischievous smile. "I'm going to make you an Urban Orgasm. It's delicious, and it's made with amaretto, triple sec, Kahlúa, Irish Cream, and a bit of brandy. This is precisely what you need." Gustavo picked up a bottle of Disaronno amaretto from the shelf and was about to pour it into a barrel glass, as always confident of his ability to know what his customers desired.

"No! Make me a Whiskey Sour, like the ones you made for me in LA," Alice ordered.

"What? No. That's not how it works. I know what you need, Alice, and you will appreciate it as soon as you taste it."

"You may know what I need, but you can't know what I want. Make me what I want, or I will leave this place."

"You can't leave," Gustavo cried out as he gently put the bottle down in front of Alice. "You can't leave until we are done with our tasks. Z. will not allow it."

"You think so. Then go ahead and make me your fucking drink and watch me disappear."

Gustavo stared at Alice, trying to weigh the veracity of her threat, but his natural urge to do the right thing won out. He picked up the bottle of amaretto again and commenced to make the drink that he was sure in the depth of his being was the right one to make.

At that moment, the door of the tavern opened sharply, and a tall woman walked in. She took a few steps away from the entrance and then stood still as the water dripped from her clothes, making a puddle around her feet. Her long baby blue dress was clinging to her, and her long hair was matted. The wind howled and pushed the rain sideways, dowsing the floor. The door was closing too slowly, so she walked behind it and pressed hard against it. The door finally shut, the howl of the wind ceased, and the red exit light turned on again.

The woman took a towel from the coatrack and dried her hair. She then looked up at the people by the bar and said, "I would heed Alice's words."

"Tess, what are you doing here?" Gustavo asked.

He then opened a cabinet behind him, took out a large towel, and handed it to Tess as she sat on one of the stools and wiped her hair and face again.

Gustavo put a glass of Irish Coffee in front of Tess and said, "Drink it, it will make you feel warm and dry."

"We didn't expect you, but I'm glad you're here, Tess," Alice offered.

She took a large sip from her glass and felt warm and dry. "I'm here because of the last-minute decision by Z. to take my voice away, as he did with you. I was devastated but hesitant to accept the invitation. Though now I'm glad I did and clearly at the right moment."

"Your timing is impeccable, Tess, as always," Death said.

Tess turned to Gustavo and said, "Go ahead and make Alice's drink then."

"Are you sure?" Gustavo moaned. "I feel it will be the death of me if I don't do the right thing."

Death laughed heartily. "Maybe so, Gustavo, but death means different things to different people. I wonder which is worse for you though, betraying who you think you should be or watching Alice walk away."

"I don't know. . . ." Gustavo said, looking desperately at Marshall for help, but he busied himself with his drink.

"We are all here for a reason, Gustavo," Alice said. "You are afraid and I am too. We are venturing to an unseen world where we can hold on to our own destiny. Even Z. admitted he doesn't know everything. I am trying to be brave, and I hope you can too."

Alice waited for Gustavo to react, but when he didn't move, she stood up and grabbed her coat from the hanger, and Death walked over and helped her put it on.

"Thank you," Alice said and then kissed Death on the cheek. "I will see you later, I am sure, but hopefully not too soon."

She smiled and started toward the door, and the red exit sign on the top of it started blinking. Outside looked dark, but the dimmed streetlights revealed the menacing, frigid night as the strong wind made the snow fall sideways. Alice opened the heavy door, causing an icy wind to fly inside the bar and a torrent of snow to wash the entrance.

"Don't!" Gustavo cried out and then again, "Please, don't."

Alice turned around but held the door open with her hand as the wind shoved her about, her eyes tearing up from the cold.

"Close the door," Marshall shouted.

Alice let go of the door and it started to close in its excruciatingly slow way. The yowl of the wind finally died down and the room began to warm again.

"I will make you what you want," the bartender promised.

"Come on, girl. You have made your point," Tess said.

Alice walked over and sat back on her chair after throwing her coat on the hanger. Gustavo looked at her, turned around, took a large brown egg, and poured its white into a metal cocktail shaker. He added aged Blanton's single barrel bourbon, fresh lemon juice, simple syrup, and shook it patiently. Next, he put in large chunks of dense ice cubes and shook it for ten seconds more. Gustavo then poured the content through a strainer into a coupe glass, dotted the top of the drink with Angostura Bitters, and used a small toothpick to make a heart shape. He looked at his creation for a second, but thought it was missing something, something Alice would want. He hooked two brandy-soaked cherries on a toothpick, put the hanging black fruits on the top of the glass, and then ceremoniously presented it to Alice.

Alice stared at the drink, and they all could see a momentary hesitation.

"I can still make what you *need*," Gustavo offered.

She shook her head and took the small glass into her hand and sipped the silky, cold liquid. "Oh, my God," she cried out, and they all stared at her with total attention. There was visible fear in their eyes.

"What is it?" Death asked.

"I tasted something I have never known existed."

"What?" Marshall asked, leaning on the counter.

"I don't know how to describe it." She smacked her lips a few times. "Would hope have a taste?" Alice asked, but she was still not satisfied with the answer.

"Make me one too," Marshall ordered with a tone that said he didn't want another beer.

"It doesn't work that way," Death said as Gustavo looked at him for guidance.

"Maybe it tasted more like freedom, if that's even possible," Alice said, more to herself than the others.

Gustavo put a pint of Younger's Special Bitter in front of Marshall, then made a double espresso for Death and poured a spoonful of hot milk on top of it to cut the bitterness. He served another Irish Coffee to Tess.

"Yes, I think that's how it feels to be able to write your own story, your own life," Alice continued. "That's the taste."

"That's why I came here, Alice," Tess offered. "We all need to tell our own stories. We've been silenced for far too long."

"Are you okay, Alice?" Gustavo asked and then, perhaps with more apprehension, "Should I make you another?"

"No. I want you to come to my side and kiss me."

Gustavo looked at Alice and the zinc bar that separated them, and though he could imagine how it might feel to cross the threshold and kiss her, he felt too paralyzed to act.

"Do it," Tess ordered.

"It will be the end of me, I'm sure."

"We went through a similar argument earlier," Death offered as an encouragement.

"Yes, but you have said it, and you have said it many times that we are all here to serve. Were you wrong?"

"This is all new to me, too," Death said. "I admit we're at a crossroads that I have not seen before. The story has taken an unexpected direction."

"So, should I do as I want or as I should?"

"It's a simple task, Gustavo," offered Alice. "We sat at your bar for days talking, and didn't you ever want to jump over the counter and touch me and kiss me?"

"Yes."

"I wanted it as well, and I thought if I played my role right and followed the rules that were given, then our stories would be told, and we would create a new environment where we were given the roles we desired. But it didn't happen, and those times were wiped clean, relegated to an unrecorded backstory of two unimportant characters. I am done with that, Gustavo. Aren't you?"

Gustavo stared at Alice as tears welled up in his eyes, and his body trembled as two forces pulled at him. Death seemed to have had enough of the drama, as he rose and stood in front of Alice.

"May I?" he asked, and Alice nodded. He kissed her, and she kissed him back. When they pulled back, Death licked his lips and his powerful eyes shone. "You taste sweet and powerful, Alice."

Alice still had her eyes closed with her mouth partly open. "That kiss felt like the first kiss one has in her life," she said. "I thought I would never get that feeling back again. How amazing to be able to have the first kiss twice in one's life. It feels like I've been born today, and everything I do from this moment forward will be new."

"Could we?" Tess asked.

Alice nodded, and Tess walked over and kissed her, too, while they held each other. Tess traced Alice's face with her hand, and Alice leaned down and kissed her while brushing her fingers against Tess's breasts. Alice pulled her closer, and they kissed again.

"Stop," Gustavo cried out, and they all looked at him. "Stop," he said again but didn't make a move, still holding onto a rag that he used to wipe the counter.

"You need to make a decision, Gustavo," Marshall said. He had been watching the drama with the curious eyes of a child.

"It's a choice," Death said.

"I've made my decision," Alice said, and she pulled away from Tess.

Death walked back and sat on his stool. Tess followed him, and the four stared at the bartender patiently. Gustavo closed his eyes for a moment and the others waited.

"If you are not going to make your move, then could you make me another Cortado?" Death asked.

Gustavo looked across the room again and cried, "Help me, Z."

They all turned around to see Z.'s response. He had stayed aloof all this time, and thus shocked them when he stood up and walked to the bar.

He held Gustavo's eyes and said, "You all want your stories to be told and are angry when some of the pages are purged and point an accusing finger at me. You haunt me in my dreams and beg me for a larger presence. But you have all that and more. I know each of your stories to the fullest, and I have envisioned the story of you, Gustavo, crossing the zinc bar, and I pondered the story of you when you did not. You don't crave merely a story but an audience for it. That's what each of you is really asking. You don't want to tell your own story; you want me to tell it for you, and when I do, you complain that I didn't do enough. So, no, Gustavo, I will not help you here."

Z. nodded to Death and walked back to his table without looking at the others.

"Well, you heard the man," Death said. "Now, what about my coffee?"

Gustavo looked at Death, then at the espresso machine, then at Alice and beamed before jumping over the counter. He stood close to Alice but didn't dare make the next move, as if now that he had crossed the threshold, he didn't know what to do. Alice stepped forward and leaned against him and held him in her arms. He was stiff at first but then relaxed, accepting what he had done, and held her as affectionately. She looked up and kissed him, and he kissed her back.

"Is it still the same?" he asked.

"It's better because I love you," she replied.

He kissed her and then more. She grabbed his hand and led him to the storage room in the back, and he followed obediently. The door was locked, so he had to get the key from the end of the bar, but he managed to open the door, and they walked in without delay and closed the door behind them.

"Are we alone?" asked Gustavo.

"Do you want to be?"

"I'm not sure. Part of me wants us to be alone and have this as our private time. But wouldn't it then become like what we had in LA? Isn't our private time our death in some ways?"

"It's a funny way to put it, but I know what you mean. We have achieved more than what we had in Los Angeles, but we can't crave privacy for it to become real and permanent. Perhaps some of each. Z. is right: we want our story to be heard. That's what makes us real."

"Is that possible?"

"Kiss me, and we will see."

Gustavo leaned forward and kissed her while holding her face in his hands, and she wrapped her arms around him. They kissed for a while longer and when he reached out to touch her breast, she put her hands onto his and squeezed it.

After a while, she stepped back and pulled her sweater over her head and then took off the cotton olive shirt. He came closer and unhooked her bra, and her breast fell into his hands. He then unbuttoned his shirt and helped her take off her long woolen skirt. The room was cold, and she shivered. He took her hand and led her to a small bed at the back of the storeroom. She crawled under the blanket, took off her underwear, and tossed it across the room. He completely undressed while standing, and she watched his meticulous movements with admiring eyes. He crawled in with her when he was naked, and they kissed again.

He kissed her neck, then chest, and moved down to her stomach and when he tried to move further, she grabbed his head and he looked up, smiling.

She smiled back and said, "Maybe we can have some privacy, or is it too early?"

"No, it's time," he replied.

An hour later, the door opened, and Gustavo and Alice walked back to the bar. The sun had come up, its light casting warm pathways through the large windows. The trees, now fully grown and branches laden with oranges and apples, were dancing under the sun. Death opened one of the windows, and a light breeze came through. They all could smell the summer flowers from the meadow beyond the bar.

Gustavo walked behind the bar and asked, "What can I get everyone?"

"I'll have a Chardonnay," Marshall said, and Gustavo poured him a large glass from a new bottle. Marshall took a small sip and nodded with vigor.

"I'll have the Cortado," said Death. "I tried to make one while you were *occupied,* but it was no good."

"I'll have another whiskey sour," said Alice as she sat on her stool.

"I'll have one too," Tess said.

"Love is a strange thing," offered Death to no one in particular, and then looking at Tess, "Will you tell us your story? Is it of love or death?"

"It's of both, and it's complicated," she replied. "Z. understood it."

"Then tell us, girl. What are you waiting for?" Alice asked.

Tess looked at each person in the bar and said, "I lied. I wasn't invited. I came anyway so I could tell you my story because I thought it deserved to be told. And I was angry with Z. for holding me back."

Alice said, "I think I can speak on behalf of everyone here as we know how it feels to be ignored and to be relegated to the background."

"We all agree," Marshall added, "So, tell us what you need . . . no, what you want to tell us."

"Thank you," Tess said, her voice turning small. "I came here to tell you about my sister and her bravery. I wanted to prove there is a dark side in each of our stories. I know certain decisions we make have grave consequences, and when they are made—when you decide to take the step to go left rather than to go right—then the other options are closed to you forever, and you must stay on your chosen path no matter what. As if there was no choice in the first place, after all. And no matter how much you wish and pray to go back, you know there are no second opportunities, no second chances. So, you live with your decision and hope and wish the next time, if there is one, you do the right thing or make a better choice."

"I know what you mean, Tess," Death said. "I remember your sister. She was indeed a brave young soul. Alice very much reminds me of her, don't you agree?"

Tess nodded. "Yes, now that you said it. She would have grown up be like Alice."

"So, tell us your story, already," Alice insisted.

"No," Tess said. "Now that I am here, I can see why Z. had stopped me from telling my sister's story. It doesn't belong to the world. I had blamed myself for years for not being a good sister and then blamed her for dying so young, depriving me of the opportunity to make it up to her when we were older. . . .

"But in her death, she gave me a zeal for life, and I became who I am because of her. I think I'm a better person because of it and the memories of my sister are a constant force to keep me on the right path."

They all nodded, and Tess continued, "I am glad I came here when I did to see Alice and Gustavo defy Z., so I don't have to hold this anger against him anymore."

Death said, "Your sister called on me some time before her appointment. I sat with her while we waited."

"Was she in pain?" Tess asked.

"Yes."

"Oh, no. The doctors told us she was comfortable and free of pain."

"They lied, or they couldn't understand her pain. But she was strong, Tess. She died happily. She died loving you."

"Did she talk about us?" Tess asked warily, finally looking up from her glass.

"In her way. As you saw, when you were sitting with her, she was not coherent. But she spoke to me at the end when the appointment neared."

"Had she forgiven me?" Tess asked.

"Yes."

Alice walked toward Tess and held her in her arms. "Think about all the amazing things you have done since then. Think of all the love and care you gave to your friends. They are better people because of you, Tess."

"Let's stop this silliness," Marshall wailed. "We all have regrets. We all wanted more voices in these stories. Well, except Death, of course, who has been getting way more than he deserves and plus he gets to kill people in horrid ways before their stories are fully told."

"Come on, Marshall. You can't stay mad at me for your plunge down the gorge," Death said. "I was just doing what I had to do, but if it makes you less angry, then I apologize, again."

Marshall waved his hand, dismissing Death's apology. "It's all fine now, but what about the story of Spenta, then? Didn't we come here for that?"

"Perhaps this *is* Spenta," Gustavo said hopefully.

"It can't be," replied Marshall. "And why Spenta? I like Beatrice, and if you don't know, it's derived from Latin Beatrix, which means she who makes happy. How lovely is that?"

"It's lovely. I also question my meeting with others on Spenta Island. It makes no sense," Death added.

"Exactly. Who wants to go to Spenta Island? Beatrice Island: now, that makes sense."

"Not really, Marshall. Neither of them makes sense. How would the story go, anyway?"

"You know Dante liked Beatrice. Dante presents Beatrice as being worthy of speaking for God. Now, that's holy. That's power. It makes perfect sense for you and the gods to meet on her island. Okay?"

"I don't know," said Death. "If Z. is looking to change the story from Spenta, then I would suggest Susa. That's where I met the other gods, anyway. We met in Susa in a little tavern that served lamb stew and had this lovely wine. Coffee was still unknown there."

"Susa! Was it as lovely as history tells us?" Alice asked.

"Yes. It was a grand city. And the tavern that I spoke of earlier had withstood so many invaders. The last time I was there, it was a joyous one, so I am dismayed that my role in the liberation of knowledge and empathy has been distorted. The only thing true of the story was the lovely young woman named Spenta. I revisited her for our final appointment years later in a far-off land in Syria. It was not a happy conclusion."

"If you are going to change the location of your meeting," interjected Marshall, "then I would like to see a happy ending for Jackie. There was no indication that it would be anything but happy, and yet Z. made it so dreary. Why? It makes no sense at all."

"I agree," offered Tess. "And I want Stock to live. I'd like to see him fight the disease and survive. I want a happy conclusion for Stock and Dalia, too. I demand it."

"Furthermore," Marshall continued, "the bus stop has to be on Spenta Circle. That's significant if you ask me."

"I agree with you all," said Alice. She turned around, looking at the back of the tavern, where a lone table was now lit with a small table lamp. Others turned with her. "I would also like to suggest a new story. And this is important to me. I want to be Zuleika, and I want to tell her story."

"And I want to be Joseph," said Gustavo.

"Do you understand what we want, Z.?" Alice asked and then, looking at Death, "It's important to tell their story, don't you think?"

Death nodded and then looked at the back of the room. "Yes, it is, Alice. I think it is as important as any other story that has been told and without it, there is no story."

Marshall walked over and sat next to Death. "I have a lengthy list of changes, and it'd be best if you would write everything down."

Death nodded. "Gustavo, could you get us a pen and a piece of paper?"

Gustavo bent down and rummaged through the cabinet underneath the cash register, and after a while, produced a yellow legal pad and a fountain pen. "That's all I have," he said.

"I love those pens," Marshall said. "Give it to me."

Gustavo put the pen and the pad of paper in front of Marshall, and the others joined in, each offering their own narrative. Marshall wrote down each suggestion, numbering each one and underlining the key points. He had ornate handwriting, and when they were finished, the pages looked like an ancient declaration.

They all looked at Z., but he was focused on his own task and continued to ignore them.

"Who will take it to him?" Gustavo asked, and they all looked at each other, their earlier bravado now diminished.

"I will," Marshall declared.

"No," Death said. "I should. I, after all, I have had a hand in where these stories have gone."

Marshall tore the pages from the pad and folded them neatly. "No, Death. This is not a task for you." He then pushed his way from the group and walked toward the table by the sidewall. He stopped a few steps before reaching it. "We have some suggestions," he said and then, finding the power within, "No, Z., we have some demands."

Z. looked up, and Marshall held his gaze.

"I do not fear you anymore. You have already upended my story." He stepped forward, unfolded the papers, and put them in front of the man. He then walked away without looking back, but instead of going to the group at the bar, he exited the tavern through the heavy door.

The group next to the zinc bar looked at each other, unsure of the next step, but then, one by one, they followed Marshall out. When the last of the group had left, and the only person was the man at the table next to the large window, the heavy door closed and the red exit sign stayed dark.

Z. stood up, grabbed the papers, and walked to the zinc bar. He leaned over and took a bottle from behind the counter, but after inspecting it, he put it back. He went behind the bar, reached on the top shelf, and brought down a Macallan 25. He poured the full-bodied scotch in a whiskey glass and took a leisurely sip as he read the list. After he finished his drink, he crumpled the papers in his hand and tossed them into the trash. He poured another drink and sipped it as he stared into the darkened sky. He finished his second drink, put the glass in the sink, and then left the tavern as the others had done—but instead of using the exit door, he used the side door, right behind where Marshall had been sitting, and he walked into his study.

ACKNOWLEDGMENTS

A man with a deep well of imagination lived in a small, rented room. He was far too timid to draw from the well, so it sat there, sealed away for many years. But one night, a wealthy friend, endowed with ensorcelling prose, gave him dozens of words as a gift and helped him arrange them along with the man's own voice in a notebook. Night after night, the friend bestowed more words, each carefully chosen, and after many months the man noted that his manuscript was almost complete. He wondered if he could sell his opus to a publisher.

I could buy a home like my sesquipedalian friend with the advance for my book, and undoubtedly when it becomes a best-seller, I would become famous and wealthy and marry a beautiful woman. And before long, I would have a family, thus needing a larger home in a better neighborhood. Then, of course, I would come back to visit my friend, and we would rejoice in our reunion, and we would check to see who might be living at my old place. The new person would be poor, but he would be honored to have a famous writer at his home. He would indubitably take out his notebook to show off his work and ask me to read a passage. I would acquiesce, of course, as famous people should be agreeable. But then I would see the poetry and beauty of this new writing, and as I read more, I would be filled with a sense of awe, but soon after anger and envy would consume me. "How dare you help this wretched creature? You should have given the words to me, a famous writer, so I could have my second book," I would cry out to my friend. And he certainly would try to calm me and say he is a friend to many people, each with their own dreams. But I would not stand for it—I would grab the notebook and throw it in the fire.

So, the aspiring author, driven by his overpowering thoughts, acted on them, and the fire engulfed his years of work, and his futile attempt to retrieve the smoldering book was rewarded with burnt fingers and the shattered hubris of his empty hands.

I always loved the parable of "The pious man, the fat and the honey," as told in *Kelileh va demneh* or even its earlier version, "The Broken Pot" from the *Panchatantra*. This story has been told and retold in so many versions and languages in the past two and a half centuries that I think it won't be too arrogant to present my version of it; I am a dreamer too. Still, I have a good sense to listen to friends, family, and colleagues who help me do better and skillfully guide my chaotic imagination into coherent, polished stories.

I am grateful to UNO Press editor, Chelsey Shannon, who, with her discerning questions and suggestions (and they were many), helped weave stronger connections between the eight stories in the book. I also appreciate the work of Jessica Brasseur (publicist), Christian Stenico (copy editor), Alex Dimeff (graphic designer), GK Darby (managing editor), and most of all, Abram Himelstein for managing the entire project. Thank you to Lori Hettler for amazing publicity work. I am also profoundly thankful to Xuxu Ariya Amoozegar-Montero for the cover illustration.

I want to thank the following people who had a hand in one or more of my stories, real or imagined: Mahbod, Xuxu, Aïda, Maryse (Beanie), Kian, Ali (Mahjoob), Glenn, Khosrow, Spencer, Pedro, Mylene, Golshid, Dale, Oscar, Tami, Marjaneh, Ömer, Babak, Majie, Peter, Carolyn, Matthew, Fariba, Patrick, Michael, Azita, Donna, Sue, Lana, Sigrid, Doug, Elizabeth, Don, Brennon, Ken, Marty, Kendra, and Randy.

Finally, I am very grateful to Maria Kawah Leung (the author of *Little Heroes of Bay Street: And How They Stay Strong in an Unhappy Home*) and María Montero for offering superb insight and edits throughout the many versions of this manuscript.